THE BOSTO
LUCA

Book Cover by Y'all. That Graphic

Edited by Victoria Ellis, Cruel Ink Editing and Design

Proofread by Rose Sharon, Fairy Proofmother Proofreading, LLC

CHECK YOUR TRIGGERS

Your mental health and emotional well-being matters to me. You can find a list of possible triggers on the book's page on my website katerandallauthor.com or by scanning the QR code below.
Xoxo

To Matt
Always my MMC. Love you babe.

CONTENTS

CHAPTER ONE
LUCA

EIGHTEEN YEARS OLD

"**D**AD, I'M HOME," I call out, walking into the quiet house. Usually around this time, the old man is standing at the stove cooking a huge dinner and the smell of whatever he's frying up permeates the air, but not tonight. My dad likes to tell me he's going to start working overtime just to pay the grocery bill that's doubled since I turned fifteen. But it's not like it's my fault that sophomore year I hit a growth spurt and the football coach took notice of my size and asked me to try out. Two-a-days take it out of me, and when I get home, I'm hungry enough to eat a horse.

"Old man," I call again. "You home?"

We live in a small neighborhood on the Central coast in California. Apparently my dad is from Boston, but he's never taken me back there to visit family. Said without my mom, there was no reason for us to visit the East Coast. She didn't have any living relatives and he didn't have any ties there. Not that it ever mattered much to me. I'm perfectly happy staying on the warmer coast.

Walking into the living room, I see my father sitting on our old plaid couch with a weathered box in front of him and photographs scattered all over the oval coffee table. I've seen the box before but never its contents. It's one he's kept hidden in the back of his closet. One day, when I was about twelve or thirteen, I went into my dad's closet to look for a shirt for picture day. I was already growing like a weed and didn't have a nice shirt that fit, so Dad told me to grab one of his, then gave me a hard time about having to go clothes shopping again. The box was hidden in the corner, and just as I was about to open it—I was a curious little brat—he came in and saw what I was doing.

"Son, there are things in a man's life he'd prefer to keep private," he told me. "I'd like to think I raised you to respect that."

I never tried to look in the box after that, assuming whatever was inside was something he didn't want to discuss. He was right, he did raise me to respect personal boundaries. Seeing it lying out in our living room all these years later is a little startling, to say the least, especially with the open bottle of whiskey sitting next to him.

"Little early in the day to be hitting the bottle, Pops."

My dad looks up at me as though he's just now realized he isn't alone. Frank Bennetti is many things, but a man who is drunk before six p.m. on a work night is not one of them.

He doesn't say anything about my appearance, doesn't smile, doesn't do anything but stare at me.

"What's going on, Dad?"

His silence is unnerving. In fact, his entire demeanor has alarm bells ringing in my head.

"Sit down, Luca," he says, pointing to the dark-brown recliner across from him.

That's the last thing I want to do. His tone and the devastated look in his eyes have me wanting to run the opposite direction and not face whatever he's about to tell me because I know, beyond a shadow of a doubt, it's going to drastically change my life. It's not a feeling I'm familiar with; more like an instinctual part of a person's mind. I'm scared, but I also know this isn't going to be something I can hide from, whatever this is.

So, I sit.

My father holds out an old picture of my mother. We don't have many. Actually, this is the only one. When I asked why we didn't have any more photos of her, he said it was because when she died suddenly in a car accident, he lost his mind for a minute and burned them all. He told me it was one of his biggest regrets because I deserved to have photos of her. I never held it against him, though. I'd never lost the one person I thought I was going to spend the rest of my life with and had a baby to care for all alone, so who the hell was I to judge?

"Ciara was beautiful," he says as I hold the yellowing photograph between my shaking fingers.

I nod and glance at the picture of the woman who shares the same blue eyes with me, then back to him. "She was. What's all this about?"

Other photos are strewn about the low table. All of

them are filled with faces I don't recognize. They're old and obviously from when he was younger. Dad's in a few, and I pick one up. My dad and the other two men in the photo are wearing suits. One holds a cigar in his hand, and his head is tipped back in laughter. I recognize my father standing to the right of him, his hand clasped on the man's shoulder, a wide smile stretching across his face. The other man is laughing with my dad and the stranger in the picture. They all look comfortable together, as though they've known each other for years.

"Old friends of yours?" I ask.

"You could say that. They were part of the life I lived before you. Before I left Boston."

"Before Mom died?"

He blows out a long breath. "I went to the doctor last week. I haven't been feeling well. Short of breath, tired, had a couple dizzy spells."

I nod as I think about the last few months. Sure, he's been a little more tired than normal lately, but the man isn't getting any younger.

"He called me today to go over some test results." He's holding my stare with anxious eyes.

Fear drops to the pit of my stomach.

"There's no easy way to say this. Fuck, I wish there was."

His eyes squeeze shut and when he opens them, the pain behind his dark-brown gaze tells me what he's so afraid to say—what I'm terrified to hear. "My heart is giving out, son. The doctor explained I've had what's called a silent heart attack. Probably more than one. With my age, he said a heart transplant is unlikely, and that's about all they can do in cases like this."

I jump to my feet. "Bullshit. With all the technology and…"

My dad shakes his head. "There's nothing they can do except medications to reduce the risk of further damage, but this is it, son. I'm being called to the mat for all the shit I did. All the people I hurt." He leans back and takes a swig from the whiskey bottle.

"What do you mean about the people you hurt?" My brows draw close together, confusion and fear battling for dominance in my head.

I've never known the man to hurt a fly. Sure, he's a big guy who may look and sound intimidating with his deep voice and a thick Boston accent, but he's a caring single father who works for the power company and comes home every night to have dinner with me. He's the man who throws the ball around with me on the weekends, who takes me camping and fishing. He's not violent or a bad guy.

He leans forward and picks up the picture of him and the two other guys that I was looking at moments ago. "I have to tell you some things. Things I swore I would take to my grave, but seeing as that day is coming sooner rather than later, I need to get this off my chest. It's been just you and me since you were a baby, and when I leave this world, I need you to know you aren't alone. That you have family out there." He waves his hand toward the front door before he tilts his head, indicating for me to sit back down.

"This is really fucking cryptic, Dad."

Usually the old man would have my head for dropping the swear words that are flowing freely from my mouth, but he doesn't comment. He rummages through the stack of pictures and finds the one he's looking for. Taking the photo in his hand, he stares at it for several silent moments, then hands it to me.

I stare at a picture with my mother holding me standing next to the man that was in the other picture with my dad.

"So this guy knew my mom and you?"

My dad purses his lips and stares me in the eye. "That's your father."

Looking back at the picture then to the man sitting across from me—the man who raised me—I shake my head slowly back and forth. "No, you're my father."

His eyes squeeze shut and a tear escapes. Never in all my life have I seen this man cry.

"I knew your father, but I never met your mother." He picks up the picture of the three men and hands it to me. "The man in the middle is Francesco Cataldi. He's head of a Mafia family back in Boston. Your father, the other man next to him, was Elio Romano. He was Francesco's consigliere."

I look at him in confusion. My father knew people in the Mafia?

"What's a consigliere?" That is seriously the least important part of this conversation.

"It's a sort of advisor to the boss. I was a capo in the organization, and when Francesco needed things handled quietly, he'd send me in."

"You were in the Mafia?" I stare at my dad. I'm surely misunderstanding what he's saying or this is going to be some horrible joke. This entire conversation has to be some horrible joke. He's not my father? He didn't even know my mother?

"I was in the Mafia until the night I met you. The night I killed your parents."

I sit stock-still, too stunned to speak, to breathe, just staring at my father, who seems to be holding his own breath, waiting for my reaction.

"This is crazy," I whisper, looking at the picture then back to the man in front of me. "This is fucking crazy!" The volume of my voice doesn't faze my dad. Or maybe I should start calling him Frank because, apparently, he isn't my dad at all. In fact, he killed him.

"You killed my parents, then stole me? For what? Were you jealous of my real father and wanted what was his?"

None of this makes sense. The last ten minutes have turned my world upside down, and I can't begin to make sense of anything he's telling me.

"I can't believe you're saying this. Fuck. I can't believe any of this is real."

I jump from my chair and pace the room, looking from

Frank to the pictures and shaking out my hands. My entire body is vibrating with wave after wave of barely contained anger crashing into me. A sickness washes through me, and I clutch my stomach as though I'm going to throw up from the force of the rage slamming into me. My head is spinning out of control, just like my life in this moment.

"Let me explain, Luca."

Facing the small fireplace in our living room, I keep my back to my dad, shaking my head violently back and forth. I want to cover my ears so I don't have to hear anything else that comes out of his mouth. It's too much. This is all too much.

"I don't know how you're going to explain any of this to make it make sense. What? Do you expect some sort of forgiveness? You expect me to tell you that it's okay you murdered my family since you took me in and raised me? Now that you're dying I have no choice but to hear you out and forgive you for *killing* my real parents?" I place both hands on the fireplace and claw my fingertips into the rough brick, taking several deep breaths in an attempt to calm the nausea swirling in my gut. It doesn't work.

"I can't expect your forgiveness, Luca. That's not why I'm telling you this. The Cataldis have no idea you're still alive, and neither does your mother's family. You can keep it that way if that's what you decide, but I couldn't leave you and not tell you that you have family back in Boston. I couldn't leave you alone in the world, son."

I whirl around and face the devastated man on the couch. "Don't call me that. I'm not your son."

"You're right. You aren't mine by blood, but the first moment I saw you—" Frank's jaw tightens for a moment before he continues, his voice rough with emotion. "I knew I was sent there to protect you. If he had sent anyone else to do the job, you would have been dead."

"Who?"

"Francesco." He leans forward and rests his elbows on his knees with his head hanging low. His fingers link together as though he's praying, asking for absolution.

He won't find any with me.

"Francesco Cataldi was not a good man. He demanded absolute loyalty from his men and anyone in his organization. If he thought anyone was lying or would possibly betray him, he'd send me in to take care of them. He would blame it on a rival organization, usually the Irish, so he wouldn't have to face any backlash from the other families or alert his capos. It was a way to foster the hate between our two organizations. Of course, there was never any proof it was the Irish, but he whispered it in every man's ear. We were always on the brink of war because of his lies, but he never gave the go-ahead to go after them. Obviously, I knew the truth, but I was loyal to the man. And so was your father."

"Then why the hell did he have him murdered?" The yell bursts from my mouth before I can contain it. Not that I care to try.

Frank looks up from his hands. "He met your mother and things changed. He had to keep her a secret, but he was so fucking in love with her."

"How would you know that? You said you'd never met her."

"When Francesco came to me and told me Elio had betrayed the family and I needed to take care of him and his side piece, I did some digging. I followed him around for about a week until he led me to her. To you." He closes his eyes again. When he opens them, he grabs the bottle and takes a long pull. "I went back to Francesco and told him Elio had a baby with the woman. He didn't care. He convinced me that Elio was funneling information to the Irish. That he was a rat. That was the worst thing to be accused of in our life."

"What do the Irish have to do with anything?"

"Your mother was the sister of Maeve Monaghan, wife of the head of the Monaghan family. They were our enemies. Having anything to do with anyone associated with that family meant death, in Francesco's mind at least."

"So my family are nothing but killers and criminals on both sides. That's just fucking great," I say with a caustic laugh as I run my hands through my hair, yanking on the strands. God, what I wouldn't give to go back in time and believe my dad was a normal working-class single father who missed my dead mom.

"I couldn't argue with Francesco. I knew if I did, he'd have me killed without question. He wanted it to look like a home invasion since he knew the Irish would be out for blood. That night, I knocked on the door—"

"Excuse me, Frank, if I don't want the details of how you murdered my parents."

He inhales a sharp breath. I'm not sure if it's a result of me calling him Frank or calling him a murderer.

"When I saw you alone after...what I'd done, I couldn't do it. Fuck Francesco and his bullshit reason for wanting your parents dead. I wasn't going to hurt a child. I never had, and I wasn't going to start then. You were crying so hard, but the second I picked you up, you looked me in the eye with those big blue ones of yours and just stared at me." He smiles and it does nothing but make me angrier that he's thinking about it as some twisted bonding moment instead of the bloodiest night of my life by his hand.

"I didn't know what to do," he continues. "I knew Francesco was out of town, but his wife, Rosa, stayed behind. I called the house, and thankfully, she picked up instead of one of the guards. I told her what was going on, what I'd done, and what I couldn't do. She was a devout Catholic and told me to meet her at the church and to bring you."

"You put an awful lot of faith in the wife of the man who ordered my parents' murder."

Frank nods his head in agreement. "I did. I don't know, maybe I thought she knew a family who would take you in. I thought she could help me figure out a way to disappear. Rosa had a goodness in her that wasn't tainted by the life we were in. I knew in my heart of hearts she would help me. I'd done something I never thought I'd do. I was betraying my boss, and I knew what the consequences would mean. I wasn't exactly in my right mind that night."

I look back at the picture of my real father with Frank and Francesco. They looked like friends. How the hell could one friend order the murder of another?

"She showed up at the church but made her guard wait outside. She was beyond distraught at discovering her husband ordered the murder of an innocent child, especially since she had a child at home. She told me Francesco was well on his way to turning her sweet boy into the ruthless man he wanted to take over for him someday. Honestly, I think if she could have run with me, she would have, but there was no way Francesco wouldn't have hunted us down and made both of us regret ever having attempted it. She brought me all the baby supplies she had on hand and a wad of cash. Told me to get as far away as I could. She said God must have put me in your path and this was my chance to make amends for all the heartbreak I caused. That getting you away from that violent and bloody life was my chance at redemption."

"I'd say taking off to the other side of the country was a good plan then."

He nods. "I was so fucking scared those first few days. Hell, the first few years. I knew there was no way Francesco wouldn't be looking for me. I kept checking online for reports of what happened to your parents. But there was nothing. No news reports or anything. Between the cash Rosa gave me and the money I had in my safe, I set us up out here with new identities."

"Why didn't you go to the authorities? If you really regretted what that guy was going to make you do, why didn't you call the FBI or something? Turn him in."

"There was nothing witness protection would have done for me that I wouldn't be able to do for myself. And I sure as hell wasn't going to incriminate myself to get them to cut me a deal. Disappearing in the wind was the best option as far as I could see at the time. And I believed Rosa when she said I was meant to raise you to be an honorable man with no ties to our life. That wouldn't have happened if we hadn't disappeared."

"Why didn't you take me to my mother's family then? You could have disappeared on your own and been done with the whole thing." The only thing I keep thinking over and over is how fucking crazy this all sounds.

How is this my life?

"I thought about it so many times. There were days I was sure you should be with your mother's family, but then I'd think about another kid being raised to live a violent life. I couldn't imagine putting you there. I didn't know the Monaghan's that well, but everything I knew, everything I'd been fed about them, told me they weren't any better than the life I took you from. I don't know; I just couldn't imagine you growing up to be a killer like me. I wanted to protect you from that life. Something intrinsic changed in me the first time I held you, Luca. It was impossible to ignore and even more impossible to explain. I never gave much thought to God or a higher purpose, but between the way you looked at me that night and what Rosa said in that church, I just couldn't hand you over to another criminal family."

"Why tell me now then?" I yell, the numbness I was feeling moments ago morphing back into anger.

"Because I'm dying. Because I feel guilty for leaving you with no one. Because I've raised you to be a good man, and I believe you'll make the right choices with your future. Choices you wouldn't have had if I'd left you on the Monaghan's doorstep. I don't know, son. The reasons change minute to minute."

I bristle at his use of the word son but don't comment.

"I can't be here right now," I say, standing from the old recliner.

"Where are you going?" he asks, worry creasing his forehead.

"I don't know. This is...this is all too much."

My legs carry me to my room, but I don't feel anything as I throw a few changes of clothes in my bag and head to the front door.

"Luca," my father—no, Frank—calls from the living room. "I love you. You have every right to hate me, but I need you to know that."

I don't look at him.

I don't respond.

I just walk out the door.

CHAPTER TWO
LUCA
TWO YEARS LATER

I'M BURYING MY FATHER today.

Standing at the edge of his grave, I stare at the casket that holds the body of the man who held so many secrets. So many regrets. And I let myself cry. I finally let it out after months of refusing to allow myself to get to this point. During the last several months, his body weakened until he needed help with everything—and I was that help. His tired heart wouldn't allow him the freedom to even make it from his wheelchair to his bed on his own.

It took three weeks to come back to the house after my father told me about my real parents and his role in their deaths. Three weeks of couch surfing between my friends' houses and fielding questions from their concerned parents. Three weeks of unanswered calls and texts from my dad. He never asked me to come home. He just wanted to make sure I was safe. I don't know. Maybe he thought I'd go off the rails and run to Boston to find my real family or something. I never answered him, though. As far as I was concerned, he didn't deserve to have that peace of mind.

I'm not sure what kept me in California. During the day, I'd pretend everything was fine. I went to class, went to football practice, and did my homework. I'd eat dinner with whatever friend's family I was staying with and pretended my dad was on a business trip, saying he was doing some sort of training at different plants. My excuse was wishy-washy as hell, but I didn't have years of practice when it came to lying, unlike some people.

At night though, I'd lie awake thinking about the story he told me, the life he led and the reasons he had for saving me that night. I never told a single soul what he confided in me. Shit, at the time, I was sure no one would believe it. I hardly believed it myself. And I didn't know how to tell anyone that the life I had was one big lie. There was also another part of me that didn't want anyone looking at my dad differently. Regardless of how he came to be my father, it didn't change the fact that he raised me. No matter how angry I was, there was still the part of me that remembered that. Maybe that's why, after three weeks, I walked back through the front door after football practice instead of going to a friend's house again.

The look of relief on my dad's face when he saw me will forever be burned in my memory.

He hugged me and told me he was happy I was home. Though something inherent changed within me the day he'd told me about Boston, I couldn't let him suffer and die alone. No matter what he did and how horrible it was, that wasn't the man I knew. The man I knew did everything to give me a safe and stable life. The truth of our past would go in a box in the recesses of my mind, just like the box of photos he'd hidden in the back of his closet. I told him I was a long way from forgiving him, but I wasn't going to punish him either.

As the months wore on, my dad's health declined. Thankfully, he had good insurance and benefits, so when he had to stop working, his company took care of him. I got a part-time job, but he insisted I take courses at the community college after graduation. There was no way in hell I was going to a four-year university on a scholarship I could've gotten with football. If it were any other situation, he would have argued with me about my decision. Instead, he was grateful for the time I was willing to give a dying man.

We were never the same after he told me about our past. I knew he wanted to talk to me about it, to check how I was handling everything, but he didn't dare bring it up out of fear I'd probably disappear again. And trust me, there were days I wanted to, days when my anger wanted to get the better of me. When I wanted to rail against him and the entire world, but I didn't. My feelings were complicated and so damn convoluted I wasn't sure I would ever make sense of them, but I couldn't ignore the eighteen years of love from a man who gave up everything to protect me.

We spent our days watching old westerns and shows about a couple guys going through people's junk and finding hidden treasures. Toward the end, Frank mostly dozed off for long periods during the day, but he insisted on sitting in our old recliner rather than wasting away in bed. He needed the company, and quite frankly, so did I.

Now he's gone. And that box I'd kept a tight lid on for the last two years has smashed wide open.

My tears fall. Hot, angry rivulets of water splash to the damp ground at my feet. The day is overcast, the marine layer hanging on tightly and blocking the sun and its warmth from my skin.

The service was small. There were just a few friends from high school I've kept in contact with and some old coworkers of my dad's who came to pay their respects. I feel the gazes of the men waiting to start filling the hole where my father's coffin lies. I know I should let them do their job. They probably have other things to do with their day rather than stand here and watch a twenty-year-old man cry over his father's grave. But I can't seem to make myself move from this spot. When I do, I'll be going home to an empty house with nothing but memories to keep me company.

When I was a kid, maybe seven or eight, I asked my dad if he was ever going to get married again, still believing he was married to my mother when she died. He laughed and shook his head, telling me he was perfectly happy living his life with the best son any father could hope for before he asked why I brought it up. He was probably concerned he wasn't enough, worried I was missing out on not having a mother. I didn't really care about that part, although I thought at the time it would be nice to have snuggles from a mom, but my dad was the best hugger in the world. No, I wanted a little brother. My dad laughed and laughed when I told him that, but I thought it would be cool. My best friend in second grade had one, and he always had someone to play with. Seemed reasonable to me. But when my dad said I'd have to share my cars with another kid all the time, I thought better of the idea. I liked having my own stuff that only I was allowed to play w ith.

The memory makes me smile, and I think about my dad and his booming laugh. He didn't sound the same after his body began to betray him. A laugh like that would've probably left him wheezing for breath and made him pass out from exertion.

I wipe my damp face with the backs of my hands and stand a bit taller, taking a deep breath before turning to face the parking lot where my car sits. My gaze briefly lands on the workers, who give me a small smile before I walk to my car to drive myself back to my empty house.

Opening the door to our one-story bungalow nestled in the quiet neighborhood that butts up against acres of farmland, the finality of the day hits me. Similar to how I felt at the cemetery, but this is quieter somehow, sadder. I look to the left, and my gaze lands on the medical equipment on the kitchen table where I spent hours doing homework. I'll have to call the hospice company again to have them pick all this stuff up. One more thing for me to take care of now that this is all...over. My dad died here three days ago. It's not as though this is the first time I've been alone in the house. The old man didn't want to go to the hospital. There was nothing they could have done for him there, he told me. He wanted a quiet passing in the home he'd created here with me. Now, I'm the only one in the home.

With the funeral over, there really isn't anything for me to do for the first time in two years. I took this last semester off from school, with my dad's health declining drastically over the last few months. My part-time job stocking shelves a couple nights a week at our local grocery store gave me the next week off for bereavement. *There's nothing for me to do.*

I toss my keys in a bowl on the slim table we have next to the front door and head into the living room. Collapsing onto the couch, I throw my head back and stare at the ceiling. Suddenly, I feel like I can't breathe. I rip the tie from my neck and undo the top two buttons on my black shirt. It doesn't help. The silence is stifling, and I feel like I want to run ten miles to get rid of all this excess energy strumming through me. With no one to take care of or funerals to plan, I feel lost, adrift in a life I wasn't prepared for.

During the weeks before my father passed, he wanted to talk about Boston. It was the first time in two years he tried to bring it up. I didn't want to know anything about his life there or the life I could have had with my biological parents, but I also didn't have the heart to deny a dying man. It was a fucked-up situation all around. Sure, there was a part of me that was curious, but again, when I came back to the house two years ago, I put it all in a box and was perfectly content not opening it.

But I let him speak.

He told me how my father was always quick with a joke and people loved being around him. He had a way that made people feel at ease, which was crucial in his position. The men respected him, especially Francesco, which is why my dad was shocked when he gave the order for his murder. He said the times he saw my mother from a distance, she was smiling at my father, always excited to see him. He told me the love they shared was obvious to any outside observer, which is what he was since he spent so much time spying on t hem.

He debated whether or not to tell Francesco there was a baby, worried that his worst fear would come true—which it did. Francesco Cataldi didn't care that there was an innocent baby involved. He wanted Elio, along with his young family, to pay with their lives for what he perceived as the ultimate betrayal. And because my father was as loyal as they came, he agreed to do the job, not that he really had a choice. He told me you simply couldn't say no to the boss. Though when he fled with me, that was the ultimate fuck you to Francesco.

He also told me that not a day went by where he didn't

regret not running before he went to my parents' house. He wished, down to the very marrow of his being, that he would've had the guts to walk away and leave Elio and my mother alive and happy with their baby. That he should have told Elio about Francesco's plans. His biggest regret was the reason he made damn sure I felt loved and safe from that night forward. He couldn't take back his cowardice, but he could spend his life trying to be the caring father he took away from me.

And when I look at it subjectively, if Frank hadn't killed my parents, someone else would have. Once Francesco got something in his head, there was no changing it, according to Frank. And if that would've been the case, that person wouldn't have spared my life.

I don't know if my father, Elio, not Frank, wanted to leave with my mother and me and get away from the criminal life. Neither did my dad—Frank, not Elio. It was confusing when I thought about the two men. Elio was my father, who I have no recollection of, and Frank was my dad who raised me but wasn't blood. And the kicker? Turns out Frank wasn't his real name and Luca wasn't mine either. Frank's real name was Constantine Barelli and mine was Elio Luciano Romano Jr.—hence *Luca* when Frank changed our names. He wanted me to have some piece of my past, even if it was just a name, and I never knew where it had originated from. I'm not sure if Frank would've told me about our shared past had he not been dying, and I didn't want to ask, too scared of the answer. Still, his reasoning wouldn't have mattered because I know now.

Frank went on to fill me in on what he knew of the Monaghans. They were the Irish mob in Boston. Started as bootleggers and made a name for themselves in the protection racket after prohibition ended, then started illegal gambling rings throughout Boston. They had legitimate businesses they ran their dirty money through, namely four bars in downtown Boston, at least when Frank left Boston twenty years prior. He wasn't sure what state the organization was in, too afraid to reach out to any of his old contacts and risk having Francesco find us. When he took me away from Boston, he told me Maeve and Cormac Monaghan had one son, Finnegan. That was all he knew about the Monaghans, not that I wanted the information. I was perfectly happy living in sweet denial.

My dad wrote the numbers to the four bars on a piece of paper that has stayed in my pocket since he handed it to me two weeks ago. He said if I wanted to get to know that side of the family to reach out, but be careful. He didn't want me going after Francesco in any way, shape, or form. And he worried that Cormac Monaghan would try to lure me in with the promises of family loyalty and all that bullshit. It was a life Frank had led, and he didn't want me to have any part in it, especially considering what would happen if Francesco found out who I was. Frank wasn't worried about himself, knowing he was going to be long gone before Francesco could do anything, but he was worried for me, worried that

Francesco would consider me unfinished business.

Though Frank never wanted that life for me, I want revenge. The feeling started not long after I came back after my dad unloaded his past on me. Even though I did a damn good job at keeping the maelstrom of emotion regarding my true parentage at bay, there were nights I would lie awake and think of the ways I could make the Mafia boss pay for depriving me of the life I could've had with two loving parents. But then the guilt would come when I thought about my dad's disappointed face. He wanted me as far from that life as he could get me and never wanted it to taint me. So, like all the other thoughts that swirled in my brain when I thought about Boston, I'd shove those feelings in a box in my mind and shut it tightly.

Now, though? They're front and center as I sit on this couch, feeling like I'm ready to jump out of my skin and having no dying father to distract me from it all. Frank is dead. My dad is gone, and it wouldn't matter to anyone if I decided to act out my plans for revenge that have been simmering since I was eighteen.

I stare at the beige wall across from me. My eyes find their way to the picture of me and my dad at my junior high graduation. It's surrounded by other pictures of various birthday parties and fishing trips. I let out a long breath, my anxiety not waning one damn bit. Scrubbing my hands over my tired face, I get up from the couch and walk into the bright-yellow kitchen that my dad said was a cheery paint color when I told him it looked more like the color of a banana. Moving on autopilot, I open the refrigerator and peer inside, looking for something to eat even though I'm not hungry. There are casseroles from neighbors that sit covered, but I can't bring myself to take them out. "Death casseroles" is what I call them. I thought it was fucking hilarious, but Mrs. Barker, an old woman who lives down the street, didn't.

I open the cabinets, looking for what I don't know, but finding the liquor bottle on the top shelf of the second cabinet gives me pause. That damn bottle of whiskey my dad was drinking the day he threw my life into upheaval. He stayed away from alcohol after that night, not wanting to put unnecessary strain on his body after learning he was in the end stages of congestive heart failure.

Taking the bottle from the shelf, I hold it in my hands. Part of me wants to smash it against the counter for no other reason other than I feel like destroying something that represents the worst day of my life. Another part of me wants to drink the rest until I'm so fucking numb that this day, the second worst day of my life, is a distant memory.

Fuck it. Option two it is.

Screwing off the cap, I toss it on the counter and take a gulp of the fiery liquid.

"Jesus Christ," I cough out, nearly hurling the second I swallow the whiskey. My eyes water as I continue to cough, but the whiskey stays in my stomach. I was never much of a drinker aside from having the occasional beer at high school parties. Being a football player meant taking care of my body. There were a couple times I had hard alcohol, but only when it was mixed with something, never straight from a warm bottle.

"Fucking gross," I say to no one as I stare at the amber liquid.

Instead of putting the bottle back in the cupboard, I grab a soda and ice from the fridge and pour a healthy amount of whiskey into a glass, topping it off with soda. Taking a sip, I nod to myself. Not bad considering I'm far from an expert bartender.

I return to the couch and grab the box that was in my father's closet. I haven't opened this since the day he showed me its contents.

Pulling out picture after picture is surreal. There are photos of his parents in there and a few more of him as an adult with various people who I don't know. No names are written on the back, which seems reasonable. No photographic evidence or any shit like that. The only people I recognize are Frank, Elio, and Francesco.

My dad told me he took several photos off the wall before he left my parents' house that night. He wasn't sure why he did it at the time; he just knew he needed to. When he went back to his apartment and grabbed the cash from his safe and some clothes before meeting Rosa Cataldi at the church, he dumped them all in a box.

One thing about my dad was he always snapped

photos of me growing up. He was hardly in any of them. I don't know; maybe he was afraid of someone finding them and recognizing him or something, but I have a ton of pictures of me growing up. Grabbing the one from when I was a junior in high school from the wall, I compare it to the picture of me with Elio and my mother holding me as a baby. I have my father's darker skin tone—kind of like a perpetual tan. Frank had the same one, but the eyes? All my mother. Dark blue with thick black lashes surrounding them. My hair is darker than hers, more like my father's. I have the same cheekbones as my mother but my father's jawline and nose. My smile is all my mother's, too. That's weird to see. Frank always told me I took after my mother, which is true, so I never questioned why I looked different from him. There were qualities Frank and I shared, sure, but when I see a picture of my biological father, it's as though I'm seeing the other half of myself.

I take a long sip from my drink and get up to make another one, this time more alcohol and less soda.

When I sit back down, I can't stop staring at the picture of me compared to my parents.

Fucking unreal.

My phone buzzes with a text from one of my friends I stayed in contact with from high school. I don't answer, though. I simply don't feel like talking to anyone.

After Frank's diagnosis and the last year being pretty bad health-wise for him, I lost touch with a lot of people from high school. I don't hold it against them in the least, though. This isn't the type of town most kids stay in after graduation. Sure, some kids from my high school still live around here, opting to work and start their lives as adults, but most of my friends went to four-year universities right after graduation. That was always my plan, too, but I refused to leave my dad. I knew his road was going to be hard, and he was a proud man who would've had a hard time asking for help, even if he needed it. Of course, he argued, but I promised when the time was right, I'd finish my degree at a university. The right time being when he was dead, though neither of us said that. We both knew there was no way I was going to leave him to fend for himself. At least not after I came back after the three weeks I spent couch surfing.

The burn of the whiskey as I guzzle my last drink matches the burn in my chest. Who the hell does this Cataldi fuck think he is? He took my parents, and then, by some ugly twist of fate, the man who raised me is gone now, too. I have no ties. They were all stolen from m e.

The phone number in my pocket feels like it's burning a hole in my damn soul. I don't know shit about Mafia politics. Hell, for all I know, the Cataldis and Monaghans get along just fine these days.

But what if they don't?

What if they're the only line I have to get back what was stolen from me? A family. Safety. A life out from under the shadows. Frank didn't want me to chase after revenge, but fuck, getting revenge sounds pretty damn good right about now. My dad told me the Cataldis were nearly untouchable. The cops, DEA and FBI have tried to build cases against them for years, yet they've never been able to stick charges to the boss, Francesco. But what if the way to take them down isn't by using the law but by some other means? Some way to get in there and destroy them from the inside. If Francesco was so worried about Elio feeding information to the Monaghans, that meant Elio knew things about the Cataldis that would destroy them. And if he knew then I can find out, too.

I pull the number from my pocket, my eyes blurry from the tears and the whiskey, and dial one of the numbers to a bar the Monaghans own.

"Clovers Tavern," the voice on the other line answers.

Am I really fucking doing this?

"Hello?" the person who answered asks impatiently.

"Uh, hi. Cormac Monaghan, please."

"Mr. Monaghan isn't here." The voice seems slightly confused. "Who's this?"

I don't know what to say. I don't know what the hell I'm doing, actually.

"My dad was a friend of his and he passed. Thought Mr. Monaghan would like to know."

That makes no sense. Frank and Cormac weren't friends. If she asks who it was, what the hell am I supposed to tell her?

"His son is here. Hold on, I'll get him." The woman's

voice is sympathetic, and I feel like shit for lying. But again, I have no idea what the hell I'm supposed to say. I need to talk to someone. I need to figure out what my next move is, if I have a move at all.

"This is Finn," a man with a deep voice answers.

I'm stunned speechless.

You called him, dumbass.

"Hi, my name is Luca Bennetti. Our fathers knew each other." Kind of true.

"My bartender said our dads were friends. What was his name?"

"I may have embellished on that a little," I answer.

"What the fuck is going on? Who the hell are you?"

Inhaling a deep breath, I decide to answer with the truth.

"I'm your cousin."

CHAPTER THREE

LUCA

ONE YEAR LATER

THE HOUSE IS PACKED up. The last year has been a whirlwind of getting my ducks in a row to move out to Boston. When I think back on that first drunken phone call I made to Finn the day of my dad's funeral, I can't believe it was only twelve months ago.

To say he had a hard time believing me is an understatement. He basically told me to fuck right off and hung up on me. I was defeated, certain my chances of taking Francesco Cataldi down had flown right out the window.

Then, a week later, I got a phone call.

"Hello?" I answer my cell phone hesitantly, recognizing the Boston area code.

"It's Finn Monaghan. Fuck, I don't know why I'm calling."

He's silent for a beat, and it doesn't seem like he wants me to answer that for him, so I don't.

"You know, my first thought was to find you and kill you myself for even suggesting something so insane, but the more I thought about it, the more I decided I was willing to hear you out."

"Okay..." I'm not sure what I'm supposed to say to that.

"So tell me who the hell you are and what makes you think you're my cousin."

"Just get right to the point. Alright." I wipe a sweaty palm down my jeans and walk out to the back porch. For some reason, sitting within four walls doesn't feel like enough room to have this conversation.

"I don't have time for bullshit, Luca Bennetti, who lives in Atascadero, California."

"How do you know that?" I didn't give him any information when I talked to him last week.

"You said our fathers knew each other, correct?"

"Yes, but they weren't friends. Not by a long shot."

"Regardless, if your father knows mine, then I'm guessing he knows exactly who my father is and who our family is. Didn't take a genius to track you through your cell phone number. Hell, didn't even take more than an internet search."

"Knew. Our fathers knew each other. Mine died."

"Right, right. My bartender did tell me that. Sorry to hear. As far as I knew, you were dead, too, so tell me how I'm talking to a ghost."

I fill Finn in on the things Frank told me. About who my birth parents were, how they came to die on Carlo Cataldi's order and how my dad saved me and ran.

"My father looked for you for years," Finn says when I finish my story. "He managed to keep the story out of the press, but he knew Cataldi had something to do with his sister-in-law's death. My mother spent years looking into the eyes of every child she passed on the street in Boston to see if she recognized you. It nearly tore her apart. Shit, for a while there, it did. You just disappeared into thin air."

"I'm sorry." I don't know what else to say. The people he's talking about don't mean anything to me. Not in any real way.

"So what do you want, Luca? Why did you decide to contact me after all this time? You knew two years ago who you were. Why now?"

"Frank is dead." It's a simple answer but the truth.

"Good riddance," Finn responds.

"Hey," I bark out. "He may not have made the right decision, but he was a good father. He did the best he could in a shitty situation."

Finn doesn't apologize, not that I expected him to. The man stole me from his family after killing his aunt. I wouldn't dare think he'd be grateful to him for keeping me safe. Hell, there are moments when I'm pissed as hell at him. But he didn't know Frank like I did. He doesn't have the years under his belt with him that I do.

"You haven't answered my question. What do you want?"

"I want that fucker Cataldi and his entire organization to burn to the ground. I want to stand over him while he takes his last breath and know I was the one who caused his destruction. I want revenge for what he did to my parents," I tell him as I stand at the edge of my back porch and stare into the field beyond.

Holy shit, I've never said that out loud. Now that I have, it feels good. It feels like the truest words I've ever spoken. Maybe that makes me a monster, no better than the people Frank was trying to save me from, but fuck if I care. That man deserves everything I plan to do. Hell, probably more.

"Okay." Finn is silent for a minute. "If that's what you want, I can make it happen. You want the whole organization to fall, then it's going to take work and patience. The Cataldis haven't survived this long on luck."

"So you'll help me?"

"I'll help you. But we do this my way. You don't know jack shit about this life. And we can't tell anyone you're related to me or who you are. I'm not going to lie, Luca. This is going to be dangerous as shit. You may not make it out alive. I'm not going to have those old wounds opened for my mother if she finds out who you are just to have you die."

I think about that for a few moments. It's not like I have any family as it is now.

"Okay. So what do we do?"

"Do you know how to shoot a gun?"

"No."

"Do you have any sort of training in martial arts or fighting? An expert thief by chance? Any skills that would make you at all desirable to a criminal organization?"

"Not really. I played football in high school, but that's about it."

"So you're a big guy with no fighting skills who's never

shot a gun? I can work with that."

"I have a question for you."

"Shoot."

"Why do you want to help me? How do you know I am who I say I am?"

"I hacked into your DMV records. You have my mother's eyes. Your mother's eyes. You look just fucking like her, man."

Considering I have the pictures to prove he's right about the family similarities, it's as good as a DNA test in his eyes.

"This is what you need to do before you come out here," Finn says, and I listen intently to his every instruction. After all, he's right. I have no clue what it takes to be a criminal in his world, but I'm sure as hell about to find out.

The ringing phone jerks me out of my memory. Finn sent me a burner phone, which I only talk to him on. He said not to call anyone else in Boston from my original phone and to disconnect it as soon as possible. He told me if we're doing this, then there can be no ties to my life in California. That part was easy. I didn't have a girlfriend, and though I had good friends in high school, taking care of a sick father and the secrets I had to keep from everyone about my history put a wedge between us. With Frank gone, I don't have anyone I care about or who cares about me enough to miss me when I'm gone. Everyone here thinks I'm getting out of Atascadero to start a life away from reminders of my dad. That I'm leaving heartbroken. But I'm not. I'm leaving with a plan to take down a dangerous man who ruined not only my life but countless others.

"Hey, what's up?" I answer.

"Today's moving day. You all set?"

"Yup. Just need to get in the car."

"You can still back out. Once you're in Boston, shit's going to get real. It won't be just an idea anymore."

Finn has made sure at every turn that I'm prepared for what life is going to look like once this whole thing gets underway. When we started this, he told me I had to get used to thinking on my feet and keeping a straight face because there's no doubt I'll see things that would otherwise make a normal person cringe.

"I'm not backing out, Finn. I've already put the work in. If anything, I'm more determined than ever to get out there and get shit started."

When I talked to my cousin a year ago, he gave me a list of things I was going to have to do. One of them, funnily enough, was acting classes, specifically improv. He said since I didn't grow up in the life, I needed to learn to think fast and control my expressions. I thought he was overdoing it, but there was no way in hell I was going to say no to him and have him back out of our deal.

He told me to learn how to shoot and get to the point where the gun felt like an extension of myself. I clocked a shit ton of hours at the gun range, learning everything I could and becoming a damn good shot, if I do say so myself.

Boxing was another class Finn insisted on. I'd never been in a real fight, and Finn was adamant I learned how to use my fists. It came in handy with the next part of the preparation plan for me. He wanted me to start hanging out in the seedier dive bars. Aside from the night I first called him, I hadn't been much of a drinker, but Finn said I didn't need to become an alcoholic to sell any of this. I just needed to make nice with some of the less desirable regulars at the bars I went to. It didn't take long for me to be involved with my first bar fight, but thanks to the boxing classes, I learned how to throw a powerful punch. I won't lie and say the camaraderie after the fight didn't make me uncomfortable. These weren't good guys. They were drug dealers and junkies, but Finn insisted I needed to be comfortable around those types of people and learn to fit in because a major part of our plan depended on it. I bought coke and pills from people and acted glad to see them every time we ran into each other at one of the three bars I frequented. I never took anything I bought off them, instead flushing that shit down the toilet when I got home, but I studied how the dealers operated.

So, after months of doing everything Finn told me to, we decided it was time for me to come out to Boston and find a way into the Cataldi organization. He said since it's not something you can exactly apply for, I'd have to get an introduction to one of the capos and work my way up from there. Considering my size, he figured they would most likely want me as a guard, but I'd need to prove myself first.

"You need to work on that patience, cousin. This isn't going to happen overnight."

That was another thing he kept hammering home. He told me countless times that something like this could take years. That it wasn't enough to go in and kill Francesco right away. I needed to get in there and figure out how and where we could weaken them so when it was time for a full-blown takeover, Finn would be the one to step in. That was the plan, at least. I'd be his inside man, and he'd make moves to take over their territory. Then, when the time was right and they were weak, that was when Francesco would be mine.

"I've been patient. For the last three years, all I've thought about is watching the old man take his last breath. I'm ready to put this in motion, Finn. Don't start doubting me now."

Finn chuckles. "I don't doubt you, Luca. I'm simply making sure you're ready."

"I'm getting in my car now. I'll see you in a few days."

"Drive safe."

Hanging up the phone, I look at the only house I've ever lived in since I was a baby. My father's life insurance included a clause that, at the time of his death, his house would be paid off. It's a small place, but the money from the sale will set me up nicely until I can get on a crew with the Cataldis and start earning.

The summer sun is beating down on me as I stare at

the old bungalow. The three-bedroom, one-story home is ready for the family that bought the place to move in. It's a nice-looking house in a quiet neighborhood with white paint and black shutters. When my dad was alive, it was painted light yellow with white shutters and matching trim, but the realtor said black and white was much more appealing. The first time I saw it freshly painted, it didn't feel like my house anymore. And as of today, it no longer is. With one last long look, I get in my old SUV, packed with a few boxes in the trunk and pull out of the driveway. I don't look in the rearview mirror, choosing to keep my eyes trained on the road ahead and the new world I'm ready to dive headfirst into.

The cross-country drive was uneventful and too fucking quiet. Frank and I never drove from coast to coast. Makes sense why, considering he was trying to stay as far from Boston as he could possibly get.

It's the first time I'm driving through the Rockies, then the plains, passing through small no-name towns with nothing but my thoughts and a few CDs I brought with me. My car is so old it doesn't have any sort of way to listen to music other than a CD player or the radio. This was my dad's car, the one he shuffled me to and from school in and all the football practices and camping trips in between. Now, I'm taking it to the one place he vowed never to return to.

My mind repeatedly drifts to how he would feel about my plans. He wouldn't be thrilled I'm putting myself in danger. Every time the idea of him being disappointed runs through my head, I remember the picture of my smiling mother with me on her hip or the look in Elio's eyes, smiling down at the woman and child he clearly loved. Then, the rage comes back in full force. One man was responsible for taking that away, making their last moments on this earth terrifying in ways I could only imagine. And that man needs to pay.

It takes four days for me to get to Boston. Four days of sleeping in cheap motel rooms and eating at greasy diners, or grabbing something from a convenience store along the highways I traveled. Four days of watching the scenery go from wide open plains to congested cities and finally reaching Boston.

I pull into the parking lot of an abandoned building on the outskirts of the city to meet Finn. If I didn't trust the man so much, I'd be pretty damn worried right about now, considering this is where it looks like a man like him would be perfectly comfortable snuffing the life out of someone. Where a man like me would come to do the same thing. Because that's who I am now. Maybe I should be having second thoughts about the path I'm on, but I can't find it in myself to turn back. Nothing is going to stop me from taking down the Cataldis.

"You made it," Finn says as I step out of the SUV.

"Did you have any doubts?"

"Nah," he replies and walks over to me, clasping me in a hug. "Good to see you in the flesh."

Finn and I have talked at least twice a week on the phone over the last year. We've had several video calls, too.

Just as he releases me, another guy steps out of the car. He isn't quite as broad as Finn, but he has a cunning gaze as he eyes me from where he stands.

"This is Cillian," Finn introduces as the man makes his way over to us. "He's my lieutenant and the only other person in Boston who knows who you are and what we're doing."

That takes me by surprise for a moment. "I thought we agreed no one would know anything," I say, looking between my cousin and Cillian.

"There aren't a lot of guarantees here, Luca. But one thing I know for certain is shit can spin on a dime. If anything happens to me, I don't want you left in the wind. I trust Cillian to be able to keep his mouth shut."

"What about Eoghan?" Finn told me all about his little brother, who is still getting his feet wet in the organization.

"I love my brother, but I don't want him to be part of this. One, he's a mama's boy, and like I said before, this could go sideways in a heartbeat. I don't want my mother going through that heartbreak again if she finds out you were living in Boston under her nose, and she lost you all over again. And two, the fewer people who know anything, the better. Eoghan can't inadvertently give up information he doesn't have."

Finn keeps his inner circle tight, which I suppose a man in his position would have to do.

Cillian walks over to me, reaching his hand out to shake mine. I notice the tattoos around his wrist and the hard look in his eyes. The scars on his knuckles tell me he's well acquainted with the violence involved in this life and has no problem doling it out when the situation arises. I'm sure Finn has the same tendencies, but he has an easier demeanor, almost as though they play the good cop, bad cop. Or maybe bad cop, worse c op.

"Nice to meet you, Luca," Cillian says in a deep, emotionless voice, as though meeting the person who's about to risk his life being a mole for his organization is as mundane as sharing the weather report.

"You too," I reply, then step back.

"Let's get to business, then," Finn says, and Cillian and I turn our gazes to my cousin, the newest head of the Monaghan family. He's a few years older than me and has been in charge since his father retired three years ago. Seems kind of young to be the head of a criminal organization, but the way he tells it, his mother, my aunt, was done worrying about her husband after his second heart attack. Finn was more than ready to take the reins, and Cormac, her husband, agreed and stepped down as head of the family.

Finn hands me a piece of paper. "Here're the addresses of a couple bars that men in the Cataldi organization frequent, including Francesco's son, Carlo. Start there." Then he hands me another sheet of paper with several addresses listed. "Here's a list of apartment buildings in Cataldi territory. They aren't exactly upscale penthouses, but they aren't total shitholes either."

I nod and take the papers from him. Finn's dark-blue eyes bore into mine. "We aren't going to be able to talk much while this is going down, and meeting face to face is going to be even tougher. If anyone sees us together, it'll put you under suspicion. If there's a chance for us to meet, I'll text you on the burner, but keep that shit hidden. I don't have to tell you what happens if you're found out."

We've already gone over all the gruesome ways the Cataldis handle moles in their organization, as though I don't have knowledge of it from Frank's stories.

"You ready?" Finn asks.

"Considering I've been waiting years to get here, yeah, I'm fucking ready."

Chapter Four

Giada

Three Years Later

"**G**IADA, YOU HAVE TO come tonight," my best friend, Bianca, whines into the phone. "Jason is going to be there, and I know you've been crushing on him since freshman year."

I let out a snort of laughter at her attempt to try to sweeten the deal.

"I'm over high school boys. He's had almost four years to make his move and hasn't done jack shit." I fall back on my bed and stare up at the gauzy, white canopy above me. God, this room hasn't changed since I was four years old and thought I was a princess living in a beautiful castle. Little did I know, it's a castle in a kingdom built on the blood and pain of other people.

"Oh please, he was scared. It's not like everyone at school doesn't know who your family is. But Chelsea told me she overheard him talking the other day at soccer practice that he's ready to shoot his shot with you. I think he just needed to work up the courage to ask you out."

"Four years, Bianca?"

"It's a long time, I'll give you that," she hedges. "But

come on, better late than never."

Being the only daughter of Francesco Cataldi has made my high school dating life completely nonexistent, thanks to everyone knowing my father runs one of the most powerful crime families in Boston. Sure, he's never been convicted of anything, but several of his capos went to prison about a decade ago, throwing our name in the press for years. When I was little, I had no idea what any of it meant, but the older I got, the more I realized what people were saying about my family. And the kicker was, it's all true. My father is notorious throughout Boston, along with my older brother, Carlo, who's got quite the reputation for being a ruthless asshole, which I completely understand. To say we aren't close is the understatement of the c entury.

Honestly, I don't know why my father cares about me going to parties to begin with. It's not as though he takes any interest whatsoever in my life. Actually, scratch that. He doesn't want me getting a reputation of being a party girl, even in high school. Apparently, the only thing my father and brother think I'm good for is making a strong alliance with another family through marriage. Heaven help me if they think I've somehow been tainted by another boy before my father picks out a husband for me.

"I'll try." Bianca squeals on the other end of the line. "Don't get too excited. Luca has been watching me like a hawk since the last time I attempted to sneak out." I'm surprised my father hasn't nailed my window shut since trying to get to a party last weekend. Unless Luca never told him, but I'm sure as hell not going to ask the man if he's keeping secrets from my father. I'm perfectly happy to live in the illusion that it's our little secret because if my father found out that A, I tried to sneak out or B, Luca kept that information from him, we'd both be in a world of hurt. And I really want to go to this party tonight.

Until the night Luca caught me, I had a pretty sweet little escape route through the garden in our backyard. It was easy enough to avoid the guards who regularly patrolled the property if I was quiet enough. And I'd gotten pretty damn good at being quiet and staying out of people's way. With a brother like mine, it was a skill I'd honed years ago. But since Luca busted me last weekend, there's no doubt he's been keeping a closer eye on my bedroom balcony during his patrol shifts. It's not going to stop me; it just means I'll have to be more careful.

"Okay, pick me up in our usual spot at ten tonight."

"We're going to have so much fun!" Bianca practically yells in my ear.

I smile widely while thinking about the little act of rebellion I have planned for later tonight. The party is all well and good, but it's shoving my father's rules in his face—even if he doesn't realize I'm doing it—that really makes tonight worthwhile for me. I didn't ask to be born his little Mafia princess with his ridiculous demands and no hope for a future I get to decide rather than my father or my brother.

"See you tonight," I tell her before disconnecting the call and tossing my phone next to me on the blush-pink comforter.

Like I have so many times before, I wonder if my life would've been different had my mother survived that car crash. Would she have been the type of mom who stood up for me against my father? Or would she have been a subservient wife like I've seen from so many of the older women in this life? Would she have saved me from Carlo's painfully sadistic pinches when he thought I was stepping out of line? The number of times I've had to wear long sleeves in this house in the middle of summer is too many to count.

My mom died in a car accident when I was five. From what I remember of her, she had the warmest smile that could chase away any bad mood or hurt feelings. I was her little shadow, and she never complained. I used to love watching her dress up when she was going out with my father to a party or some other event. I'd sit on the floor of her huge walk-in closet surrounded by her long dresses and play with my dolls, dressing them up in gowns like the ones my mother wore. When it was time to put her face on, as she called it, she'd set me on the white marble counter of her vanity while she did her makeup, and then I'd try to copy what she was doing in the mirror. Of course it never looked as good as hers, quite the opposite in fact, but she'd tell me I was the most beautiful girl in the entire world.

Until the last few months of her life, she always had a wide smile on her face, but before she died, I'd sometimes see her staring off into nothingness and ask her what was wrong. She wasn't smiling or twirling me around in her bedroom, dancing to some silly songs like she always did. But as soon as she'd see the concern in my eyes, she'd plant little kisses all over my face and pretend it was nothing. But it was something. I knew it, and it makes me so sad to think she wasn't happy in the last days she was here.

After her accident, my father never spoke of her. I don't know if it was because he was completely heartbroken over losing his young wife and had to raise two kids on his own or what. Maybe it was the way men in this world dealt with a grief so deep they couldn't put words to it. When I'd cry to him and tell him I missed my mama, he would get a hard look in his eyes as though my saying that made him angry. He told me she was gone and there was no use crying over someone who was never coming back. I was five fucking years old, and I never forgot the look he gave me. That was the last time I brought her up.

It's Saturday night, and per usual, Carlo and my father aren't home. They're probably at one of their casinos or brothels the family owns throughout the city. They think I don't know how they make their money, but I'm not stupid. Being a girl in this house means I get overlooked most of the time, but I have eyes and ears.

I've seen and heard plenty here in my eighteen years, and not all of it pleasant. I've witnessed men come in bruised and bloody with fear in their eyes. I've heard about the whores—their words, not mine—that were too old to earn and needed to be disposed of. Hell, I've even seen a man they brought through the property once with a knife sticking through his gut from my bedroom window before they took him into one of the outbuildings I was warned never to enter. So yeah, I'm no dummy. It's not the press that makes up lies about my family being criminals. They are, in fact, much worse than what's been reported in the news, even if no one has been able to pin anything on my father. Not a day that goes by when I don't wish someone would come knocking on my door and haul my brother or father away in handcuffs. That's a shitty thing to think about your family, but they deserve to pay for their crimes, and I deserve to be free from the thumb my father keeps me firmly under, crushing my dreams and hopes for a future away from the Mafia.

Sitting up, I jump off my bed and head to the narrow staircase usually only used by our servants that leads to the kitchen to grab myself something to eat. I'm not a huge drinker, but it's my senior year. I think after surviving the last four years at one of the most pretentious and exclusive private high schools in Boston, I deserve to do a little partying. But waking up with a hangover after drinking on an empty stomach is not how I'd like to spend tomorrow. Learned that lesson the hard way. Of course, I'm not celebrating getting into a university like several of my friends. I wasn't allowed to even apply. My father doesn't see the need for a higher education when all that's expected of me is to marry the son of another powerful man. He's allowing me to take a trip to Italy this summer as a graduation gift, though. Who knows, maybe I'll get lost in the Italian Riviera and never make it back to Boston. It's a fun fantasy but highly unlikely, especially if Luca is tasked to be my guard for the trip instead of one of my family's other men.

Luca came to work for my family about two years ago. I swear, the second I laid eyes on him, my sixteen-year-old heart nearly exploded out of my chest. His dark hair was longer at the time, as though he didn't have the time or care to get a proper haircut. The way it fell into natural waves that he tucked behind his ears made him look like a rock star or something in my eyes. All the men in my father's employ kept their hair short and perfectly styled. Luca was a breath of smoky air that called to my rebellious nature, even at that age. When his piercing blue eyes landed on me, a warm blush crept up my neck and over my cheeks. I'd never experienced such a visceral reaction before in my entire life. God, and when he said hello to me, his voice was deep and a touch raspy like he's just woken up after a long night of doing whatever it was someone who looked like that would be up late doing. I didn't know what that necessarily would have entailed; I was only sixteen and had lived an extremely sheltered life, but I knew he was different. Or so I thought.

Then my brother found out about my crush. He was being his usual asshole self and barged into my room one afternoon as I was writing in my journal—not a diary because those were for kids—and found me writing about the future I'd longed to have with the scruffy bodyguard I'd met just weeks before. He grabbed the notebook out of my hand and started reading it out loud then ran down the stairs with it. Carlo continued reading what I thought about Luca's blue eyes and the way he smelled like sandalwood and cedar mixed with nicotine. About how I'd never liked the smell of cigarettes, but on him, it was alluring.

Right in front of Luca.

I'd never been so mortified as I was the moment Liuca turned to me. My brother was finishing a particularly private line about me wanting him to be my first kiss and wondering if his lips would feel as soft as they looked. Carlo was laughing so hard he was having a hard time catching his breath, and Luca didn't say anything for a moment. Until he laughed right alongside my brother and made some stupid comment about being irresistible to all the ladies. My brother grew serious and told him under no circumstances was he to ever touch me. Luca laughed it off and said he'd never be interested in a spoiled little princess, and I was just an obnoxious brat with delusional fantasies anyways. If you could hear a heart break, mine would have sounded like the crystal vase in our foyer shattering all over the tile floor.

From that day forward, I hated the man who ripped my heart to shreds with his callous laughter and cruel words. Soon after, he looked just like every other guard in my house with the short hair and stone-cold expression they all wore on their faces. But because I'm apparently a glutton for punishment, I occasionally remember who he was the first time I saw him and allow myself to miss that version of him and myself. The version of me who thought life could hold something more with someone who wasn't the cookie-cutter Mafia asshole.

After cleaning up from my solo dinner in my empty kitchen—the staff takes a break when Carlo and my dad are out—I head back to my room and pull out a pair of black skinny jeans and black motorcycle boots from the depths of my closet, hidden behind my school uniforms in a large old doll house. I haven't played with dolls in years, but it makes a great hiding spot to keep the nosy maids from tattling to my father about the clothes I have stashed in here. I even have a fake ID tucked away in here, not that I've had the opportunity to use it. There're too many people in Boston who know my father and brother who would surely run to them if they saw me in a bar drinking. High school parties are one thing, but I haven't been brave enough to take my fake ID for a test drive.

Sliding the jeans up my legs, I pair them with an old

midriff T-shirt and slide my feet into the boots. I tug my long, dark hair into a messy ponytail and outline my eyes with coal-black eyeliner, making my amber eyes stand out even more than usual. Slipping into an old black moto jacket I also have buried in the recesses of my closet, I give myself a once-over in the mirror and smile, feeling the thrill of escaping my gilded prison, if only for one more night.

The years of dance classes I'd been forced to endure have given me strength and control I doubt I'd have otherwise, which comes in handy as I throw a leg over the second-story balcony and shimmy down the drainpipe, landing quietly behind the shrubs next to the house on the soft ground. I stay still for a moment to catch my breath from the adrenaline rush I always feel after successfully scaling down the side of the house. When I'm sure there's no movement from around the property, I make my way to the garden, keeping to the shadows.

Passing through the garden undetected by the guards who roam the grounds at night sends another thrill through me. It's like a little game I play, but I'm the only one who knows we're playing. I've spent the last couple years tracking the guards' movements, and at this hour, they're switching with night duty and going over anything they need to inform the overnight guards about. That means they're in the gatehouse at the front of the property before they start their patrols back here. And since Luca was on the day shift today, he'll be up there and about to head home.

I've never given much thought to what would happen if I got caught; I'm that confident in my abilities to go through the property undetected. Until last weekend, it had never happened, but knowing the only guard who's ever caught me is on his way home, I'm not worried about it tonight. I've gotten good at making myself blend into the background. Not that I've ever really needed to. No one pays attention to the little Mafia princess in the first place. I'm just a stupid girl with no backbone of her own.

Being ignored and underestimated has worked in my favor.

The fence lining the property is in sight. A couple years ago, I found one of the bars hanging loose on the fence. I probably should have let someone know, but I didn't. Instead, I walked through the gap and felt my first taste of freedom. No sirens went off; nothing happened other than an excited thrill running through me at knowing there was an escape route if I wanted one. The next day, I came back and tied a wire to the loose post to make it look like it wasn't falling off to anyone who would have happened upon my little secret. It's how I've been sneaking out the last year.

A smile tilts my lips when I kneel to untie the wire, knowing that Bianca is waiting for me at the edge of the property, and sweet freedom is moments away.

"Hey, princess."

I yelp and fall backward hard on my ass, staring up

into the blue eyes of Luca.

"Son of a bitch," I whisper-yell. "You scared the shit out of me."

Luca steps away from the large tree trunk he was hiding behind and studies me as I jump up from the ground, my hand going to my chest. Taking several deep breaths, I try to calm my racing heart.

"Get back to the house, Giada. I'm assuming you can get back to your room the way you snuck out."

He's so damn dismissive of me.

"If I wanted to spend another night cooped up in my room, then that's where I'd be. Fuck off, Luca."

His eyes narrow as he takes a step toward me and I take one toward the fence.

"If I have to take you back to the house kicking and screaming, that's what I'll do, princess. Do not test me." The growl in his voice stirs something inside me. Vengeful defiance. That's what I'm going to call it.

I stare at the tall man in front of me. He should be terrifying me at this moment. I should be scared he's going to tell my father or brother he caught me trying to sneak out. But this isn't the first time he's caught me trying, and I know, as sure as the sun will rise tomorrow, that he never told them he caught me the first time. That little fact gives me some collateral here.

"You never told my dad or Carlo you caught me before, did you?"

His jaw tics, and I keep going. "So no, Luca, I don't think you're going to carry me back 'kicking and screaming.'" I tilt my head to the side. "You know exactly what will happen if I go back and they find out I left in the first place. I'll tell them both you caught me once. Then you can explain to them why you never brought that information to their attention to begin with. I'll make sure they know that you"—I point a finger toward his heaving chest—"knew there was a breach in security and didn't do anything about it. Who do you think is going to get in more trouble here? You or me?"

I tap my chin as though I'm contemplating what I just asked. It's a shitty threat, especially because I know what they would probably do to him if they found out he was keeping something from them. But dammit, I don't want to get in trouble either.

"What are you suggesting then?" he asks.

"Let me go."

"Absolutely not. You're not going out by yourself in Boston. Do you not understand what could happen if the wrong person got their hands on you? There's a reason you aren't allowed to go into the city without your brother or father."

"I'm aware, but I seriously doubt it's for my protection." If I had to guess, it's so they can keep an eye on me and make sure I'm not doing something inappropriate that would be unbecoming of a chaste and pure Mafia princess. After all, if I allow another man to ruin me, what good would I be to my family?

"Either let me go or come with me. Those are your two choices," I tell him.

His head rears back while his lip curls in disgust. "Go with you? To where?"

"A party. If anyone finds out, I won't rat you out. I'll tell them you tracked my phone or some shit and found me at the party and came to take me home. I'll take the fall." I mean, if we get caught, I don't see the point of dragging him down with me, but the likelihood of that happening is pretty low. It's not like this is my first rodeo. The other kids at my school keep everything under wraps. No one wants to get busted at a party drunk or high by the cops or angry parents. That's a surefire way to ruin our party spots.

Luca runs a hand through his short hair. God, I miss the long, wavy hair he had when I first met him. Now he looks like every other asshole bodyguard we've ever had.

He is, Giada.

"Fine," he eventually breathes out. "I'll go with you to make sure you don't get in trouble. But for fuck's sake, Giada, this needs to be the last time. This is fucking dangerous for both of us."

A giant smile spreads across my face, somewhat shocked that my threat worked.

Before he has a chance to change his mind, I squeeze through the bars and he follows but has a harder time getting through. When we get to the other side, I don't say anything as we walk to the road along the other side of the property where Bianca knows to meet me.

"I mean it, Giada. Last time." There's that growl again.

My gaze travels to the man walking next to me, who looks wholly uncomfortable with this entire situation. "Relax, Luca. It'll be fine. I do this all the time."

"That doesn't make me feel any better," he mumbles before we reach Bianca's Mercedes idling on the side of the road.

She gets out of her car, looks at Luca then back to me. "What's going on?"

"He's coming with us."

Bianca's eyes widen as Luca walks to the driver's side of the car.

"And I'm driving," he tells her.

She nods quickly, scrambling to open the back door of her car. "O-okay."

When we get settled in the car, I feel her eyes boring into the back of my head, silently trying to telepathically communicate something along the lines of *what the hell's going on right now?* "Luca busted me, and we came to an understanding. He wouldn't let me go alone, so here we are. It'll be totally fine," I tell her.

Bianca scoffs. "Yeah, showing up with a bodyguard to a party in the middle of the woods won't look weird at all."

She's right. Luca's shoulders are tense as he maneuvers the car back onto the road. There's no chance he'll blend into the crowd at a high school party. Hell, I don't think there's a crowd anywhere he wouldn't stand out in.

"Can you not look so..." I try to think of exactly how

to put my thoughts.

"So what?" he asks, never taking his eyes from the road or looking like anything other than an intimidating killer behind the wheel. Shit, he probably is, for all I know.

"So murdery," I finally finish.

"No," is all he says as we drive in silence.

I can tell Bianca is unsure if going to this party is still a good idea.

"Hey, look at it this way." I smile widely and turn in my seat to face her. "At least we have a DD for the night."

"Don't push it, princess," Luca says.

Okay, so maybe this isn't one of my more brilliant ideas, but the night is young. As I've told Luca and Bianca, I'm sure everything is going to be fine.

Chapter Five

Luca

I'M AT A FUCKING high school field party. Well, not a field exactly. We're in the middle of the woods, but it's pretty reminiscent of the few parties I went to in high school, right down to the giant bonfire in the middle of the clearing that's filling my nose with the scent of burning wood. I wasn't much of a partier in those days, knowing my coach would have my ass if I got busted for underage drinking, not to mention I didn't want to disappoint my dad. I was one of those people who never wanted to disappoint anyone, really. Always believed in staying aboveboard. That was my old life, though. The one I rarely think about, aside from reminding myself why I go through the hell of having to face the man who had my parents killed on a daily basis.

Finn's plan for me to introduce myself to Carlo and, by extension, his father took about a year to come together. I spent time hanging out in the few bars frequented by that asshole, Carlo, and found my in one night when a fight broke out. I was there in time to save Carlo from getting stabbed. Of course, I took a slice to the ribs, but after getting stitched up by the "family" doctor, Carlo decided to repay me by asking if I needed a job. Said he'd made a few calls and liked what he heard about me. It didn't hurt I'd made friends with a couple of the guys I knew who did some penny-ante work for him. I was their "muscle" a few times when shit went sideways. It took nearly six months to get an introduction to Carlo, and then another six of drinking with him and stroking his inflated ego like all the other wannabe gangsters he surrounded himself with before I saved his ass in that fight. He was in need of a few guards at his house and asked if I wanted in. He appreciated that I was willing to put my life on the line for him. Said if I wanted to make some real money, he would see to it that I would get on a crew if I proved loyal. I guess when you beat a man bloody with a knife sticking out of your ribs, you prove your worth.

And somehow, that led me to a high school party in the middle of the woods on a Saturday night.

When I caught Giada trying to sneak out of her room a couple weeks ago, I never in a million years imagined she'd try again. Would it have changed my decision not to tell her father? No. If I'd told him, he would no doubt tell her brother, and Carlo is an asshole of the highest order. He couldn't give two shits about his sister. And Francesco is about as checked out as a father as I've ever seen. There's no one who actually cares about that girl in the house. Not saying I do, but I know a desperate girl who hates the confines that her position as Francesco Cataldi's only daughter has her tied in.

It's a fucking shame what they expect of women in this life. Finn swears up and down it's not like that in his family, and I have to believe him. Not like I'd know any different.

I've met plenty of Francesco's capos through the last few years and their wives as well. Most of them are shadows that trail their husbands at parties. The same husbands who I've seen at the brothels when Carlo needs an extra body to follow him. It's not often I leave the grounds, Francesco and Carlo have had the same personal guards since I've been here, but there's been a handful of times. And that was plenty for me.

When Carlo found some diary his sister was keeping, he read it out loud in front of me. Giada had a crush on me when I first came to the house, made evident by what she wrote. Watching her grasp for the notebook Carlo held over his head as he read its contents out loud told me everything I needed to know about what kind of brother he was. He didn't care that doing that to a sixteen-year-old girl was probably one of the cruelest, most embarrassing things to have happened to her in her short life. I thought it was a dick move, and it put me in a position I never wanted to be in. Of course, I knew she had stars in her eyes. Giada wasn't as adept back then at hiding her feelings as she is now. And I reacted the way I knew a man in this life would be expected. I laughed and acted like she was a stupid little kid, saying things about her to make her hate me and make her brother think I was a heartless bastard like him. She was crushed, and I felt like a complete asshole.

Ever since that day, she's barely looked at me unless it was to sneer at me behind her brother's back. She's gotten pretty damn good at hiding her true feelings under the mask she wears in front of her brother and father. Good for her. She should hate me. She should hate every man in this life who would treat her like a nuisance or a person who doesn't deserve respect. She'll likely be married off to some asshole who isn't much better than her brother or father, but I like seeing that rebellious fire in her eyes. It'll be a sad day when it goes out. And it will. It looks like it has for just about every wife or girlfriend I've met in my time with the Cataldis.

That's probably why I'm standing in the middle of the woods keeping an eye on Giada and her friend. Let her think she has a say in her life while she's still young. I don't need to be the one to burst her bubble when she realizes how short-lived this part of her life is going to be. It won't be much longer, a few years maybe, before her father signs her life away in a marriage contract. Knowing what I do of the Cataldi men, he's simply waiting until another family makes him an offer that's too tempting to pass up. There's already been a couple, but nothing that comes close to benefiting him in the way he thinks marrying the only daughter of the head of a powerful Mafia family should.

Hopefully I can bring the old man down before it comes to that. I thought being in the house would clue me in how to make that happen, but I haven't been able to find anything I can take to my cousin yet. I'm still earning my stripes, as they say, and haven't been privy to the private meetings in his office or overheard any useful information. But I'm patient and know that at some point, I'll be moved to a crew. Then I can start digging in. Not at first, though. Nothing says *mole* like being the new guy and things going to shit from the start, but eventually, I'll start hitting these fuckers where it hurts—their wallets. Spending time in the house, it's become more than apparent the only two things that hold any merit are money and power. Without the money, they don't have the considerable power they've amassed throughout the years. So, that's where I'll start.

Giada and her friend are in a circle with a couple other girls, talking and laughing. I told her and Bianca under no circumstances were either of them to drink any alcohol tonight, and thankfully, I haven't had to knock any cups out of their hands. The last thing I want to worry about is if Giada can get back into the house undetected or her friend driving home drunk. There were plenty of mumbles in the car about me being a wet blanket and maybe trying to take the stick out of my ass for once, but I just turned my hard stare at the girls and they both shut the hell up.

My gaze sweeps the crowd again. No one has paid me much mind. It's not unusual for these kids to be around security since this is a party of kids who attend Giada's overpriced and privileged-as-hell private school. I'm the only guard in attendance, but everyone here is so accustomed to seeing bodyguards they look right past me as though I'm simply part of the scenery. Rich little pricks.

When my eyes land on a group of boys Giada and her friends were talking to earlier, I catch one of the little punks drop a tablet in a beer he just poured from the keg and swirl it with his finger, a smarmy grin covering his smug fucking face.

Oh, fuck no. I don't care who the intended target is; that shit will not be happening on my watch. I begin to make my way over to the little asshole who's about to feel what it's like to have his jaw broken when he beelines toward Giada and her friends. I watch as he walks straight up to her and tries to hand her the cup. She shakes her head, not accepting it, but he's a persistent little shit and tries again.

I see fucking red.

"Come on, babe. Just have one drink with me."

"I'm not drinking tonight, Tyler. I already told you."

When Giada sees me, her eyes grow wide at what I'm sure is an absolutely murderous expression on my face.

"You drink it," I say to Tyler as I come to stand next to Giada.

He looks at me then back to a confused girl at my side.

The little shit gives me a withering look as though I'm the hired help and shouldn't deign myself important enough for him to respond to.

"It's for Giada, not me. Here, babe."

"Why do you want me to drink it so bad, Tyler?" she asks the boy, suspiciously looking from him to the cup.

I feel her eyes on me as I stare at the side of Tyler's face. She's a smart girl. She knows something isn't right. This isn't the first time tonight someone has offered her a drink, but it is the first time I've intervened.

"Forget it," Tyler says. "Bianca, you want a beer?" He holds the cup to Giada's best friend, who stands silently watching the scene.

"How old is Tyler?" I ask Giada.

"Just turned eighteen."

As soon as the words are out of her mouth, I knock the cup from his hand and send it flying into the grass several feet from us. Before Tyler has a chance to react, my fist flies into his stomach and he doubles over.

I don't know if his being underage would have stopped me from teaching this kid a lesson, but it seems reasonable that I could potentially find myself in less trouble if he's an adult.

With him hunched over in pain, I take the opportunity to smash my fist into his jaw, which sends him flying back and landing with a thud on the ground. I don't waste a second and grab him by the front of his shirt as I rain blow after blow to his face. Screams and cheers barely register as blood flies from the punk's face with every punch I land.

When I stop, Tyler's face is a mess of blood, snot and tears, but he's still conscious. Barely.

"Listen to me, you little fucker. If you ever try that shit on another girl, I'll find you and finish the job. And believe me, I will find out. You've just landed on my radar, Tyler. Lucky you."

"My father will have your job for this," he groans out.

Kid's got balls; I'll give him that. Too bad he's so fucking stupid.

I pull him closer to my face, and with deadly calm, I tell him, "You just tried to drug Francesco Cataldi's daughter. Do you honestly think your father can do anything about it? If he finds out, not only will you never be heard from again, but neither will your parents. You want to risk that?"

The last thing I need is Francesco or Carlo finding out I was here with Giada. She said she'd take the blame, but I'd rather not have to deal with figuring out how to smooth anything over, especially if they find out this wasn't the first time she's snuck out.

"I'm willing to show you mercy and let you live. Francesco Cataldi will not."

All bravado drains from his eyes with that last statement. I'd like to think the idea of losing his parents would be a factor, but I have a feeling he's the type of asshole who doesn't give a shit about anyone but himself. Hell, he could very well be hoping his parents are out of the picture soon so he can inherit everything. Nothing surprises me about these fucking rich kids anymore. But when I told him Francesco would make sure he dies a bloody and painful death, well, that changed things for him.

"I won't do it again, I swear," he coughs out.

I slap his face a few times and smile like a psychopath. "I knew you'd make the right decision. Take care, Tyler."

When I release my grip on his shirt, everyone is staring between me and the boy on the ground, groaning in pain.

I find Giada's eyes, and what I see there startles me. It's not hate, far from it. It's the same way she used to look at me before her brother read me her diary, and I laughed in her face with him. Shit. I sure as hell don't need this kind of complication inside the family.

"Let's go." I turn, expecting her and Bianca to follow, which, thankfully, they do. When we make it back to the car, Bianca silently gets in the back, and I drive us to the edge of the property, where she'd picked us up.

Turning to face Bianca, I pin her with a stare. "No more fucking parties in the middle of the woods. You two are prime targets for assholes like that one back there, and I won't be there to protect you next time."

Bianca's smile makes me uneasy. She's looking at me like I'm some knight in shining fucking armor. Jesus Christ, if watching someone beat a person to bloody hell does it for her, she's in serious trouble. Neither of these girls should find anyone in this violent life appealing. Least of all, someone like me.

Giada opens the door, and I get out as well, allowing Bianca to get in the front so she can get the hell home.

"I'll call you tomorrow," Bianca calls before taking off.

Giada stands on the side of the road with the same look in her eyes as she had when we left.

"Let's go," I say, stomping past her to the fence line.

"Thank you," she says, having to walk a little faster to keep up with my long strides.

"I didn't do anything someone with a shred of decency wouldn't have done."

"That's not true. Those guys were more than willing to watch him drug me."

I stop abruptly and she nearly collides with my chest when I whirl around. "Like I said, anyone with a shred of decency. Those assholes don't have any. They're spoiled rich fuckers who are used to getting their way and not having to answer to anyone. Case in point—they tried to drug the daughter of a very dangerous criminal and thought they'd get away with it. Stay away from them, Giada."

She nods her head jerkily, like one of those toys you stick on your car's dashboard. "I will. I swear. I honestly didn't think that would happen. I mean, I've never heard of it happening."

"You really think just because you haven't heard about it, that means it's never happened? Wake up, Giada. This kind of shit happens all the time in this world. You need to watch your back. I'm not going to be there to always do it for you. If I wasn't there tonight, he would have drugged you and done God knows what to you. I'm sure he's done it before, but probably threatened the girl somehow so she wouldn't talk. That's the kind of world we live in, and you need to be a hell of a lot more careful if you're going to survive in it."

I'm so damn frustrated. At her. At that asshole. At myself. The fact that young girls even have to worry about shit like this pisses me the hell off.

"I'm sorry, Luca. I'll be more careful."

"No more parties," I tell her through gritted teeth.

She nods once. "None." Her eyes soften and lose the remorse she had, to be replaced with a glint of something sweet. And fucking dangerous. "I've never seen you so mad," she says with a breathless whisper.

For fuck's sake.

This is what happens when a girl is starved for attention from the men in her life. I'm certainly not the one she needs to be doing any sort of pining over. I did what I did because that's what my dad taught me. You protect women. When you see shit that isn't okay, you handle it. If it means with your fists, then so be it.

It's a habit I shouldn't have, considering I'm supposed to be blending in with the pricks around me. None of these guys give two fucks about a woman in trouble. Hell, they'd be more likely to take a turn and record it than do anything to stop it. And Giada needs to think I'm the same as these assholes.

"Let's get something straight, *little girl*." I emphasize the last part to hurt her, and judging by the look on her face, it works. "The only reason I beat that kid to hell was because I work for your father. If anyone thinks they can mess with this family, then we're all fucked."

"Oh, please. If it had been another girl, you would have done the same thing." Her hand rests on her hip as she challenges me. "You aren't like my brother and the rest of the goons around here, Luca."

"That's where you're wrong, princess. I'm exactly like them. If it had been anyone else, I would have let those boys have their fun. But seeing as it was my boss's daughter, I put a stop to it."

I fucking despise the words coming from my mouth as well as the look on her face.

She holds my stare for a solid minute before shaking her head and letting out a huff of humorless laughter. "You all make me sick."

"Good."

Let her be disgusted with what I just said. It's safer for me if she doesn't harbor any notions that I'm a good guy. Those thoughts won't do anything but bring suspicion to my doorstep if she walks around with hearts in her eyes and someone notices. The last thing I need is anyone thinking I'm indulging her crush in any way, shape, or form.

"Get back to your room. I've had enough of your shit tonight." My voice is cold, and though it isn't a particularly chilly night, Giada shivers at my tone.

She spins on her heels, and I watch her walk back to the property. Fuck, I was just supposed to be doing one more round before I went home to my shitty apartment for the night. I wasn't supposed to get tangled up in this bullshit.

The next day, I'm up bright and early and back at the house when I'm called into Francesco's office. I haven't seen Giada this morning, but since the guards weren't gossiping about finding her outside of her room, I assume she made it back in without being detected. It's not like she hasn't had practice. I don't for one second believe the first time I caught her was the first time she's snuck out.

"Luca," Francesco greets when I step inside his office.

"Sir." I bow my head to show respect to this asshole even though that's the last thing I feel for the man. In every interaction, every smile I've given the man, I've had images of me putting a bullet between his eyes playing on a loop. He thinks it's respect behind my eyes when, in reality, it's murderous thoughts of the day I get to have him on his knees with my gun pressed to his forehead.

His office is pretty standard of what you would expect to find in any mafia boss's office. Dark leather furniture and dark-red carpet coupled with wood-paneled walls make the space seem like the den of a supervillain. I'm sure Francesco wants people to think he's some sort of criminal kingpin, which at the moment he is, but every villain has a weakness. I just need to find his so I can get the hell out of the expensive hellhole I find myself in every day.

One of his capos, Alberto, rises from the leather club chair in front of Francesco's oversized mahogany desk. The man has obviously been living the good life if his portly belly and cigar-stained fingers are anything to go by.

Alberto holds out his hand, and I take his meaty palm in a firm shake. "Hi, Luca. Come sit."

I have a seat next to him as Francesco's beady eyes scrutinize me. "You've always been a good guard, Luca. Loyal."

Fuck, maybe Giada got caught and that's why I didn't overhear the guards talking about it. Maybe they didn't want to give me a heads-up that shit was about to go down.

"I appreciate that, sir."

"I hate to lose you," Francesco continues.

Double fuck.

"But I like to reward loyalty. Never let it be said I'm not a fair man. Right, Alberto?"

"Absolutely, boss," the man next to me replies.

Francesco leans back in his seat. "Alberto needs a couple guys on his crew. Wanted to know if there was anyone within the organization who deserves a leg up. Someone loyal who keeps their mouth shut and does as told but isn't afraid to get dirty when the situation calls for it. I remember how you came into my employment, Luca. You saved my son's life even when it could have cost you your own. You know what Alberto and his crew do?"

I look at Alberto and nod. "He runs the whores."

Francesco and Alberto dip their chin in confirmation..

"Among other things," Alberto says. "How would you like to come work for me? It pays better than being a guard, that's for sure. And the perks aren't half bad, either." The dark chuckle that comes from both men raises the hairs on the back of my neck.

"Gotta start them somewhere," Francesco says before turning to me. "I'm giving you a promotion, Luca."

My lips tip up in a grateful smile, but it's not for the reasons they think. Maybe now I'll finally be able to get some useful information about the organization so I can pass it to Finn and take these bastards down.

"Thank you, sir," I say with restrained excitement, completely for their benefit. "I won't let you down."

"You'd better not," Francesco says, nailing me with his hard gaze. His mouth splits into a smile, taking the sting out of the not-so-subtle death threat.

"See, Alberto. Reward your men. That's how you keep them loyal." He turns to me again. "The second Carlo brought you to me, I knew you were more than just a guard. But I had to make you prove yourself. Make sure you were going to stick around." A.k.a., didn't fuck up and get a bullet to the head. I didn't end up six feet under, so I guess in this life, that's proof enough that you're ready for bigger things. "Alright, Get out of here. I'm sure Alberto is ready to show you the ropes. You have a lot to learn."

I stand and shake Francesco's hand. "Thank you for the opportunity, boss."

"Do me proud, son."

There's no doubt I'll be doing someone proud with this new position, but it sure as hell won't be him.

"Of course, sir."

"Go on and grab some breakfast. I need to go over a few things with Alberto."

I nod at the two men and leave the room, shutting the door firmly behind me. When I look up, Giada is leaning against the wall a few feet from the door.

"Listening in?" I ask.

She shrugs noncommittally. "So you're out of here."

"Yup," I say, heading toward the kitchen.

Of course the little princess has to follow.

"Well, congratulations. You get to run a prostitution ring with Alberto," she says snidely.

I look at her with surprise, and she rolls her eyes. "Oh, please. It's not like I don't have eyes and ears."

"You need to keep what you hear to yourself, Giada. If the wrong person hears you talking..."

She rolls her amber eyes once more. What the fuck is with eye rolls and teenage girls?

"I sincerely hope your parents are proud of you, Luca. I'm sure being a glorified pimp was your mother's dream for you. See ya around." Giada spins and walks away from me.

I stare after her for a brief moment.

I wouldn't know what my mother's dream would be for me. Your father had her killed.

And I have every intention of making him pay.

Chapter Six
Luca
Four Years Later

I FUCKING HATE THESE warehouse meetings. They're fucking dangerous and too many variables mean I could end up dead. Every time I have to drive Alberto out to the middle of nowhere to meet some shady asshole, the thought crosses my mind that the reason he's taking me along is because they found out what I'd been up to. I've covered my tracks so well the last four years I've been on his crew. There were times I almost had myself convinced I belonged with these pricks. That's what living a double life does to you. Makes you start believing what you're trying to convince other people of. It eats at your humanity, bite by sickening bite.

This meeting, in particular, is the side of Alberto's business that, until recently, I wasn't to take part in. We're meeting someone to buy a girl. It's the second time he's included me in a purchase. The first time was only a few months ago. I felt so disgusted with myself I went home and threw up then proceeded to drink myself into oblivion. I called Finn and told him what happened. He was glad Alberto had finally deemed me worthy to take part in that side of his business.

I'd been collecting from the girls he had on the streets and shaking down the pimps that were on Alberto's payroll the last four years or so since I was moved to his crew. No one cares about prostitution, and that certainly isn't going to bring down a criminal empire. But this skin trade shit? Yeah, that made a shit ton of money for the Cataldis, and Finn has decided that's how we're going to take them out. It's risky as hell selling women. Seems a substantial amount of their take comes from it now. Topple that, we cripple the entire organization. I just hope to hell I get enough information before I have to sit through any more of these meetings.

I texted Finn the location we were at. Not because we're ready for a full takedown but because the girl they're bringing in is connected to the Black Roses, an MC my cousin does a lot of business with. Word is this girl, Charlie, has some information that could help the Cataldis take out my family. Her "handler," as Alberto calls him, is some piece of shit that did some work for Finn in the past, but this asshole decided getting high on the shit he was supposed to be unloading was far more important.

The only reason he isn't six feet under is because he's Cillian's cousin. In a rare show of loyalty to anyone other than Finn, Cillian asked for Jace's life to be spared when it was obvious that Jace was coming up short on money and product. I don't think it had so much to do with saving his cousin rather than saving his mom the heartache. His aunt died years ago, and the kid was raised with his dad, who apparently was a complete asshole. Cillian's mom tried to take Jace, but his father refused. She always felt guilty about the distance she allowed to be put between them, especially seeing who he'd become. I guess she held out hope that Jace would turn his life around. Hate to be the one to break it to her that it's most likely going to be a very short one. Jace was keeping tabs on drop locations and safe house sites that he had in a handy-dandy little notebook his ex-girlfriend stole from him. She ran with it after one of the enforcers for the Black Roses MC beat the shit out of him for abusing her. The girl got away, and Jace ended up in the hospital with a grudge the size of Texas.

When Jace found her, he wanted the book and revenge on the Black Roses, which led to him getting in contact with the Cataldis.

Pulling up to the abandoned warehouse in the middle of nowhere Massachusetts, I spot a beat-up old car but nothing else.

"He must be inside," Alberto says next to me in the luxury sedan with blacked-out bulletproof windows. "Keep sharp. This guy is a fucking tweaker and jumpy as a stray alley cat. Not to mention he's willing to sell out his cousin to the highest bidder. I don't trust him as far as I can throw him."

"Got it, boss." Gee, he doesn't trust a criminal. Shocker.

We exit the car along with Fausto and Ernesto, the other two goons he brings everywhere with him, and head into the warehouse, our eyes constantly scanning our surroundings. The warehouse smells musty, as most forgotten buildings do. Flecks of disturbed dust float through the air, illuminated by the sun streaming in through holes in the broken painted windows.

"Alberto, there you are. Glad you got my message."

My eyes land on a greasy man who looks as though he hasn't slept or showered in at least a week. Next to him is a girl in a red bikini tied to a chair with blood oozing from a cut above her brow and a blackening bruise around her eye. Charlie's gaze scans the four of us, and though her eyes hold anger, they're still unfocused as she realizes the predicament she's in. He must have drugged her with something to keep her compliant.

"This is the girl, then?" Alberto asks, walking over to the girl strapped to the chair, studying his newest acquisition. Though the plan wasn't to buy her from Jace, Alberto knew he had her and was more than willing to cut a deal for her and the notebook when we got here.

"Never let an opportunity to put a few extra dollars in your pocket pass you up," he said on the way over here.

"Yeah, man, this is her," Jace replies. I can tell the informal way Jace is addressing Alberto is getting under his skin. I have to hide the chuckle that threatens to escape. These Mafia assholes like to think of themselves as some sort of royalty, so I always get a kick out of it when they're talked to like any common street thug by someone who doesn't know better.

"Where's the notebook you promised us?" Alberto asks, circling the girl and most likely counting the cash he thinks he's going to get from the sale of her.

"Well, that's the thing," Jace starts. "She doesn't have it. The dumb bitch gave it to Ozzy, so it's at the clubhouse. But I'm sure we can work something else out since you've been helping me."

With the promise of getting information on my family and the Black Roses, who do business with the Monaghans, Carlo has been keeping Jace hidden until he can get the notebook back. Too bad for him, his ex found herself under the protection of the Black Roses, and it's taken a little longer. Now, it seems impossible since she handed it over to the club's president, Ozzy.

"That was not our deal," Alberto says, irritated that the plan isn't going according to what was promised. "You were supposed to bring me the notebook, then we would pay you accordingly for the information. All you've brought me is a bruised-up girl and trouble from not only the Irish but the Black Roses."

I see where Alberto's going with this. He wants Charlie, but he's going to try to undercut her sale price under the guise of him being inconvenienced.

"Right, yeah, but you know, sometimes things don't work out like we planned." Jace is starting to fidget and sweat, as he should, considering he wasn't able to deliver on what he promised. Alberto isn't known as the forgiving type. "I can't get you the notebook, but what about her?"

And there it is. He's desperate to prove he's useful to the Cataldis, and Jace, the stupid fuck, just played right into Alberto's hand. Charlie's blue eyes widen into saucers, realizing her ex-boyfriend is about to sell her into human trafficking. Fuck, I hate how scared she looks. I want to sneer at the asshole standing in front of me, both of them, then grab the girl and get the hell out of here. But I can't blow my cover, not when I'm finally in a position to get what Finn needs. Fuck, my cousin better hurry the hell up.

"I've heard you guys deal in more than blow and guns. You could get a pretty penny for her on the auction block, no?"

Alberto looks like he's considering Jace's offer, but I know it's all for show. "Yes, she would do nicely, I think. What do you think, Luca?"

I cast a lascivious grin in Charlie's direction and hate myself for it. "We would make a pretty penny off her, boss."

The tweaker nods his head, looking between the scared girl and Alberto. "There you go. With a little training and a strong hand, I'm sure she could fall in line. She always did for me."

The hardest part of this undercover bullshit has been having to stand by and watch shit like this happen. When I was a guard in the house, I didn't see it as much as being on the street, but the abuse they inflict on people they deem weaker is fucking atrocious, especially with women. I hated the way I saw Carlo and Francesco treat Giada, but it's nothing compared to what I've seen during my time with Alberto. The things I've had to participate in. It makes my fucking skin crawl.

I think of Giada then and the last time I saw her outside of her father's office. The way she looked at me like I was going to be just like every other asshole in her life. I thank God she doesn't know the half of what really goes on behind closed doors. She may have to deal with her father and brother treating her as though she's nothing more than property to be auctioned off to the highest bidder in marriage, but at least she's never been sold for a few hundred dollars for a couple hours on the street, or sold off as someone's sex slave. The fire in this girl's eyes reminds me of Giada's. I hope like hell neither of them ever loses it.

"And what do you expect out of this new deal?" Alberto asks, shaking me out of my thoughts.

"Just a finder's fee. I understand if she isn't worth as much as what we originally agreed on, but I think something in the ballpark of ten thousand is fair, don't you?"

Dumb fuck could have asked for double and Alberto would have paid.

"Fine, fine," Alberto agrees as though he's being magnanimous in settling for the girl he planned on buying anyways. "Luca."

I step forward and hand Jace the cash from the inside pocket of my jacket. I don't allow myself to look at Charlie, sure that if I do she'll see the disgust I feel over this entire transaction. Buying humans makes me sick to my fucking stomach, along with the men currently negotiating for the price of her life.

Jace walks over to Charlie and unties her from the chair. They speak a few words to each other, but I can't hear them over the blood rushing in my ears. Where the fuck is Finn? I can't go through watching another girl be handed over to the monster who just paid for her, and if I step in, I'll blow my cover.

Jace roughly grabs the girl by the arm and hauls her toward Alberto. "Pleasure doing business with you."

Before Alberto can make a move toward Jace and Charlie, the door to the warehouse flies open, and three men walk in, opening fire.

Finally. Finn, Cillian and some other man who I don't know are here. I quickly duck behind one of the stacked pallets and begin returning fire, purposely aiming away from my cousin and the rest of his crew. It's absolute melee in the warehouse. One of Alberto's men goes down, and I see the blood pouring from his unmoving chest. One more piece of shit I don't have to worry about.

"Did you sell us out, you fucking cunt? How the hell did the Irish know you were here?" Alberto yells.

A smile crosses my lips. He thinks Jace called the Irish. Wrong, asshole.

I hear Alberto yell something else at Jace but don't catch his exact words before another shot rings out. I duck low and see Alberto lying dead on the floor with a bullet between his eyes.

"We're getting the fuck out of here," Jace calls just before a metal door at the other end of the warehouse opens and light pours in.

I catch sight of Fausto when he pops around a large cement pillar off to the side of the warehouse he'd thrown himself behind when the shooting started.

"Get the girl!" he yells to me as he returns fire.

"On it," I call back and head toward the door. When I'm behind Fausto, I lift my gun and put a bullet in the back of his head.

This isn't the first time I've killed a man in my time with the Cataldis, and just like the other three times, satisfaction washes over me. One less piece of shit walks the planet today.

"Clear," I call to my cousin as I turn to head toward the door Jace hurried Charlie through. Just as my hand reaches the knob, a gunshot rings out on the other side. I open the door, praying I don't see a dead girl on the other side.

Charlie is bent over Jace, her shoulders shaking as she cries over his prone body. Just then the thunder of several motorcycles reaches my ear, and I quickly shut the door. The Black Roses are here, and I know they'll take care of her. No one is supposed to know who I am. My cousin trusts the MC, but the fewer people who are aware of my involvement in this, the better. Not to mention that girl still has a gun in her hand, and there's no doubt if she shot her ex, she'd have no problem turning the gun on me in a heartbeat.

Turning around, I see my cousin walking up to me with his gun raised, still playing the part of my enemy.

"Declan and Sean, go outside and see if Ozzy needs any help. I'll take care of this piece of shit."

Both men holster their guns, walking past me.

When they've cleared the building, Finn and Cillian lower their weapons.

"That was fucking close," Cillian says.

"Your cousin is out there with a bullet to his gut," I tell him.

Cillian nods and looks toward the door. There's no remorse or sadness in his eyes over the fact that his cousin is probably lying dead in a gravel parking lot. "It was always going to end up this way," he says, turning his back toward the door.

Finn clasps Cillian on the shoulder then turns to me. "Well, this is a shit show."

"Yeah," I agree, looking around the warehouse at the three dead men.

"It might be time to pull you," Finn suggests.

I thought about this when I put a bullet in Ernesto's head. There's no easy way for me to stay with the Cataldis. It would be far too coincidental if I ran back to them without a scratch on me. Plus, I'd look like a coward in their eyes if I came back unharmed.

"You need to shoot me," I tell him.

Both he and Cillian turn an incredulous gaze to me.

"Come again?" Finn asks, his eyebrow quirked in question.

"Think about it. If I walk back into that house unharmed, they'll be suspicious immediately. It needs to look like I ran for my life after trying to save Alberto. The way I look at it, I'll take a shot to the arm and tell them we were outgunned and I watched Alberto and the other men fall. Then I'll tell them I got away when you were running after Jace to get him and the girl."

"Fuck, Luca. I don't know if that's going to work. What if they get suspicious? The first place to look for a mole is at the one person left standing."

"That's why you need to shoot me, Finn. It sells it."

"We could pull you now—"

"No." My voice is resolute and leaves no room for argument. "Listen, I hate those fucks as much as you, and believe me, I'd love nothing more than to get the hell out of there, but the skin trade is booming and the Cataldis play a large role in it. Taking out Alberto is the tip of the iceberg. All that did was take away one man who was helping Carlo. It's not enough. We need more information. With Alberto and the other two gone, he might move me up in his place."

"That's a big 'might.'"

"It's all we have right now."

"He's right," Cillian says. "If Luca comes out now, we could very well be screwing ourselves in the long run."

Finn looks anything but convinced as he contemplates the possible outcome of pulling me from the Cataldis too soon.

"Fuck," he says, running a hand through his disheveled dark hair. When his gaze flicks back to me with eyes eerily similar to mine, I see the decision in them.

"Let the record show I hate this idea."

"Noted," I reply as he raises his gun and fires.

Once I'm a good distance from the warehouse, I call Carlo.

"Fuck, man! They knew we were there. It was a setup. I think that asshole Jace double-crossed us. The fucking Irish showed up then the Black Roses. I barely made it out."

My arm hurts like a bitch and I'm getting blood all over Alberto's car, but all in all, I think I'm selling my bullshit pretty well.

"Where's Alberto?" Carlo barks.

"Dead, boss. Everyone's dead."

"Shit," he hisses into the phone. "Okay. Are you whole?"

"I got shot when they barged in. It's just a graze, but fuck, it's a good one."

At least that part I don't have to fake. Finn refused to

shoot me through and through, insisting a deep graze would be enough to sell it. Considering I've never been shot, I'd have to agree.

"Jesus. Okay, where are you?"

"About two hours north of Boston."

"I'm going to send you the location of one of the docs we use out there. You have any cash on you?"

"Yeah. Jace only had half on him when the Irish showed up."

"Alright. Give the doc five grand then bring me the rest. That should be enough to buy his silence."

Should be, but not will be. Glad to know my staying out of the prying eyes of the police is so important to him.

"Where's the girl and that fuckwit Jace?"

"She got away with the Black Roses. Pretty sure Jace is dead." If he's not now, he will be soon.

"Shit. The Black Roses are about to be even more of a pain in my ass than they were before," he mumbles. "Get stitched up then meet me at the house."

"Got it, boss."

We hang up and my phone chimes with the location of the doctor a minute later with a message that he's expecting me.

Thirty minutes out. Thank fuck.

After getting stitched up, I get back in the bloody car and head to the Cataldi compound. Carlo meets me at the door and looks me over, noting the scrub shirt the doc gave me, considering mine was a bloody mess.

"Let's go into my office."

I haven't been here but once since I went to Alberto's crew. The house looks the same. Same gaudy marble pillars and marble tiled floor. The staff keeps it looking clean with fresh flowers in the entryway, but the inhabitants are dirtier than ever. It was Alberto's men who worked the human trafficking for Carlo. Carlo made it clear he didn't want the other crews involved. I think it was because not everyone in the organization had the stomach for it, but Alberto was a twisted fuck who had no qualms about seeing the fear and desperation on young girls' faces. In fact, he got off on it. That and he was making more money for the organization and himself than any of the other capos.

We step into Carlo's office, which is significantly different from his father's. Instead of the dark reds and old world feel his father's office had, Carlo's is cold and lifeless, much like the man himself. Modern black leather furniture with a glass-topped chrome desk fills the space along with large black and white photos of the Boston skyline hanging on dark gray walls. There's almost a sterile feeling to everything. Maybe he thinks it makes him look more modern, like he's taking the family in a new direction, stepping away from tradition.

He walks behind his desk and leans back in his chair before he waves to the square, low-back leather seat in front of him, signaling for me to sit.

"I'm putting a pause on the trafficking operation," Carlo informs me.

My brows shoot up in surprise before he continues.

"My father isn't happy with the heat we're sure to get from the Irish and the Black Roses. He's not interested in a war at the moment."

The look of disgust on Carlo's face tells me he doesn't agree with his father, but since Francesco is still the head of the family, he can't say shit about it.

This also puts me back to square one. The hope I had that Carlo and Francesco would put me in charge of a crew now is dead, right along with the three assholes at the warehouse.

"I'm putting you back on guard duty until this shit with the Black Roses and the Irish blows over. It won't be forever, but you know how things worked with Alberto. As soon as I can convince my old man that pausing operations is a stupid way to handle things, you'll be on a crew and earning again."

"Anything you need, Carlo."

"Your loyalty is noticed here, Luca. Don't ever think we don't see how you've always been willing to do what we ask without complaint. There's been plenty of guys who come and go who don't share the same work ethic you do."

By go, he probably means a bullet to the brain. That's the only way you leave this life.

More than anything, I want to be the one to wipe his and his father's existence from this planet. But again, I plaster a fake smile on my face like his praise means the world to me and quickly come to terms with the fact that I'm going to be stuck with this family for the foreseeable future.

"Thanks, boss."

Carlo dismisses me with a nod.

I exit the door and remember the girl who was waiting on the other side of a different office the last time I was here. She had such fire, such rebellion in her eyes every time I saw her, much like the girl Jace brought to the warehouse today.

It's been years since I've seen or heard anything about Giada Cataldi. I know she hasn't married yet, so she's still living in the house. Hopefully, she doesn't act like the same bratty eighteen-year-old I left here four years ago. Then again, knowing what I do of her, I have a feeling that hope is going to die in vain.

CHAPTER SEVEN
GIADA

AFTER GRADUATION FOUR YEARS ago, my father didn't know what to do with me. I knew he was going to be marrying me off at some point, but no one had come to him with a marriage proposal he deemed worthy enough for a man in his position. My lack of a husband has nothing to do with me or what I want, only my father's ego. Which suits me just fine. I wasn't allowed to go to college. Carlo told my dad why waste money on an overpriced education when the only thing I was really good for was marrying the right man and having kids. No matter how many times I brought it up to my dad, he shot me down. I fucking hated my brother for that.

Thankfully, my father has been content to forget about me these last few years. It's hard to find a "suitable" match when you're the most powerful family in the state, shit, maybe even the entire country, for all I know. But it won't last forever, so I've been living life to the best of my ability while I can. That means I spend as little time at the house as possible. I discovered a love for travel and have spent the last five months in Europe, visiting all of my favorite places, especially Italy.

The first time I visited my mother's family there with my bodyguard, who thankfully wasn't Luca, I was apprehensive, to say the least. I haven't spoken to them much through the years. My grandmother never wanted my mother to marry my father, but she didn't have much of a choice. Her husband worked for my grandfather, who was just as cold as my father. My father wanted her as a wife and that was that. My mother's father died before I was born and after my mother died, my grandmother moved back to Italy to live the rest of her days with her family there. I never blamed her for leaving me; we weren't close. My father rarely allowed her at the house. From what I remembered of her, she never had a kind word to say about the man and he wasn't going to allow anyone in his house to say a cross word about him.

When I knocked on my grandmother's door after so many years without seeing her, the reunion was full of tears, yet joyful. She kissed my cheeks over and over, barely believing I was there. It was the first and last time I was able to spend time with her. She passed away between my trips out there, but I never stopped visiting the family I met on my first trip. The second year I went to Italy, my cousin Isabella and I decided to travel through Europe together. We ate, drank, and shopped our way through Italy, Spain and France. It became a yearly tradition, and this year was no exception—only this time, I extended my trip to five months instead of the usual three.

Before I left, Isabella made an innocent comment about me just moving to Italy and living with her in the large apartment her parents bought for her after she graduated university. I laughed, but the cogs started turning in my mind. What *if* I moved to Italy? Technically, I'm an adult and don't need my father's permission. Even now, sitting in the car that was waiting for me at the airport, I know whether or not I can legally do as I please my father still needs to give me permission. There's no way he'd allow me to stay if I took off without it. Determination steels my spine. This is the year I convince him to let me go, to let me live the life I want and not the one he's mapped out but is completely disinterested in.

Pulling up to the giant house, a weight of sadness drops into my stomach. Coming home is always sad for me, and that's a bitter pill to swallow. I hate feeling out of place in my own home, but this house has never felt welcoming. It's a prison that feels suffocating to come back to, especially after spending time away.

The car stops in front of the looming house with tall ivory pillars in the front built to make it look extravagant and rich, much like the people living inside. It's all a show, all an act. Sure, we're richer than any family I know, but the cost was paid by the blood of others. The ivy reaching to the roof adds to the rich, stately feeling that my father wants people to see, but all I see is a cold mausoleum where happiness goes to d ie.

God, I really didn't want to come back here.

"Welcome home," one of the guards says after opening the door for me.

"Thank you." My voice is soft and meek, like I've been trained to keep it since I was a young girl. Nothing like the woman I was allowed to be in my time away. Yes, I'd had a guard with me, Benny, but with only the one around it was easy to pretend I was some rich heiress on vacation instead of being under my father's thumb. Plus, Benny liked his wine with dinner and was usually in bed by ten o'clock. It didn't exactly take stealth of any kind for Isabella and me to sneak past his room and have a night on the town here and there. It was nothing like being in the States and having guards constantly roaming the property. Not that that was able to stop me when I was in high school.

After the night of the party in the woods, when that guy attempted to drug me, I never snuck out to one of those parties again. Not because Luca demanded it of me, but because after he beat the hell out of that kid, no one hardly looked at me. I was persona non grata for the rest of my senior year of high school. If there were any more parties, I certainly didn't hear about them. The only person who would still have anything to do with me was Bianca, but since she went away to university, our time together has been limited, to say the least. I see her when she's home on winter break, but that's about it since I've been spending my summers anywhere but here. Bianca graduated college this year while I was away. I can't believe it's already been four years since we were in school and we were sneaking out to go to high school parties. It will be a nice change of pace to have someone to spend time with outside of the house while I'm home.

Walking into the house with the ornately carved marble table in the foyer, I spot a huge vase of calla lilies sitting on top. Though I love the beautiful flowers, they always remind me of a funeral. White calla lilies were strewn over my mother's casket at her funeral. It's a reminder that beautiful things come to die in this house and this life.

While the other guards bring in my bags, I take a little detour into the kitchen to grab myself some water before going to my room and unpacking. I'm not surprised my dad or brother didn't come to greet me when I walked through the door, but I'd be lying if the stark reminder of the difference between the warm family I've come to love in Italy and the coldness of the one I have here didn't sting just a little. I've long since given up the illusion that I'm anything more than a bargaining chip for my father, but I never feel it quite as sharply as when I first walk through that door after months away. I just chalk it up to the little girl I used to be, wanting to do everything to make her daddy love her and pay attention to her.

The bright yet silent kitchen greets me as I make my way to the stainless steel sink and pour myself a glass of water. A brief memory flits through my mind of my mother kneading bread on the white marble countertop, flour all over the front of her apron and a smudge of it on her nose while I sat on the counter next to her with one of my dolls. She gave this kitchen life when she was alive, always singing and a lot of times dancing with me while we waited for whatever she was baking to be pulled from the oven. It's one of my favorite memories because of how important she made me feel by allowing me in her space. She'd always have a smile on her face as I rambled about whatever nonsense a four-year-old girl came up with, never making me feel like a nuisance.

Startling out of my memory with the slam of the back door, I turn and see the one person I never expected to lay eyes on again in this house.

Luca Bennetti.

"Well, look who finally came home to her castle." His voice is still rich, with a deep timbre rolling off his tongue. He doesn't have the typical Boston accent since he didn't grow up here. I think I overheard someone calling him the California kid at some point, but he doesn't sound like someone who grew up on the beach surfing every day, either. With great irritation, I have to admit the last few years haven't been unkind to him. He seems to fill out his suit even better than the last time I saw him. My eyes appraise him from the tips of his expensive black leather shoes, trailing up his long legs and over his midsection, where the only bulge I see is the one of his gun under the dark suit jacket. It's when I get to his eyes that I realize the toll the last several years have taken on him. When I knew him before, he had a dark-blue stare that seemed to scrutinize everyone and everything around him. Now his blue gaze looks almost...haunted, as though he's seen some things that have changed him to the very marrow of who he is. With one blink it's gone and quickly replaced by a smirk and, dare I say, a challenge to rise to his little dig about me being some sort of princess.

"Wow, it's a real treat to be greeted by one of Alberto's glorified pimps on my first day back. Slap around any hookers today?"

"Nice to see you still have a mouth on you, Giada." For a brief moment, I swear there's a glint of pride in his gaze, but that can't be right. Luca is like every man in this organization. To them, a mouthy female is anything but something to be proud of or even tolerate.

"What are you doing here, Luca?" I set the glass in the sink before pinning him with my amber stare. "Are you here for some business with my father as one of Alberto's little lackeys?"

Years ago, I eavesdropped on the conversation he and that lecherous old man had with my father. I was worried Luca and I would be found out after I blackmailed him into following me to a party rather than telling my dad what I was up to. Turns out my father wanted to reward him for his loyalty to the family and put him on a crew that dealt in the prostitution side of the family's business.

"Alberto's dead," he says with no regret behind his words. "I'm here until things...settle."

I have no idea what that means, and honestly, I don't care. Having my teenage crush in the house again isn't going to affect me in any way. Nope. Not at all.

"Well, you have fun around here. I'm sure it's not as exciting as what you've been up to the last four years but don't worry, I have no doubt you'll fall right back into a routine."

"We will," he says with a small smirk playing on his lips.

"Excuse me? What do you mean *we*?"

"Your father wants you to have a personal guard, and I drew the short straw."

Welcome home to your own personal hell, Giada.

I shoot Luca an obstinate look, my eyes narrowing on his smug face. "We'll see about that."

Stalking past the man in front of me, I stomp out of the kitchen in search of my father.

"He's in his office," Luca supplies as I head in that direction.

"Thank you." My tone is prim and doesn't express any sort of gratitude for his input.

Two quick knocks and my father calls for me to enter. When I open the door, what I find on the other side stops me in my tracks. My father sits behind his desk, pale as though he hasn't stepped out in the sun for years and skinnier than I've ever seen him. In the last five months I've been away, he looks like he's aged ten years.

He looks from the paperwork on his desk to me, then flips a page over and goes back to reading whatever I interrupted without showing any emotion on his gaunt face.

"You made it home," he says indifferently.

"I did. Uncle Louis sends his love."

He doesn't respond. It's as though I'm not even standing here.

"I wanted to talk to you about having a personal guard."

My father finally looks up from his oh-so-important papers and nods to the man standing behind me. "Close the door, Luca."

I turn my head and see Luca standing in the doorway before he dips his chin and does as my father asks, like the good little lapdog he is.

"Father, I've never had a personal guard. There really isn't any reason for me to have one now."

"You had one in Italy."

I don't bother telling him that Benny's only mission in Italy was to get drunk at dinner and promptly pass out, allowing Isabella and I to do whatever the hell we pleased until the early hours of the morning.

"Right," I concede. "But that was different. I was away from home and—"

My father slams his bony hand on the desk and meets my gaze, nothing but anger behind his eyes. "And nothing, Giada. I want you to have a guard, so you will have a guard. There is no room for argument or discussion. You don't decide what's best for this family. I do. You seem to have forgotten that in your time away. Maybe I need to rethink my leniency on such matters. It seems I've given you too much freedom."

He hasn't given me anything but an opportunity to be out from under the oppressive life that I'm unfortunately tied to for a few brief months a year. A life I never asked for and don't want.

"No, Father. You don't need to do that. I think I'm just tired from the travel." The last thing I want is for him to suddenly decide that to make Luca's job easier, he's going to confine me to the house. "I'm sorry."

My father studies me for a moment before returning his attention to the papers on his desk. "You're too much like your mother, Giada. It was a tragedy what happened to her. See to it you don't make the same mistakes."

I'm stunned silent. My mother died in a car accident. Why would he say that to me?

"Is that all?" he asks, annoyance rippling through his tone with the fact I'm still standing in front of his desk.

"Yes. I'll see you for dinner, Father."

"You won't. I have a meeting that is going to run late."

I nod, though he doesn't lift his head to notice and turn to leave. Straightening my spine, I walk toward the door and Luca opens it for me. When he steps out of my father's office and shuts the door firmly behind him, he grins at me.

"Didn't turn out how you planned, did it, princess?"

I want to rage, to tell him to go to hell with his smart remarks and devastating blue eyes. Instead, I roll my eyes and cross my arms. "So you have to trail me everywhere like a puppy?"

His jaw clenches. In fact, his entire body seems to tense before he narrows his eyes. "Yes."

A wide smile stretches across my face. "Good. Be ready to leave the house at ten."

"We aren't sneaking out again, princess."

I shake my head from side to side while my cunning smile remains. "Of course not. I don't need to sneak out anymore, Luca. I'm a grown woman now, or haven't you noticed?" His eyes flare for a moment. "I'm meeting Bianca later, and since you're my new shadow that means so are you."

I turn on my heels and brush my long, dark-brown hair over my shoulders. This is going to be so much fun.

The club Bianca and I are at is packed with sweaty bodies dancing along to the loud music. The place is dark minus the light coming from the DJ booth and, of course, the bar. It's a typical Boston party spot and one I knew would irritate the hell out of Luca. When I called Bianca to have her meet me here after talking to my father, she was more than a little surprised this was the one I picked.

"Girl," she says, leaning into my ear as we stand at the bar waiting to order our drinks. "Luca does not look happy."

I look at the man in question and feel a certain sense of satisfaction. He looks just as unhappy now as he did when I met him at the front door in my tight white bodycon dress that dipped low in the front and was held together by silver chains in the back that reached well below my waist. Nor was he happy when I pulled a flask from my small jeweled purse and took a long pull of vodka before leaving the driveway.

"That's just his face, Bianca. Tragic, if you think about it."

I plaster a fake pout on my face, and Bianca laughs.

After getting our drinks, Bianca and I toast with the cheap plastic cups and take a sip.

"I'm honestly surprised you wanted to come here. This really isn't your scene," Bianca tells me.

"I wanted something a little different." I shrug a shoulder, not wanting to be honest about why this is where I chose tonight because, honestly, it's a little juvenile. But I can't seem to help from acting like the brokenhearted teenager who wants to prove some point to Luca rather than the woman I've grown into and recognize he's just doing his job. It's never felt like that for me, and I fucking hate it.

"Hi." A man who looks like he's spent a few too many hours at the gym and way too much time doing his hair slides between Bianca and me. "I saw you standing here and thought to myself, that girl looks like she needs to dance."

Ugh.

"Do I?" I say coyly instead of brushing him off like I normally would. You know, if these were normal circumstances. "With whom?"

His too-white smile broadens as he moves a tad closer. "Me, of course. Come on, legs. Dance with me."

Legs? God, this guy is a douche. Not that it matters right now.

Another man, who seems to have spent an equal amount of time at the gym working on his arms, is trying to chat up Bianca. She doesn't look impressed.

"Sure," I tell the guy in front of me. I set my empty cup on the bar and catch Bianca's gaze before tilting my head toward the dance floor. Seeing my intent, she rolls her eyes but allows the meathead she's talking to lead her to the floor.

We stay at the edge where Luca can keep an eye on us, the one concession I gave him without argument, as the man wearing far too much cologne grinds against me. Who the hell told this guy, or any other one for that matter, that dancing with a girl like you're trying to fuck her in front of everyone is attractive? I try to back up, but he keeps pulling me back to him. After a few more songs pass, I'm ready to call it quits since this guy can't seem to keep his damn hands to himself. He leans in and shouts in my ear, "I'm gonna go take a piss. Don't go anywhere."

He smiles down at me, and I force a plastic one on my face, having no intention of following his command.

Satisfied with my reaction, he smacks his hand on his friend's shoulder and signals toward the bathroom. His friend nods and leans into Bianca, probably giving her the same line.

They leave and Bianca comes over to me, rolling her eyes. "These guys are fucking douchebags, Giada."

I throw my head back in laughter. "I know. Let's not be here when they get back."

"Agreed," she replies.

I turn toward where I last saw Luca standing and find the spot empty.

Jesus, for someone tasked with my protection, he's doing a bang-up job already.

Bianca and I dance for another song sans the leeches that were attached to us, and Luca isn't back yet. "Let's go get another drink," I suggest.

We get our cocktails, and as I turn toward the dance floor again, Luca comes from the direction of the bathrooms.

"We're leaving," he says when he approaches.

"Uh, no. We're not. Bianca and I are waiting for a couple guys to come back from the bathroom."

His eyes darken as he takes the drink from my hand and places it on the bar. "They aren't coming back." Luca turns to Bianca. "I've called you a car to take you home since you've been drinking."

"Um, yeah." Her eyes dart between Luca and me. "Okay, thanks."

She never could stand up to him even when he was being an unreasonable Neanderthal.

"We'll walk you out," Luca tells her and holds his arm out, signaling for us to walk in front of him to the exit.

I give him a hard glare before turning my head toward where he came from and see the guy I was dancing with tumbling into the crowd with blood all over his crisp white button-down, holding his bloody nose.

My head whips to my asshole bodyguard. "Seriously, Luca?"

"Let's go, Giada. Now." His tone leaves no room for argument and since Bianca is already on her way out, I decide to follow rather than cause a scene.

When we get outside, the chilly night air cools my heated skin. Luca takes one look at me and takes his jacket off to cover me.

"I'm fine," I grit out as he hands the valet his ticket.

He walks back over and leans in close, his lips nearly brushing my ear when he whispers, "That may be, but I'd rather not every person in downtown Boston see the shape of your hard nipples in that dress."

I quickly look down and see my nipples poking through the dress that I'm not wearing a bra with before closing the jacket around myself.

"Thank you," I reply with a tight voice.

Bianca's car pulls up to the curb just before the valet returns with ours.

"I'll call you tomorrow," I tell my friend and unwitting partner in this little scheme to make Luca's time guarding me as painful as possible before leaning in for a hug.

"I'm so glad you're back," she says, returning the embrace. "It'll be like old times with both of us home." When she pulls away, I give her a grateful smile. It will be nice to have someone to hang out with now that I'm back in the States for the next several months.

With Bianca safely in the car and on the way to her parents' house, Luca directs me to ours and opens the door for me.

"Such a gentleman," I say with a sarcastic bite.

"Get in the damn car."

The second my feet are inside, he slams the door and stalks to the other side, opening his door and getting in. He puts the car in drive with an angry tug on the gear shifter and pulls out in traffic to take us back to my house. With his hands on the wheel, it's then I notice the slightly swollen red knuckles across his fist and my anger spikes.

"What the hell is with you punching that guy? Just because he was dancing with me? That's taking it a little far, even for you." Honestly, I don't know what would be considered too far for him since I haven't been around him in years.

Luca shakes his head and lets out an exasperated sigh. "I swear to Christ, Giada. I don't know how you do it, but you manage to find yourself surrounded by the worst possible men."

"Present company included."

Luca tilts his head side to side and cracks his neck but doesn't comment.

"We were just dancing." I let out a very mature huff of annoyance.

"What you think you were doing and what those assholes thought you were doing were two entirely different things."

"Did you ask them before you decided to act like a caveman and break that guy's nose?"

"I didn't have to ask him shit, Giada. When they were in the bathroom, they were practically high-fiving each other, convinced that they were going to take you and Bianca home, regardless of whether or not you came consciously. At least that's what it sounded like they were saying. It was hard to tell between the lines of coke they were snorting up their noses off the fucking bathroom counter."

I take a breath and stare out the window. It was a dumb idea to go to that club. The place is notorious for assholes like that hanging out and girls getting way more fucked up than the couple of drinks they remember consuming would be responsible for. But I knew Luca would be miserable standing there all night among the sweaty gym rats looking for a quick lay.

There isn't anything for me to say. He's right, but I'm far too stubborn to admit that to him.

The next twenty minutes are spent in silence on the

way back to my house. When we pull into the long driveway, we're confronted by a sea of police cruisers, some unmarked but all with their bright red and blue lights flashing.

"Luca," I choke out, my panicked gaze colliding with his.

He parks behind one of the unmarked cars and turns to me. "Stay here."

Just as he gets out of the car, several figures emerge from under the portico. I slowly emerge from the vehicle, my eyes never leaving the man the police have in handcuffs.

My father.

I look at Luca, whose jaw is tight, as my father is led to one of the cars, a hand going to his head before being shoved into the cruiser.

Luca turns to me, my eyes wide with disbelief. In all the years I've been alive, my father has never been arrested at our home. I hold Luca's stare as thoughts race through my head. What are we supposed to do? What am I supposed to do? Does Carlo know our father is on his way to jail?

The moment that last thought crosses my frazzled mind, I see my brother standing on the steps that lead into the house, a small smile ghosting his lips. I know that smile, remember it quite well from our childhood, and I know damn well it doesn't mean anything good.

Before anyone can stop me, I'm running toward my brother. A few officers shout, but I pay them no mind.

"Carlo, What the hell is going on?"

My brother gives me his signature bland look. The good thing about being in Italy nearly half the year is I don't have to deal with the asshole standing in front of me.

"Oh, you're back."

"Yes Carlo," I begin with a bite to my voice. "I got back this morning. Are you going to tell me why our father is being shoved into a police cruiser?"

"I would think it's obvious, Giada. He's being arrested." He looks back toward the driveway where the cars are pulling out as though the fact that I'm standing here hardly registers in his thick skull.

"Jesus *fucking* Christ, Carlo. I'm not an idiot. Where are they taking him? Have you called his lawyers?"

He lets out an annoyed sigh and looks behind me. I turn briefly and find Luca at my back, his gaze flicking between Carlo and me. "You couldn't have kept her in the car?" he asks my bodyguard.

"She ran off before I could stop her. Do we know anything?"

"They're taking him to the station. The feds showed up about thirty minutes ago with a warrant. I'll know more when I talk to his lawyers."

The fact that Carlo is answering Luca's questions and treats me like an annoying fly buzzing around sends rage coursing through my body.

"Talk to *me*, Carlo. Tell *me* what's going on. I'm his daughter, goddamnit."

He finally looks back at me. There's still annoyance in his cold gaze, but something else, too. Something darker. "What's going on is our father has been arrested, most likely never to see freedom again. What that means for you is I'm now in charge of the family. What I say goes, and right now, you need to go to your room and stay there until you can calm the hell down. I don't need your grating voice in my ear."

He turns and walks back into the house, effectively dismissing me like he always did when we were growing up. To say Carlo and I have a strained relationship is putting it mildly. Even when I was a kid, he never had patience for me, often screaming at me to get out of his way or physically pushing me away. I never understood why he seemed to hate me, but there was never a time when he didn't treat me like the gum on the bottom of his shoe. Now, he expects me to ask how high when he tells me to jump?

Well, screw that and screw him. I refuse to lie down and let my brother dictate my future.

Chapter Eight
Luca

GIADA IS LEFT STANDING under the portico after her brother unceremoniously dismisses her by turning his back and walking away. If the furious look in her eyes is anything to go by, I'd say Carlo is pretty damn lucky there are no sharp objects within his sister's reach. She looks about five seconds away from stabbing him in the back.

"Maybe you should let me take you up to your room," I offer.

Her angry gaze swings to me. "Well, looks like you have a new master to bow to, Luca. Please don't let me keep you waiting. Run along after my brother." She waves her hand in the direction of where her brother walked off.

Why the hell I thought this girl was going to accept any form of help from me is anyone's guess. When I saw her face as they were putting her father into the police cruiser, the devastation written in her amber eyes, I couldn't help but feel sympathy. I know damn well what it's like to have your world turned upside down. Different circumstances, sure, but for a brief moment I saw a side of Giada I'd never witnessed before and I wanted to help, to be here for her. I certainly won't make that mistake again.

"Whatever, princess. Have it your way."

Turning on my heels, I leave her standing outside and go in search of Carlo. I find him sitting in his office with a glass of scotch in his hand and his phone to his ear. He motions for me to have a seat while he listens to the person on the other end, humming his agreement a few times before thanking whoever he's talking to and disconnecting the call.

"Scotch?" he offers as though this is simply a friendly little chat and we didn't just witness his father being hauled away in handcuffs. I'm not particularly surprised. I've come to know Carlo as an ice-cold asshole. I don't know if the man feels any emotion whatsoever or if there's just a black hole in the center of his chest that craves to be filled with power and other people's pain. It seems to me the latter rings true for most, if not all, days.

Playing along with his relaxed attitude, I nod and he pours another drink from the bottle sitting on his desk.

"Is my sister in her room?"

"Yeah." At least, that's where I'm assuming she stormed off to.

"There's going to be some changes around here happening a hell of a lot sooner than I planned," Carlo tells me while taking a drink of his scotch.

"I'll say. Did the lawyer give you any insight?"

"Nah. He won't know much more than what the warrant says until the arraignment on Monday. It's a hell of a thing. I was hoping we still had some sway in the US attorney's office. We should have known something."

The fact they had any sway at all is news to me. Though not surprising. Considering all the shit Francesco's been responsible for, I'm shocked the man wasn't put away years ago.

"Giada being here is gonna be a headache," Carlo tells me. "Too bad the old man didn't marry her off years ago. Now I'll have to deal with that shit, and let me tell you, finding anyone that wants to take her on is going to be a pain in my ass. Who's going to want a wife with a father in jail and what looks to be a crumbling organization?" The way he sighs and looks into his glass of scotch, as though somehow the liquid will hold the answers to his question, is laughable. He truly expects me to sit here and feel sorry for him that he's going to be the one to deal with it.

"No matter," he says, straightening. "When we have more details after Monday, I'll see if I can persuade the attorney in the case to lose some evidence. Shouldn't be too hard. Usually, a little threatening goes a long way with those guys. Fucking pricks." He sips his drink again, and I take a healthy swallow of my own.

"What do you need from me?" I ask.

Carlo tilts his head back and forth, considering my question. "I want you to keep an eye on Giada. Make sure she doesn't get herself into trouble."

"Any trouble in particular you're concerned with?"

He shrugs. "She's too headstrong. Did you see the way she demanded answers from me? She would've never dared with our father, especially with cops all over the place. I need her to stay out of my way. If the wrong people see her mouthing off to me, they're going to think I'm not fit to lead if I can't even handle my own sister. The truth is, Luca, my father wasn't going to be head of the organization for much longer as it was. This moves up the timeline and actually may work in our favor when all is said and done."

"I didn't know the boss was retiring."

Looking like the cat that ate the canary, Carlo leans in with a grin on his face. "My father is dying, Luca. No one knows except me, him, and his doctors. So if he gets convicted, the feds will think that's the end of the Cataldi organization. And he won't be in prison long before the cancer finishes him off. If he doesn't get convicted, then he's dead in the next year anyways. And the feds will think the same thing, at least for the next few years. He's always been the face of the family, and they'll assume we'll be in shambles. It buys us time for me to take the organization in the direction I've been working on without raising any red flags with the law."

There's no way to hide the surprised look on my face at Carlo's admission. The old man is dying. It also makes sense now why Carlo isn't worried about him being in prison. He knew he was going to be taking over sooner rather than later. Too bad it won't be my bullet that wipes his father from this earth.

"I had no idea he was sick."

"No one did."

"Not even Giada?"

"He was going to tell her after he secured a marriage contract, though that plan has been put on hold until we see what side he falls on after his trial. There are a few things up in the air until we see whether or not he beats the charges."

I consider everything Carlo's just told me, but he seems to take my silence as disappointment that I'm not more involved.

"Don't worry, Luca. I'll make sure to bring you in once everything is set up. We're doing this how my dad wants, for now, so keep your mouth shut about the cancer, yeah?"

"Of course, Carlo. My lips are sealed."

He nods and finishes his scotch. "Think I'll head out for a while. Work off some of this stress." His lascivious grin tells me he's going to visit one of the brothels. "I'd like for you to stay on the property until shit gets sorted. It'll make it easier for you to keep an eye on Giada. If she needs to leave the estate, I want you on her at all times."

"Is there some sort of threat we should be worried about?"

"Not yet. But the last thing I need is the feds trying to talk to her or another organization vying for power and trying to use my sister to do it."

That would certainly ruin his plans to do the same shit. I suppose, in his mind, he has the right since she's now going to be his property, along with everything else his father is sure to give him control over.

Taking that control may be a bit more difficult than Carlo realizes. Part of my job for my cousin is to keep my eyes and ears peeled for anything he can use. I've heard the whispers from other capos about Carlo. I've seen the eye rolls behind his back. If I were a betting man, I'd put money on the other capos wanting to take over in the power vacuum that's sure to come with Francesco no longer heading the organization. They'd never dare with the old man at the helm, but Carlo? Yeah, I'm damn sure he's in for a fight.

"Alright. I'll head over in the morning and grab a few things before Giada gets up."

I stand to leave, but Carlo stops me before I make it to the door. "Things are going to be changing around here, Luca. All the assholes that thought we were dying out are in for a rude fucking awakening." His smile is so damn smug I wish I could punch it off his face.

"Can't wait." Things are going to change, and I, for one, am looking forward to watching the entire Cataldi organization crumble from the inside out.

I wake before the sun and head to my shitty little

apartment in Boston. The only reason I like this place is because no one asks questions. This isn't the type of building where anyone is interested in getting to know their neighbors, which suits me fine.

The first thing I do is grab my burner phone from the crawl space I cut into the ceiling of my closet. It's as good a hiding spot as I could figure out in the small one-bedroom apartment.

It's early as shit to be calling Finn, but I don't know the next time I'll have a chance. I don't think it's safe to bring the phone to the estate. It's not as though there's reason to believe Carlo is suspicious of me, but on the off chance that he or someone else goes through my things when I'm not around, it'd be pretty damn hard to explain away a phone with only two numbers on it belonging to my cousin and his lieutenant, Cillian.

When I dial Finn's number, he answers in a groggy voice, "Luca. Everything good?"

"Yeah. Did you see the news yet?"

"Fuck no. I just went to bed two hours ago. What's going on?"

"Francesco Cataldi has been arrested on RICO charges."

Finn releases a low whistle. "Well, that's something. What's Carlo saying?"

"A lot of talk about him being in charge now and things changing, but he hasn't told me anything specific. Just said when the time is right he'll pull me in. He also confided that the old man has cancer and doesn't expect to make it more than a year."

"Shit. Well, that's definitely news. This is the first I'm hearing about it."

"They didn't want anyone knowing. Carlo was saying if his father goes to prison, it gets the heat off him, and even if he doesn't, he'll be dead soon. So no matter what, Carlo will be running things."

"Wow, he sounds real broken up about losing his old man," Finn comments with disgust ringing in his tone. That's the thing about my cousin. Family means everything to him. Nothing like what I've seen from the Cataldis. Especially where Giada is concerned.

"Yeah, here's the thing, though. He wants me at the house to babysit Giada. I'm keeping my apartment, but the phone is staying here. I wouldn't put it past him to search his employees' rooms or some shit."

"Makes sense. Need me to come water your plants or something?"

I bark out a laugh. "No, asshole, you don't need to water plastic."

After I moved into my apartment, my cousin thought a little housewarming gift was in order and got me a fake plant to stick in the corner to make the place feel more homey, he said.

"See, it was the perfect gift," he says, chuckling into the phone.

"Yeah, yeah. Anyways, if you don't hear from me for a while, that's why. I don't know when I'll be able to make it to my place or how often."

"Alright, cousin. Stay safe and keep your ears open. If Carlo starts making moves, I want to know everything you can find out. Sounds like we'll have you out of there soon."

"I fucking hope so."

"If it was getting to be too much, you'd tell me, right?"

"We've gone over this shit. Francesco is on his way out no matter what, but the way Carlo makes it sound, they'll rise from the ashes like a fucking phoenix or some shit. The plan stays the same for now. I stay inside so we can take them out and make their organization nothing more than a cautionary tale."

"If you're sure..."

"I'm fucking sure." I'm not throwing away years of work.

"Alright. Listen, I need to get a few more hours of shut-eye. You good?"

"Fine, Sleeping Beauty. Get your rest," I reply.

"Fuck you, asshole."

"Love you too, cousin."

I disconnect the call and pack a bag before grabbing the large envelope where I keep the only evidence of my past. Pulling out the stack of pictures, my eyes land on the first one of me and my dad, Frank, taken at the lake we used to camp and fish at. I was eight and had just caught my first "big one." My dad's smile is beaming, and I look so damn pleased with myself as I grin into the camera. It was a great day. The one beneath it is of my mother and father holding me when I was just a few weeks old. The look of love and pride was evident on both their faces. They had no idea that less than a month later, they'd lose it all. Both are pictures of families ripped apart by death before their time. Both pictures remind me of why I'm doing this, of why I'll watch the Cataldi empire burn to ash at my feet.

When I get back to the house, Giada is in the kitchen dressed in a pair of black slacks matched with a green sweater, her amber eyes shining with determination.

"You're up early," I say, walking to the coffeepot to grab myself a cup.

"I need you to take me to the police station." She leans against the counter and brings her coffee cup to her lips, taking a long sip.

"Turning yourself in?"

She sets the cup on the counter and cocks her head, her eyes narrowing at me as I lean against the counter opposite her. "That's pretty fucking tasteless considering we just watched my father be arrested last night, Luca. I want to visit him."

She's right. It was tasteless, but I have no sympathy for the man sitting in jail. Not when my parents are buried six feet under at his command. Looking at the pictures at my apartment this morning has all the anger I felt when I came to Boston boiling too close to the surface. It's not Giada's fault, but I'm finding it difficult to look at her and not see the sins of her father. Fair? No. Honest? Yes.

"I doubt they'll let him have visitors other than his lawyers yet."

"I'm going down there, Luca. With or without you."

I have a feeling this falls under the purview of my keeping Giada out of trouble. She's liable to march in there and make demands, possibly landing herself in a cell next to her old man for throwing a temper tantrum if she doesn't get her way.

I let out a frustrated breath and take several healthy swigs of my coffee before setting the cup in the sink. "Fine. Let's go."

When we pull up to the station, where we've been told by her father's lawyer he is being held, Giada's jaw clenches as she looks at the front of the building.

"You alright?"

"Carlo thinks he's in charge. Did he tell you that? Now that my father is in jail, he thinks he can run my life. Thinks he can make decisions that affect me without caring one way or another how I feel about it. That I don't need to know anything about what's going on with my own family."

"So, what? You're here to get it from the horse's mouth? Do you think your father is going to let you go and live however the hell you want just because he isn't around? Giada, you're smarter than that."

A humorless huff of laughter escapes her lips. "Not

according to Carlo." She releases a heavy sigh. "I don't know. I just want someone to tell me what the hell is happening."

Giada is desperate for answers, but if she thinks she's going to find any here, she's dead wrong. Francesco Cataldi has never felt the need to explain anything to anyone, certainly not his daughter.

"Okay, let's go," I say and exit the car before rounding the hood and opening her door for her.

Giada walks into the police station and to the front desk with her head held high. "I'm here to see Francesco Cataldi," she tells the male officer manning the front window.

He looks her up and down, a bored expression covering his face. "And you are?"

"His daughter."

He looks something up on his computer. "No visitors allowed," he tells her.

"May I speak to your superior please?"

The annoyed officer tilts his head to the side and gives her a hard look. "He ain't gonna tell you anything different. No visitors," he reiterates more firmly than the first time he denied her.

Giada lays her hands on the counter and leans closer to the glass partition separating her and the officer. "Excuse me, Officer White, but until your supervisor comes out and tells me I'm being denied access to my father, I'll be waiting right over there." She points a slim finger at the chairs in the lobby. "And I won't move from there until I get an answer."

The bored officer rolls his eyes then looks back at his computer. "Suit yourself. Have fun wasting your time." He doesn't look at her again for a few moments and she rightfully takes it as the dismissal it's intended to be.

Giada walks to the plastic chair and sits, crossing her legs with her hands folded on her lap, sitting tall as though she wasn't just told to get the hell out.

I have a seat next to her, but she doesn't acknowledge me, instead staring at the wall opposite us.

"Do you really want to sit here all day? I don't think he's going to budge." I realize trying to reason with the woman is futile, but the last thing I want to do is be stuck in a fucking police station all day.

"If you have other plans, then by all means, don't let me stop you."

"You're a real peach this morning," I mumble, leaning back in the chair.

"Excuse the hell out of me, Luca. I'm so sorry if my attitude isn't to your liking after my father was arrested, and I'm being told my life is now in the hands of my asshole brother."

Before I can utter another word, a man in an expensive navy suit walks through the door, his gaze zeroing in on the two of us in the uncomfortable plastic chairs.

Giada stands, and I follow suit when the man walks over to us, holding out his hand. "Giada, what are you doing here?" he asks.

"Thank God you're here, Mr. Dratch. I want to see my father and the unhelpful officer"—she says loud enough for him to hear—"won't let me through."

Officer White rolls his eyes but doesn't take them off the computer screen.

"Your father doesn't want visitors, Giada. I figured Carlo would have told you that."

As if she told her brother what she was doing.

"I wanted to at least try. I need to speak to him." She conveniently leaves out the fact she most likely didn't discuss this little outing with Carlo.

"He won't see you. He's only allowing counsel. I'm sorry."

If I wasn't watching Giada as closely as I am, I would have missed the slight slump in her posture at his words. It's minuscule, but I know it means she's realizing she won't get her way.

"Will you tell him I was here, and I'd like to speak to him, please?"

"Of course. I know this is stressful for everyone. Why don't you go home and take a nice bath or get a manicure. I'm sure that would relax you, sweetheart."

Giada's lips thin into a straight line. "Thank you for your concern about my grooming habits, Mr. Dratch. I'll take that under advisement." She spins on her heels and marches to the door, roughly pushing it open. The clueless lawyer catches my eye and rolls his before turning toward the front desk and speaking to Officer White.

Following Giada outside, I spot her walking toward our car, her hands clenched into fists then releasing over and over. I make it to her before she crosses the street.

"That fucking prick," she grits out through her hard-set jaw.

"Officer White or Mr. Dratch?" I ask, unlocking the door with the fob in my hand before opening it for her.

"Both." She sits in the car and jerkily grabs the seat belt, tugging it across her chest.

When I walk around the hood, I see her through the windshield having a very angry, one-sided conversation with herself. Opening the driver's side door, the last word I hear is asshole.

"Home?" I ask, starting the luxury sedan.

"I have a better idea." She slides her sunglasses over her angry eyes. "I need a bar and a jukebox."

I should insist on going home. It would be the sensible thing to do. But all Giada is going to do there is stew and scheme. Her brother needs me to keep her out of his hair, and there's a part of me that feels bad for the girl. Her father and brother are the assholes. Giada was just born into the wrong family.

"I know just the place."

CHAPTER NINE
LUCA

THIRTY MINUTES LATER, WE pull up to a hole-in-the-wall bar in a small town outside of Boston. It's where Finn and I would occasionally meet when he wanted a face to face. I think he liked to remind me in person that I have family and I'm not completely alone even though I'm essentially in enemy territory playing the part of a heartless criminal. Finn has made it clear on more than one occasion that if it gets to be too much, I can leave at any time, but doing this, bringing down the man who ordered my parents' murder, hell, wanted me dead, too, is the driving force that keeps me going back to that house every day. Just because Francesco's in jail doesn't mean my work is done. Finn wants Carlo gone. He wants the Cataldis to be a cautionary tale of what happens when you fuck with the Monaghans. That's what keeps me firm in my resolve to see this through.

"This place looks...interesting," Giada says, peering at the red brick building I've parked across the street from. "Is this the part where you make sure I go missing for being a pain in the ass? If so, you've picked a good spot where no one will care about a woman screaming her head off."

The bar sits in the middle of a commercial building. *For Sale* signs that have been there since the first time I met Finn here sit in the windows of the businesses on either side.

"Don't be a snob. The place has a good music selection and cold beer. And no one here will give a shit that they saw your father's face all over the news this morning." The story has been on every local news station today, and no doubt a few national ones too.

Giada lets out a long sigh. "Yeah, I suppose my family is going to be the talk of Boston for some time."

I nod in agreement. "Most likely. But not here." I jerk my head toward the building. "Come on."

Giada gives me a small, nearly imperceptible smile and nods, opening her door and climbing out of the car.

As we're walking across the street, her heel gets caught in the cracked pavement and she nearly topples face-first into the road. My arm shoots out, and I grab her around the waist before she falls, smashing her body into mine.

"You okay?" I ask, looking down at her wide eyes, my arm still banded around her middle.

"Uh-huh," she pants out, and I see the vein in her neck pulse violently beneath her skin. "Damn heels."

Making sure she's as steady as she can be, with one foot in her shoe and the other balancing on her tiptoes, I kneel down and pull the heel of her shoe from the deep crack in the pavement. Her hand moves to my shoulder to steady herself while she lifts her foot and slips it back into the heel I'm holding for her.

"Thank you," she whispers and my gaze collides with hers. A charged moment passes between us, completely catching me off guard. Her amber eyes are glued to mine. For some reason, I can't seem to tear my hand from the soft skin of her ankle, even though her shoe is back in place.

"If you stay down there much longer, people are going to think you're proposing," Giada says, a half smile gracing her lips.

I stand and swivel my head dramatically like I'm searching for something. "What people?" A grin tilts the corner of my mouth when I offer her my elbow. "I'd rather not have to take you back home with a busted lip." Giada gives me a flat look but loops her arm through mine just the same.

It's impossible not to feel the warmth of her body as she walks next to me. She allows me to open the door to the bar before moving my hand to the small of her back to lead her to a table in the corner. The place is dark and narrow with old wood paneling covering the walls that have booths running the length of the building and several scarred tables with worn vinyl chairs down the center. The bar has one man behind it sipping from a coffee cup who looks less than thrilled to have patrons this early. The reason Finn likes it here is because it has no affiliation to the Cataldis or the Monaghans. Here, we were just two guys catching up. That doesn't mean

I'm going to sit in the middle of a bar with my back exposed, though.

"What do you want to drink?" I ask Giada as she slides into the corner booth.

"Vodka and cranberry please."

I quirk a brow.

"What?" she asks.

"That's just so...girly."

Giada rolls her eyes. "I like what I like. Girly or not."

Shrugging my shoulders, I walk to the bar and order her a drink and myself a soda water before fishing a twenty from my pocket and getting change for the jukebox.

"Here you go. They didn't have any umbrellas," I say, handing her the drink.

"What do you have against my drink?"

"Nothing. It's exactly what I thought you'd like."

"Well, what are you drinking?"

"Soda water. I'm technically on the clock."

Giada shoots me a sad smile. "Pretty pathetic that I'm sitting in a bar at eleven in the morning drinking with my bodyguard the day after my father was arrested."

I shrug and sit across from her. "Depends on who you ask."

"I'm asking you."

I lean back and sip my soda. "I'm not judging you, Giada. It was a shit night followed by an even shittier morning. If you need a minute to gather yourself, this place is as good as any. Here." I set the stack of ones on the table and nod toward the opposite corner where an old jukebox sits. "Have at it."

This time her smile is happy as she grabs a couple bills and heads over to pick out some music.

When she returns an old song from the sixties is playing through the bar. She slides back into the booth and sips her cocktail.

"Not what I expected," I comment.

She rolls her eyes. "What? You don't approve of my music selection, either."

"I didn't say that. I actually like the oldies. I didn't think you did."

"You don't really know me all that well, do you?" Her brow rises in a challenge for me to disagree.

"I don't suppose I do."

"I know what you think of me, Luca. I'm just some little Mafia princess who doesn't have a brain or thoughts of her own. That I'm oblivious to what my father and brother do. Or that I don't care because it keeps me in expensive clothes or some shit."

"Whoa," I say, holding my hands up in mock surrender. "I never said that."

"You didn't have to. That's what all the men in my father's organization probably think about me. Little Giada does everything she's told. Smiles when she needs to, is only good for marrying whoever her father picks out for her so he can have more power, and having little Mafia babies who'll grow up in the same life doing the same thing."

"I've never been under any misconception that you're one to do as you're told, Giada. If you recall, I used to catch you sneaking out of your room in the middle of the night to go to parties. And I believe it was just last night you made me go to a horrible fucking club with you so you could do God knows what with God knows who. That doesn't scream submissive little princess to me."

"Yeah, that club was pretty bad, huh?"

"Are you kidding? It was terrible. Why the hell did you want to go to a place like that to begin with?"

"Truth?" There's a slight wince on her face.

"Always," I reply.

She groans and takes another sip of her drink, nearly swallowing the entire contents of her glass. "I wanted to piss you off."

My head tilts to the side, staring at her as she chews her bottom lip. Something I've noticed she does when she's nervous.

"It's so fucking dumb, Luca. Especially considering the last twelve hours. I was pissed my dad said I needed a full-time bodyguard, and I wasn't exactly thrilled it was you."

"Why?"

She looks down into her empty glass and mutters, "I can't believe you're going to make me say it." Her eyes meet mine and she holds my stare. I don't know if the alcohol she just consumed in less than five minutes is giving her courage—not that she needs any around me—but she speaks in a clear and sure voice. "You had to have known I had a huge crush on you when I was a teenager. Well, seeing you again, I don't know; I guess I went back there in my mind and remembered the last day I saw you." She shakes her head, remembering the morning in the hallway when I was told I was moving on to Alberto's crew. "I was so worried we'd been caught and you were going to get fired or something." I don't bother telling her that if I'd been caught sneaking her back into the estate, my "firing" would likely have left me with a bullet hole. "Anyways, I heard you talking with Alberto and my father and realized you were going to work for him. I knew what he did and it pissed me off that you turned out to be like every other man in this business." Giada looks at her glass then me. "I need another drink."

I sit still, stunned at her admission. Not that I didn't suspect that was the reason for her behavior last night, just that she's admitting it now.

"Same thing?" I ask, nodding toward her glass.

"Maybe make this one a double."

Two hours later, Giada isn't feeling any of the sadness or hurt she walked in here with. Her hips sway back and forth in front of the jukebox as she feeds more money into the machine. I have to say, I'm impressed with her musical tastes. They range from old country to some ear-splitting pop hits mixed with a lot of songs from the sixties and seventies. Ordering another drink from Jay, our unimpressed bartender, I ask him to make this one heavy on the juice and light on the vodka.

I sit back down at the booth and Giada dances her way back to the table, picking up the refilled glass and taking a sip.

"My mom used to love dancing to this song." It's one of the older ones I appreciate much more than the newer shit she was playing. "She used to dance around the kitchen while she baked bread or was making homemade pasta. She'd twirl me around and we'd sing and sing." Giada's smile is bright as she's caught up in the memory of being a little girl with a loving mother. Something I never had.

"Before she died, she enrolled me in dance classes. It was obviously different from our kitchen dancing, but I loved it."

"I don't remember you dancing when I came to the house."

"I'd quit by then in a fit of bratty teenage rebellion."

I give her a flat look.

"Hey." She points an unsteady finger at me. "I know what that look means."

"I think we've established that you actually can't read my mind."

Giada laughs, but I'm not sure what she's finding so funny.

"You're not like I thought, Luca Bennetti, I'll give you that."

I tilt my head to the side, a question in my eyes.

"I mean, how many other bodyguards would be here

with me while I drink my problems away in the middle of the afternoon? If it were anyone else, they'd have called my brother, and he would've come storming in here and dragged me out for being an embarrassment to the family or some shit. Like I'm the one who's the embarrassment."

It never occurred to me to make that call. She needs a minute to wrap her head around everything that's going on, and someone needs to look out for her. It's not as though her asshole brother gives a shit, and neither does her father, for that matter. I certainly remember how they treated her when I first came to work for the Cataldis. It was just as Giada described earlier. They brought her out and pranced her around like a show pony then put her back in her ivory tower until the next time they needed her.

"I learned a long time ago it's better to go along with your plans than tell you no and have you sneak off without protection."

Her hips stop moving and she looks at me through glassy eyes. "Thank you," she says sincerely. "For stopping that boy all those years ago and for last night. Those assholes thought they had a sure thing in their pocket." She giggles and takes a swig of her drink. "I would have loved to see you smash his face."

"Violent little thing, aren't you?"

"Surprised?"

Considering who her brother and father are, no, not really.

"Nah, but most girls would freak out over a little blood."

Giada shrugs. "It's not the first time I've seen blood, and I'm sure it won't be the last. That's the thing about being the girl everyone forgets about. I'm like a tiny fly on the wall that no one notices."

She turns and raises her glass to the bartender. "Jay, another drink please," she calls and sets her glass on the table before sitting down next to me. Jay meets my eyes, and I nod before he pours her a weak vodka and cranberry.

Giada telling me that no one notices her makes me wonder what she's heard and seen living with Carlo and Francesco. And what information she has that could help me and my cousin bring down her family. I never considered she would be privy to anything useful, but now I'm wondering if I've been working this entire thing from the wrong angle.

"Thank you, Luca," she slurs next to me.

"You already thanked me."

She shakes her head back and forth. "No. For today. For bringing me here and listening to me ramble. There isn't anyone I can talk to about any of this. My family in Italy isn't involved with this side of our life at all, and other than Bianca, I don't really have any friends in the States. Not that I would ever tell her any of this. Hell, I don't even know why I'm telling you any of it, but here we are." She lets out a dramatic sigh and closes her eyes. "I think I'm drunk."

"I think you passed drunk an hour ago."

A huff of laughter escapes her. "You're right. Maybe it's time to go home."

"Yeah, princess. Let's go."

When we return to the estate, her brother isn't around, and Giada continues to drink and play her mom's old records that she brought down to the family room.

"My dad doesn't like anything that reminds him of her. Maybe that's why he hates me. I look just like her," she drunkenly confides in me while she's splayed out on the floor next to the old record player. The record ends and she rolls toward the player to change out albums. When the first song begins playing, she hops up from the floor and starts dancing around the room like she didn't just share one of the saddest truths of her life.

A few hours later, after switching between dancing and lying on the floor or couch listening to another song with a sweet smile on her face, she decides she's hungry, so we head into the kitchen. I'm not sure why I don't just leave her to herself and go to my room to unpack the things I brought back earlier, but I don't. Maybe I feel bad for her. She's contending with too much for a girl her age to have to deal with on her own. It reminds me a bit of when Frank told me about my true parentage. I didn't have anyone to turn to, and I was so damn angry. Hell, I still am. Neither of us deserves the shit hand we've been dealt.

Giada pulls a bag of chips from the pantry and opens them, shoving a messy handful into her mouth. While she's chewing, she grabs a loaf of bread and some peanut butter and jelly.

"I'm going to make you the best thing ever."

She grabs a pan from one of the lower cabinets and sets it on the large six-burner range. After slathering the peanut butter then the jelly on the bread, she butters each side and sticks them in the pan.

"What on earth are you doing?" I'm horrified at the sight in front of me.

"Trust me. This is the best way to eat PB and J."

I shoot her a dubious look, which makes her laugh, the tinkling sound causing the organ in my chest to beat a little faster. It's one thing to feel sorry for her and want to be there for her when she has no one else to turn to. I can sympathize with that. But this is an entirely different emotion that I absolutely need to shut down. There's no room for the daughter of my enemy in my heart or anywhere else, for that matter.

When she finishes grilling the sandwiches, I look at the messy concoction with jelly and peanut butter oozing from the sides as she takes a huge bite from hers.

"They're so good this way, right?" she asks as I take a bite of mine. "My mom used to make these for me." She bites down on another messy mouthful. "Do you have a favorite thing your mom used to make?"

I shake my head. "My mom died when I was a baby." The familiar anger at the thought of what she must have gone through in her last moments on earth rages through my body. I can't blame Giada for the sins of her father. It's not her fault he was responsible for my mother's murder. Hell, she wasn't even born then. But that doesn't mean I'm comfortable seeing the look of pity in her eyes when it was her father's order that took my mother and all the memories I could have had with her.

"That's a really shitty thing to have in common, huh?"

I nod, not wanting my voice to give away just *how* shitty this entire situation is.

"You're from California?" she asks around a mouthful of the gooey sandwich.

"Born and raised." Partially true.

"So it was just you and your dad?"

"Yup."

"You're really forthcoming with the details, huh?"

I shrug as she watches me expectantly. "I grew up in a little town with my dad. He did the best he could with what he had." It was pretty damn great, in my opinion, but I can't exactly divulge too many details.

"When was the last time you went out to visit him?"

"I don't. He died before I moved to Boston."

And that look of pity is back in her eyes. "You're alone in the world," Giada says, her eyes growing watery.

Something cracks in my chest. This girl, who has no one in the world who cares for her, has to live with who is probably the worst brother and father I've ever met. She has to navigate through a world where she has no hope for personal autonomy and she's in tears over me losing my family. She doesn't know the truth, that I'm here because of my family, but that doesn't change the fact that I want to take some of her sadness away. I don't deserve her sympathy, just like she doesn't deserve to be collateral damage in this war.

I send her a soft smile. "I'm far from alone right now, though. And you're right about these sandwiches. They're fucking delicious." I take a huge bite and hum in satisfaction.

My reaction brightens her sad eyes and she smiles wide. "I mean, I'm not going to say I told you so, but..."

"I would expect nothing less. I also wouldn't say no if you wanted to make another one for me."

She laughs and the sound lifts a bit of the weight that's been sitting in my chest.

"I've created a PB and J monster."

She hasn't created a monster, but she's gone a long way in calming the one that's been living inside me for the last six years.

After finishing our grilled sandwiches, it only takes another thirty minutes for her to pass out on the giant couch in the living room. I consider leaving her there, but if her brother comes home and finds her passed out drunk on my watch, I know he won't be particularly happy with either of us. The last thing I need is to ruin my chances of getting off babysitting duty. So I take her to bed, lay a trash can next to her just in case and shut the door behind me before going back to my own room.

The next morning, when I step into the bright kitchen, I find Giada sitting at the small table next to the large bay window. She has sunglasses covering her eyes and her dark hair is in a messy bun on top of her head. At some point in the night, she must have gotten up and changed into sleep pants and a sweatshirt because that's not what I put her to bed in. A small smile plays on my lips at her disheveled appearance. I've never seen her less than completely put together, even when she was a teenager in high school. This is the look of a woman who had far too much alcohol coursing through her veins the night before and is paying the price this morning.

"Morning," I say cheerily, grabbing myself a cup of coffee.

"Hey," she croaks out, raising her glasses from her bloodshot eyes. She scrubs a hand over her makeup-free face, something else I don't think I've ever seen and clears her throat. "Umm, thanks again for putting up with me yesterday. And for putting me to bed. I was...not in a good place."

"Don't mention it," I reply, waving off her concerns.

"I was thinking about something I told you yesterday. About how I used to take dance lessons."

I nod, not only remembering her telling me but also her dancing around the bar and then the living room last night.

"I think I'd like to start again. There's a studio—"

"You look like shit, Giada." Carlo walks in and sneers at her disheveled state.

"Fuck off, Carlo," she throws back.

He stops and looks her dead in the eye. "You'll need to start thinking twice about how you speak to me. Remember, Dad's not here anymore to protect his little princess."

It takes effort, but I manage to hold in the eye roll. That man never protected Giada from anything.

"You can go jump off—" she starts.

"Giada was just telling me she wants to start dance lessons again," I cut in. It's too damn early in the morning for the Cataldi siblings to start World War III. Plus, Giada doesn't know it, but Carlo's patience with his sister is thinner than it's ever been, and I don't know what will happen if he lays a hand on her in front of me. Not after last night and seeing another side to the girl sitting at the table trying to hold the remnants of her life together.

Carlo laughs. "Why? You think you're going to be a ballerina or some shit?"

I chuckle at his stupid joke, pretending like I think it's a dumb idea, but we should just go along with it, all the while imagining my fist flying toward his face. "Can't hurt anything. Keeps her occupied and out of trouble."

I shoot him a look that says that's what he wanted in the first place.

"Yeah, alright." Carlo turns to Giada. "Find something, but Luca goes with you and stays the whole time."

She gives him a sarcastic salute, but thankfully, before he can lay into her for her disrespect, his phone rings.

"Yeah," he barks and leaves the kitchen.

"Well, that's settled," I say, turning back to Giada, who is glaring daggers at my face. "What?"

"I just love being talked about like I'm not in the room. Thank you so much for getting permission from my asshole brother for me to do something that should be my decision and none of his concern. Really, I'm glad you two are okay with me staying 'occupied.'"

She stands from her chair, nearly knocking it over.

"Giada," I call, but the only sound is her stomping up the stairs. What can I really say though? I have to play the part of asshole bodyguard in front of Carlo. He needs to see me as the careless prick because that's exactly what he is. Nothing about last night changes the real reason I'm here. But I can't explain that to her. I'm having a hard enough time keeping up pretenses as it is. She may hate her brother and hate how her father treats her, but she's still a Cataldi, and blood will always be thicker than water.

CHAPTER TEN
GIADA

THE LAST TWO MONTHS have both flown by and seemed to drag at a snail's pace. My father refuses to see me while his trial is well underway. I showed up the first day and was told by his attorney during a recess that he didn't wish for me to be there. He didn't explain why, so I lifted my chin and walked out. This type of treatment from him is harsher than I've ever dealt with before but not so out of character that I'm surprised. Hurt? Yes, but not shocked. This is Mafia business, after all. And the last thing any woman in this life is allowed to do is involve herself.

Utter bullshit.

Carlo has become more and more unstable since my father's been away. He thought it was going to be a smooth transition, him coming into power. It's been anything but. What I told Luca the day after my father was arrested still rings true. I'm a fly on the wall that no one pays attention to, and I see everything that happens in this house. Carlo has tried to set up meetings at the house, and it hasn't gone well. He's flat-out ignored or treated like an insolent child. *Join the club, brother.*

His mood has been volatile, to say the least, and the men he has coming to the house give me the same creepy feeling as Alberto did when he'd come to talk to my father and Carlo. Their leering gazes send chilly tingles up my spine every time we're in the same room. Thankfully, Luca stays close when they're around. The way my brother's associates, Roberto and Pauly, stare at me seems to have his instincts kicking into high gear as well.

"Are you ready to go?" Luca asks as I'm filling up my water bottle in the kitchen.

Even though the way Luca and Carlo irritated the hell out of me when they discussed my decision to take dance classes again, I didn't let it stop me from doing so. Though I'll admit, it's a hell of a lot harder than I anticipated. I guess the old saying if you don't use it, you lose it has some merit to it. I found a studio not too far from the house, and three times a week, Luca drives me to classes. I was only allowed to take ballet when I was younger, but since I don't have anyone looking over my shoulder, I've decided to go with something a little more contemporary and modern.

"Yeah," I tell him and follow him to the garage, where he opens the car door for me.

We haven't been the same since the day in the kitchen when he and my brother discussed me like I wasn't sitting there, not that Luca and I were ever on the best of terms. The day after my father was arrested and Luca took me to that bar was the anomaly, not the distance that has always been between us. But there have been a handful of times over the last couple months when I've had a particularly bad day that I feel Luca holding himself back from...what, I'm not sure. It's almost as though he senses the doom I feel in my heart and wants to say something to alleviate the frustration and anger I carry. But he never does. He keeps the respectable distance that a guard in his position is expected to. I don't know whether or not to be happy about it, and that pisses me off to no end.

I feel like a complete fool for thinking one drunken night of me sharing things about myself, things I hadn't shared with anyone else, would change anything between Luca and I. Honestly, I'm not even sure I wanted them to. Carlo thinks he'll be controlling every aspect of my life like our father did before he went to jail—and probably prison in a few days if the reports coming in about how his trial is going are any indication. Though he still refuses to see me, it doesn't mean I'm going to give up, and it certainly doesn't mean I'm not going to try everything I can to get out of this life. My father is likely going to be convicted and no one wants anything to do with Carlo. The Cataldi organization is crumbling, and I want out. Out of this house and out of this life. I want to move to Italy with a family that cares about me. I want to have a life away from any and all people in this life, and that'll include Luca. As soon as I know where my father will be residing after the trial, I'll be paying him a visit and he'd better see me. It's a long shot, I know, but maybe, just maybe, he'll give me permission to leave.

The hope that he'll go to prison has been weighing heavily on me. That's not what a daughter should pray for at night. But I do. I want an escape, and if my father is convicted, I'll at least have a shot. No one from a powerful family is going to want to marry the daughter of Francesco Cataldi. It wouldn't be advantageous for them, and in this world, that's what marriages are for. There's no reason to think my marriage contract will be worth what it once was. My only hope is that my father will see it that way. Even if Carlo doesn't agree, I doubt he'll have the guts to argue with our father, hopefully.

"I want you to be careful around the guys your brother's been bringing around," Luca says, jarring me out of my thoughts.

"You warning me away from other criminals is almost laughable, Luca."

It's not like he's some upstanding citizen.

"There're criminals, then there're men like your brother has working for him," he retorts.

A caustic laugh escapes me. "You work for my brother."

"You know what I mean, Giada. There's something off about those two. I don't like the way they look at you when your brother isn't around. Hell, when Carlo is around, they don't seem to care much about being caught ogling you either." If Luca wasn't wearing sunglasses, there's no doubt I'd catch a dramatic eye roll.

"I can take care of myself. You seem to forget I've grown up in this life."

"The problem with that theory is you have no sense of self-preservation when it comes to dangerous men."

I almost feel as though he's referring to the conversation we had when I was drunk. From what I remember, I told him a few things I probably should've kept to myself. Nothing bad per se, but if he tells my brother that I know more than I let on or that I'm pissed he's trying to claim dominion over my life now that our father's in jail, Carlo will be none too happy. Not that Carlo isn't well aware of how I feel in regard to him trying to take over every aspect of our family. But it's an entirely different story if I go to his employees and start complaining. He expects a show of family loyalty, even if it's fake as hell.

"I've survived this long, Luca. Even without you warning me about the people my family associates with." It's not as though I've never been leered at before by a few criminals. And my brother or father never gave a shit either way.

"Can you just please make sure you aren't alone with those two?"

"Well, with the way you're always around, I don't think it will be an issue."

"I may not always be around, Giada. That's why I'm telling you this. Jesus, can't you just say okay and leave it at that? Everything always has to be a fight with you."

We've pulled up to the dance studio, but I haven't made a move to get out of the car yet.

"What do you mean 'always a fight'? I've barely talked to you for months. Not since you proved once again that you're a good little puppy towing the company line."

"What company line?"

"The one where Giada needs to be handled. Keep the little princess occupied and let the men handle her life. It's the same bullshit I've been dealing with my entire life." I shake my head and blow out a breath, completely disappointed in myself. "I was stupid enough to think maybe there was another side to you, but you're all the same. So, excuse me if I think your warnings are laughable. Those men may be pigs, but it's not like they hide it. And my brother may not care that they can't keep their eyes in their heads, but they won't touch me. It would be disrespectful to Carlo and my father."

"You're fucking naive if you think that's going to stop them. And I'm not sure your damn brother would care all that much either way."

"Why do you care?" I shoot back.

Luca opens his mouth to answer, but the words die in his throat. He lifts his sunglasses from his face and pins me with a stare. "You think I like the way I see women being treated in this life by men like your brother? You think seeing those men follow every move you make, playing disgusting fantasies out in their twisted minds when they watch you, doesn't make me want to rip their eyes from their heads? I've never *not* cared about you,

Giada. I may not be able to show you how much, but that doesn't mean I don't."

I open and close my mouth like a fish underwater as I search for the words to say. "Luca..."

"Forget about it, Giada. You're going to be late for dance."

He adjusts his glasses back over his eyes and stares in front of him, not speaking another word. I nod numbly, completely taken aback by Luca's admission and open my car door, grabbing my bag from the back seat before heading into the dance studio. What did he mean by not being able to show me that he cared? I could tell there was more he wanted to say, but for some reason, he wouldn't let himself. And I can't lie and say the remnants of my teenage crush didn't spark back to life briefly. But it doesn't matter about any stupid crush or teenage fantasy I used to wish so hard could be a reality. It can't be. He works for my father, he's my bodyguard, and he's part of a life I don't want.

Two days later, Luca, Carlo, and I are sitting in front of the television, listening to the reporter on the screen in the family room.

"Francesco Cataldi was found guilty on all charges, including racketeering, conspiracy to commit murder, and fraud. This is the first time Mr. Cataldi has been convicted of any crime." The reporter continues her story and the three of us stare at the TV.

"He's going to prison," I whisper, looking at Luca with tears in my eyes. To anyone, it would look like I'm devastated by the news that my father is never coming home, but deep down, I'm so fucking relieved. This is my chance to escape. All I need to do is convince my father that no one is going to want to align himself with Carlo, and I'll be free. Who in their right mind would want to marry a girl from an empire that's disintegrating right before our eyes?

"That fucking bitch!" Carlo shouts and throws the glass lamp against the wall next to the TV screen. He turns and stomps out of the room before I hear the door to his office slam shut.

The noise barely registers as Luca holds my gaze.

"It'll be okay, Giada. I'm sure they'll appeal or something," he says, mistaking the meaning behind my tears for sadness.

"You don't understand. This means I have a shot of being free, Luca. With my father no longer in charge, maybe I can convince him to let me leave, let me move to Italy with my family there—or anywhere, really. What good is a marriage to the daughter of a man who has no power?"

"What are you talking about?"

"Don't you get it? No one will want to be tied to a dying organization, and that's exactly what this is if my father gets put away. That's all I've ever been good for in the eyes of my father and brother. Just someone they can marry off to form an alliance with another family. But now I have a chance to get the hell out of this life."

"Be careful of what you say, Giada. If the wrong person hears what you're talking about they might see it as betrayal to your family."

"Fuck my family," I shout, jumping from my seat. "What the hell have they ever done for me? All I've ever been to them is a pawn in their games. The organization is dying, Luca. You've seen the way my brother is." I wave my hand toward the broken lamp. "No one wants to work with him. It won't be long until other capos start gunning for him and anyone who stands in their way."

Luca's eyes dart around before closing the double doors to the family room and walking over to stand in front of me. "You need to be quiet. Your brother is in the house," he says in a low voice.

"I'm going to see my father; make him see reason. I want to move the hell away from here. There's no reason for him to keep me locked up here like I've been my entire life. If he agrees, Carlo can't say anything about it."

"And if Carlo decides he doesn't need to listen to your father?"

"Then I'll figure it out. I have to try. I have to get out of here. I don't want this life." Tears spring to my eyes again, thinking about being chained to some asshole my brother picks out for me. It could be anyone, and he won't care about what it means for me so long as he gets what he wants.

That thought has always terrified me with my father. If my brother has the right to negotiate a marriage contract on my behalf...I don't even want to consider it.

"Please don't tell my brother," I beg Luca. He works for my brother now and no doubt feels loyalty to him. And I could very well have just ruined my chances of getting free from these ties by confiding in him. *Real smart, Giada.* "Let me talk to my father first. If Carlo finds out, there's no doubt he'll try to sabotage me before I have a chance to speak to him."

Luca stares at me for a moment before nodding his head. "We never had this conversation."

Just like all the other conversations we've never had but I can't seem to forget about.

Three days have passed, and I haven't been able to see my father yet. Apparently you can't just walk in and they let you through. I've filled out the paperwork and now I'm just awaiting approval from the warden or whoever signs it, saying I'm allowed to visit.

My brother has been MIA since the conviction. He's probably out running around with whatever flavor of the week he has or simply drowning his sorrows at some brothel my family owns. Who the hell knows? He's never bothered to explain his comings and goings to me—or to anyone else, for that matter.

I'm curled up with a book in the family room when I hear a commotion coming from my brother's office. He's back and we need to talk.

I walk in and watch as he pulls a few weapons from the safe in the wall behind his desk.

"Carlo, what's going on?" I ask, my brows rising at seeing him load the magazine into his gun before he starts cramming bullets into a few spare magazines in front of him.

"Nothing. I have some business to take care of. What do you want, Giada?"

He doesn't look at me or give me any of his attention. *Typical.*

"I need to talk to you about what happens next."

"Our father is going to spend the rest of his life in prison. That's what happens next."

I take a breath, shoring up the courage to tell him my plan. "I want to leave, Carlo. To go to Italy and live there. There's no reason for me to stay. Our father's in prison. I'm not any sort of asset to this family."

Carlo stops what he's doing and spears me with his glare. "You aren't going anywhere. You're still part of this family, and you're still required to fulfill your obligations as Francesco Cataldi's only daughter."

I let out a disbelieving laugh. "Our father isn't going to ever see the outside of prison walls again. You know that as well as I do. What further obligations could I possibly have?"

"Just because he's in prison doesn't mean I can't find you a suitable husband."

"For what? No one is going to want to marry me with a father in prison and a brother who..."

His icy stare stops me midsentence. "Who what, Giada?"

"I'm not stupid, Carlo. I see how hard it's been since Father was arrested. The other capos don't want to follow you."

In two steps, he's towering over me. "You know nothing."

"I know what I see. I'm not some little girl you can boss around anymore." I stare into his erratic gaze with a steely glare of my own, refusing to back down.

The noise of his slap registers moments before the sting of the blow brings tears to my eyes. My hand covers the burning flesh of my cheek as I stare at him with wide eyes as his glower bears down on me.

"Make no mistake, Giada." He roughly grabs my arm and brings me closer to his face, speaking through gritted teeth. "Whether or not those spineless assholes want to follow me, I'm still in charge of this family, and that means I'm in charge of where you live and who you marry. You think you can walk away? Think again. I own you just like I own everything else that was our father's. You aren't going anywhere."

Luca walks into the room and sees the tear making its way down my face and Carlo's rough fingers digging into my arm.

"Hey, Pauly and Roberto are waiting for you. They said something about needing to get to the docks."

Carlo glances at Luca then back to me. "If you try to leave without my permission, I will hunt you down and drag you back here. Anyone you run to will die for helping you. I won't be undermined by my spoiled bitch of a sister. Do you understand me?"

I jerkily nod, and he tightens his grip on my arm once more before releasing it.

"I'll be back tonight," he says to Luca as he passes him on the way out of his office. "Keep an eye on her."

Luca nods, but his stare stays fixed on me. The front door slams and it takes all of my strength to stay upright and not fall to the floor in utter defeat. It would have made leaving so much easier if Carlo would've agreed. But he's still under some delusion that our lives or that the organization our father has built isn't crumbling beneath our feet.

Luca is next to me in two long strides. "Are you okay?"

My laugh at his question holds no humor as I wipe the moisture from my cheeks and try not to wince with pain. "I'm anything but okay." I look him in the eye. "But I'll be damned if Carlo thinks this fight is over."

Carlo never came home the night after our argument in his office. It's been two weeks since I've had word from him or seen him stomping through the house. I asked Luca to look into his disappearance, hoping like hell he was dead in a morgue somewhere, though I'm sure I would have been notified if that were the case. He left me for the first time in weeks to check in with some contacts but made sure to tell me if I see my brother or the other two goons who've been working with him to call him straight away.

When Luca knocks on my bedroom door a few hours later, his face is grim. "Seems your brother pissed off the Irish and an MC they work with. He's disappeared, and either no one knows where he is, or they aren't telling me."

It's not surprising to be honest. Carlo seems to think he's untouchable even without my father standing behind him. It's clear he hasn't accepted that the Cataldi name doesn't mean what it once did, and now he's hiding under some rock like the snake he is.

"Thank you for looking into it," I tell Luca as he stands awkwardly in my doorframe.

"Listen, Giada. If you still want to leave, I'm sure your family in Italy will take you in. This might be your chance to—"

I'm shaking my head before he can finish his sentence. "You heard him. If anyone takes me in, they're as good as dead. My brother may be a complete asshole, but he's never not followed through on a threat. I can't risk it. I have to convince my father that me leaving makes sense. He can't possibly be under the same delusion as Carlo that anyone is going to want to marry the princess of a dying family."

Luca nods, but I can tell there's something else he wants to say.

"What is it?" I ask.

Before he can answer, the alarm on my phone goes off, signaling it's time for me to get my things together to go to the studio.

"Get ready for dance, I'll wait for you downstairs." Luca turns and walks away before answering my question.

With my father awaiting sentencing, he's still being held downtown. I've been going there every week like clockwork, and every week, he refuses to see me. Three months after his sentencing and he still won't have anything to do with me. The pitying looks from the deputies were almost too much to bear, but I kept my chin tilted high every day while I waited for them to call my name. They never did though. I've been iced out by my father for my entire life, but that stung just a bit more. He doesn't have anything occupying his time. There's no reason he couldn't see me, except for the fact that he doesn't deign me important enough to deal with. I've written him letters asking for his help with Carlo, begging him to let me go to Italy where I can start a new life without my brother's interference.

Then, last month, all of my hopes that I could see him or get through to him were cut off at the knees when his attorney delivered a letter my father had written to me. He said there was no reason to come to the jail to try to see him. He was never going to get out of prison. My brother was in charge, and all the power my father held was now Carlo's. If Carlo wants me to stay, then that's what I'm to do. He basically gave my brother carte blanche and he doesn't want to hear any of my petty concerns. He said he's been sick and has terminal cancer and the only way he's leaving prison is in a body bag. The organization was out of his hands and that was that.

My father told me he was dying in a letter. A *fucking letter*. Not even facing his mortality can make him have any sort of compassion or sympathy for his daughter. It was the *fuck you* I'd always expected but prayed wouldn't come. My father has never shown any concern for me or what I want. But goddamnit, would it have killed him if, just one time, he acted like a father and not some heartless asshole who's apparently washed his hands of me so easily?

Things between Luca and I aren't strained, per se, but there's been tension between us since the day in my brother's office. My brother was in too much of a rage to notice the look in Luca's eyes, but I did. He looked three seconds away from pulling his gun and shooting Carlo between the eyes. There's no doubt in my mind that Luca is aware my brother struck me that day. That's not uncommon in this life or in this house. Something shifted between Luca and me. Something I'm not even sure he's aware of or can put a finger on, but we've fallen into a routine these last few months. It's so different from when I came home from Italy and wanted to make his life hell for the fact he was appointed my bodyguard. At the time, I wanted nothing to do with him, but now I can't imagine being stuck in this house with anyone other than him. When he found me the day I got the letter from my father, sitting at the edge of the pool, he sat right next to me. He never tried to comfort me, didn't give me empty platitudes. He simply stayed next to me while I cried, when I raged, and when I was silent in utter numbness. He was exactly what I needed without having to ask.

There've been so many times I've considered sneaking out with nothing but the clothes on my back and finding a way to get the hell away from this house, from this life. I've thought about Luca's offer to get me to Italy, but Carlo's threats still play over and over in my mind. If anyone helps me, they're as good as dead, and I can't live with that on my conscience. Hell, if Carlo found me, who knows if he would let me live at all?

I feel truly defeated for the first time in my entire life. There's no one I can turn to that can help me out of this mess, not unless I want to worry about whether Carlo is going to find them and end their life. I held hope that my father would help me. Why? I'm honestly not sure.

Maybe I was looking for something that's never been there in regard to how he felt about me. But his letter confirms he views me as nothing but a pawn to be used however he sees fit, or my brother, now that our father has been forced to step down as head of the family.

I've tried to call Carlo so many times, but his phone goes straight to voice mail. Every time. He had to have known about the cancer. I'm so damn furious he didn't see fit to tell me. But what's one more thing to add to the pile of shit that is my brother?

The knock on my bedroom door pulls me out of my thoughts. It's nine in the morning, but the passage of time doesn't really mean anything to me anymore. I'm just a prisoner in this house, waiting for my brother to decide what to do with me. Not unlike how I lived my life when my father was in charge, but this feels heavier. More inescapable.

Nina, the house manager, pokes her head in. "Your brother called and said you were to be packed and ready to leave the property in two hours." Her face doesn't give much away; it never has, but I see sympathy in her eyes, which instantly has me on edge.

"Where am I going?"

She walks in and closes the door behind me. "He didn't say much except a man named Nikolai Petrov was sending a car for you and he expects you at his estate in New York."

"New York?"

Nina nods.

"The only Petrov I've ever heard of in New York is…"

I jump out of bed, grabbing my thin robe and throwing it over my small sleep shorts and tank top.

I pick up my phone and dial Carlo's number, hoping he finally picks up.

"I suppose Nina told you that you were leaving?" he asks by way of greeting.

"Carlo, what the hell is going on?"

"I've found you a husband, dear sister. Congratulations," he answers, sounding annoyed and completely put out that I'm calling him.

"To a Petrov? How could you? Father would've never condoned this. He hated the Russians."

"Father isn't in charge," Carlo snaps. "I am. The Petrovs have been gracious enough to help me with a couple things recently and my organization will benefit greatly from their continued support on one condition."

"Let me guess. If I marry one of them."

"Nikolai isn't so bad. Could have been worse. Could have been his father."

"I can't believe you would sell me to our enemy. This is low, Carlo, even for you." There's no mistaking the absolute disgust in my voice when I spit those words at him.

"I don't give a shit what you believe or how much you whine to me about how unfair your life is. It's not your decision to make, nor was it ever going to be. Our family needs this, Giada."

"Now it's *our* family? Just a second ago, it was *yours*."

Carlo is silent for a few moments, and I can clearly imagine the vein above his right temple pulsing with anger.

"You will be ready in two hours, and you will get into that car, Giada. If you don't, I'll come back to Boston to make sure you end up as a face on a milk carton. Am I clear?"

Hot, angry tears pool in my eyes, but I refuse to give Carlo any sign that I'm about three seconds from breaking down. "Crystal."

"Good. See you in a few hours." He disconnects the call, and I stare at the blank screen for several long moments.

"Where's Luca?" I ask Nina, throwing my phone on my unmade bed.

"Luca?" Nina's brows draw together in confusion. "In his room, I think."

Throwing the door open, I run down the stairs, leaving Nina in my room. The only time I've heard the name Petrov muttered is when my father would be yelling something or other about the "fucking Russian Bratva."

When I reach Luca's door, I rapidly knock, whispering to myself, "Please be here. Please be here."

The door bursts open, and Luca is standing there shirtless in gym shorts. "Giada, what's wrong?"

The defined cut of his chest barely registers before I push him inside the room and slam the door shut.

"Tell me what you know about the Petrovs." I cross

my arms over my chest and wait for him to say what I already know.

When his eyes widen at the name I just gave him, it confirms I was right about my assumptions.

"Giada, how do you know that name? Why are you asking?"

My heart is racing, and my breaths come out in quick pants, partly from running from my room to his faster than I think I've ever run in my life, but mostly from the very real and very desperate fear of what's happening.

"Tell me what you know," I demand.

Luca nods. "Okay...the Petrovs run the Bratva in New York. They aren't particularly active in Massachusetts, but I've heard rumblings that they're trying to find a foothold in Boston." His voice trails off when his gaze slams into me. "Why do you need to know, Giada?" He asks the question as though he already knows the answer.

"Nina got word that I need to be ready to leave in two hours. That Nikolai Petrov was sending someone to collect me." Tears pool in my eyes, and I see a thousand thoughts flick through Luca's with the information.

I sit on his bed, shoulders slumped as the first tear falls. Luca is still standing in the middle of the room, speechless. I might think he was uncaring about the situation I've found myself in, except for the harsh tic in his jaw as he stares at the wall behind me.

"No." His eyes find mine again. "No."

The finality of the word only makes the tears come

faster.

"There's nothing I can do, Luca. My father has given Carlo free rein." I look around the small room, regretting coming in here, regretting that I'm once again putting him in a precarious and dangerous position by running to him with my problems. What can he do to help me? He's as much a prisoner of the whims of Carlo as I am.

"I'm sorry. I shouldn't have involved you." I stand and try to walk past him, but Luca steps in front of me before I make it to the door, his strong hands grasping my silk-covered shoulders.

"Do you trust me?"

His eyes implore me to answer yes. To let him help me, and God, I'm so desperate right now not to be shipped to New York that I answer him honestly and pray he has a way to get me out of this. "Yes."

He nods and blows out a breath, the scent of mint gliding over my face.

"I'm going to tell you some things that are going to be hard for you to understand, that are going to sound absolutely impossible to believe. But I need you to trust me, then we can leave this house and never come back."

"Where will we go where Carlo won't be able to find us, Luca? He has contacts all over. If I leave instead of getting into the car, he'll hunt me down—*you* down—and kill us both. You know it's true." Hope, desperation, and nearly paralyzing fear war for dominance in my mind.

"That's the thing. He'll know where we are. But he

won't be able to take you."

My brows scrunch as I look into Luca's sincere blue gaze, a little afraid at this point that he's lost his damn mind.

"What's going to stop him?"

"My cousin."

CHAPTER ELEVEN
LUCA

G IADA'S WIDE EYES AND stunned silence allow me to continue, though I'm not sure how well she's going to absorb everything I have to say. When she walked in here three minutes ago and told me that her brother had arranged for her to leave with the Russians, a plan began to form in my head. Finn told me Carlo had been working with the Russians, and he had intel that if Carlo could drum up some support, the Russians would help him in taking back control of the ports. I knew of the Russian involvement and knew the plan had failed when Finn found the man who was helping Carlo, Orlando Farina, the son of another powerful Mafia family in Massachusetts and killed him for trying to take Finn's wife. No one wanted any part of trying to take down the Monaghans after finding out what Finn had done to Orlando, except apparently the Russians.

"If you're married to me, it will offer you some protection. They'll think twice about taking you."

"It won't matter if we're married, Luca. When Carlo finds out, he'll kill you. We'd be running for the rest of our lives, and heaven help us if he finds us."

"We'll go to my family. Trust me, he won't dare come after us."

"What are you talking about? Who's your family?"

"The Monaghans."

Giada backs up a step, and I allow my hands to fall from her, her eyes staring at me as though she has no idea who she's looking at. I suppose she doesn't, not really. No one in this house does, and I'm about to let her in on a secret that would surely get me killed if anyone outside of this room hears what I'm about to divulge.

"H-How...what..." she fumbles out.

"We don't have a lot of time, Giada, and I swear to God I will explain everything to you—"

"I think now's the time to try, Luca. Especially if you're proposing marriage."

I'm not going to lie, the way she straightens her spine, demanding answers from me, is a relief. She walked in here so broken, so defeated. Her brother is essentially selling her to the Russians to garner support since his plan a few weeks ago went up in flames. At least, that's what I'm assuming. It's not as though he's opposed to the idea of selling women. And if Francesco told him he has control over Giada's future, selling her to the highest bidder with the most for him to gain isn't out of the question. But now I'm seeing the inner strength I've always admired in the way she tilts her chin, her gaze demanding answers.

I take a step back, allowing her more room.

"Before I tell you my truth, I need to ask one thing of you."

"Are you really in a position to be asking me for anything?"

"Are you really in a position to not hear me out?" I shoot back.

Her brow quirks and she waves her hand, motioning for me to continue.

"If, after hearing me out, you decide I've betrayed you and your family to the point that there's no way you can trust me, please give me a little time before you sound the alarm. What I'm about to tell you, Giada, will no doubt make your brother or any other person in this house want me dead. Please, for the sake of the girl whose secrets I kept, promise me you'll give me a chance to leave."

She blows out a breath and the long column of her neck bobs as she swallows. "I can do that."

I wipe my hands on my shorts and grab a shirt, throwing it over my head, and begin a rushed explanation. "I didn't happen to meet your brother in a bar seven years ago. I planted myself there to figure out a way to get into his organization. But not because I was some low-life criminal looking to get an in with the Mafia. I wanted in because before I came to Boston I was told some things about my past. Some things that were kept from me when I was growing up with my father, who, turns out, wasn't my biological father. My parents are from Boston and your father had mine killed for falling in love with a woman from the Monaghan family. He took it as a betrayal of loyalty, and when the man who I thought was my father was sent to wipe my real father and his family from the earth, he couldn't finish the job. He took me and ran."

She takes a deep breath, looking around the room as if someone is going to jump out at her. "Luca...this is..."

"I know, Giada. It sounds like something out of a book that no one could possibly believe would happen in real life. But it did. It happened to me. Frank, the man who raised me, found out he was dying and came clean about all of it. I have pictures of our fathers together. Frank was a capo who handled things for Francesco when he didn't want anyone to know. Francesco played a major role in his capos hating my family for murders that Francesco ordered, not Cormac Monaghan. He's the reason the two organizations have been at war for all these years. Why Frank never told me where I really came from. He didn't want this life for me but couldn't stomach the idea that when he died, I'd be left alone in this world." I let my mind wander to that conversation, the betrayal I felt in being lied to for all those years. It's similar to the betrayal written all over Giada's face. "After Frank died, I was so fucking angry. I wanted revenge for the lives your father had taken from me. I contacted my cousin, Finn, and we came up with a plan that would get me my revenge and get Finn the control he wanted in Boston."

"Are you the reason my father went to prison? Were

you feeding the feds information? Was it part of your plan to make me trust you so you could somehow get information from me to give to the prosecutor's office?"

"No," I reply firmly. "You were never part of any of it. I won't lie and tell you the thought didn't cross my mind, but I couldn't do that to you, Giada. The US attorney's office built its own case. I didn't want your father in prison. I wanted him to lose everything, and I wanted it to be because of me, because of what he did to my family."

A knock sounds at my door, startling me and Giada.

"Luca, is Giada in there?" Nina asks from the other side.

Giada takes two long strides toward my door and pulls it open. Fuck, she's going to tell Nina everything I just told her and Nina is going to run to one of the guards.

"Nina, I need a couple things before I leave. Would you mind running to the pharmacy for me and filling my birth control prescription? I don't know when the doctor will be able to transfer the prescription to wherever I'm going."

Nina looks between Giada and me with suspicion and question in her brown eyes.

"It could take days to transfer and I don't have that kind of time, Nina. Please."

Honestly I'm not sure if Nina believes Giada's need for her to leave the house, but she nods her head and walks away before Giada closes the door.

"Hopefully my brother isn't too hard on her when he finds out I've escaped."

Ah, she gave the woman a reason for missing her walking out the door.

When she leans against the closed door, Giada's eyes find mine and I see hurt warring with anger in them, but her gaze holds steady with mine. "I need you to be one-hundred-percent honest with me right now and look me dead in the eye when you answer, Luca. Was it part of your plan to get me to fall for you and use me as leverage against my father or brother?"

"No." I shake my head and take a step toward her, but the way she fuses herself to the door halts me in my tracks. "You were never part of the plan, Giada. I just...I can't watch your brother give you away to Petrov. He's not a good man. I can't stand by and watch another woman be sold."

That's why I've concocted this insane plan that hinges on her saying yes and leaving with me. Knowing what the Russians are capable of, knowing they view women similarly to her brother and father, there's no way I can let her go from one prison to another with no one caring whether or not she's safe. Here, I was able to keep an eye on her. There, she wouldn't have anyone who cared about her, certainly not Nikolai, if the rumors about the Petrovs are true.

"It doesn't seem I have much of a choice then." Her eyes are filled with defeat. "I guess you're the lesser of two evils."

My head tilts to the side. "Giada—"

She lifts her hand to stop me from speaking. "It doesn't matter, Luca. You offered me a way out and I don't have a choice but to take it right now. I can't be traded to the Russians so my brother has a partner in whatever plan he's come up with. I won't. But make no mistake, I won't be a pawn for you to use, either. If you want to go through with this, if you truly want to help me, then you need to know I won't be used for information for your family to take mine down. I may hate my brother and my father for what they've done, not just to you but to everyone else, including me, for God's sake, but I deserve a chance. I deserve a shot at living a life where being the daughter or sister of a Mafia boss doesn't define me. I'll go with you because it's my best choice at the moment, regardless of how angry I am. But don't think for one minute you'll control me and rob me of my freedom. If that's even a thought in your head, then you're no better than Carlo or my father."

"I would never—"

"I never thought you would lie to me, and look where we are. I would've never guessed you were this entirely different person than what I believed. I'm going with you because I don't see another way out." Her eyes implore me to see her and listen to her. "Please don't make me regret trusting you now."

"I won't, Giada. I swear to you, you'll be safe."

She lets out a sad huff of laughter. "I'm a girl born into a world ruled by men who only care about power and revenge, Luca. I'm beginning to realize I'll never be safe."

She opens the door, but before she takes her leave, she turns to me. "I'll marry you, Luca, but I'll never trust you." Then she shuts the door behind her.

That fucking stings more than I have time to dissect at the moment. Right now, I need to figure out a way to get Giada off the property, and the only thing I can think of is not going to go over well with my soon-to-be wife.

"The trunk?" Giada hisses as we hurry to one of the cars parked inside the garage.

"It's the only way to get you off the property. Who knows if Carlo already spoke to the guards at the gate? We have to assume he has and that he told them to expect a car in"—I look at my watch—"sixty-three minutes to take you. It's a thirty-minute drive to my apartment. That gives us time to switch cars and be on the road to New Hampshire before the Russians get here. It's not much of a head start, and the longer you stand here arguing with me, the more time we're wasting."

I want to reassure her that everything will be fine, that she can trust me to keep her safe, but I know such assurances will fall on deaf ears. And they'll be worthless if she doesn't get in the damn trunk.

She closes her eyes and her lips move as though she's reciting some sort of prayer.

"Giada, I know you're scared," I begin, setting the duffel bag with her things in it between us. "But I just need you to trust me for thirty minutes until we get to my place."

Her eyes open and her lips form a thin line. "Okay."

She looks in the trunk, and I hold out my hand to help her climb in. The fear in her amber eyes when she looks up at me tears me apart inside. She doesn't trust me at all, but she knows she's backed into a corner with only an hour to be long gone before her brother and the Russians start ripping the place apart to find her. "Thirty minutes." I shut the trunk of the sedan and send a prayer to whoever is listening that we make it out of this alive.

Leaving the property was the easy part. The guard at the gate simply nodded to me as I drove away. There's a sense of relief that I won't ever have to come back here. I've hated the last seven years playing nice with men who I'd rather see buried six feet under than share a beer with. By the time all of this is over, I won't be surprised if that's where several of them end up.

When we pull into the small garage under my building next to my old SUV, I immediately pop the trunk, allowing Giada to see where we are. I rush to the back of the sedan and help her out.

"Can't say I've ever been shoved in a trunk and driven across town, but I can say I'd rather never do that again."

I smile down at her, but she doesn't return the gesture.

"I have to grab a few things, then we need to get out of here." I grab her bags and toss them into my vehicle. It's old as shit, but it's all I got, and I know for a fact the Cataldi cars have trackers on them. I don't particularly care if they find the car here after they realize I've disappeared with Giada. This is another place I don't ever plan on stepping foot in again.

"Come on up." I guide her to the small stairwell that leads to the apartment I've kept even though I'd been staying at the Cataldi estate.

When we enter the apartment, she looks around at the bare walls and the sparse furniture the apartment had when I moved in.

"How long have you lived here?" she asks.

"About seven years, but I haven't stayed here in four months."

"If you have your own place, why were you staying at the estate?"

"Your brother wanted me there to keep an eye on you. Make sure you stayed out of the way and stayed put. When those two assholes your brother started working with came around and leered at you any chance they got, I was so fucking thankful you weren't in that house unprotected. It's the only time I've been grateful to your brother for making sure I stuck around after your father's arrest. Guess it didn't work out how Carlo had hoped, though."

Her gaze drops from mine as she absorbs the truth I gave her. "Get your things, Luca. We need to get out of here before anyone realizes we're both gone."

"Right."

Giada isn't ready to hear the lengths I've gone through—the lengths I'll go through—to make sure she's safe. I'm still the man who came into her life under false pretenses. The man whose sole purpose of being at the house was to find anything I could to destroy her family.

Walking into my small bedroom, I head to my closet and open the crawl space to grab the box with the few things I brought with me from my past and a few other essentials. I take all the cash, guns, and the letter-sized envelope that contains pictures of my life with Frank and the pictures of my parents.

Giada is standing in the doorway when I turn around in the closet and she eyes the box in my hands.

"Can I show you something?" I ask, setting the box on the bed and opening it.

She nods and walks closer to me as I open the box and pull out the envelope of pictures. Reaching into the old manilla envelope, I pull out a picture of our fathers together and one of my real parents and me when I was a baby.

I hold the picture of the three men out to her first. "That's Frank, your father, and my real father, Elio." Then I hand her the other picture. "And that's my mother, Ciara Byrne, Maeve Monaghan's sister."

She studies both briefly, her eyes darting between

mine and the picture of my mother. "You have the same eyes." Her voice is soft, and it's the first time I've felt anything from her other than distrust mixed with a healthy dose of rage since I told her who I really am.

"That's what Finn said. Told me my aunt has the same eyes, too."

I offer a small smile, but Giada doesn't return it, the walls slamming shut once again behind her eyes. "I'll wait for you in the other room," she says, handing the pictures back to me before spinning on her heels to walk away.

After throwing several changes of clothes into a bag, I walk back to the living room and find Giada still standing there. Well, at least she didn't take off. *That's something*, I tell myself.

Grabbing the keys for my SUV from the beige parquet countertop, I leave the keys for the sedan I drove here.

"Let's go." I open the door and allow Giada to step out before shutting it and locking it behind us.

"Where are we going?" she asks as I lead her back down the stairs.

"New Hampshire."

"What's in New Hampshire?" Her voice is breathless as we hurry back to the garage.

"There's no three-day waiting period in that state like there is here. We have time to get there, get a marriage license, and see the justice of the peace."

"Wow, and all before lunch."

"The faster we do this, Giada, the faster you'll be safe

from your brother. I'll call my cousin when it's done, and we'll figure it out from there."

"What if he decides it's too much trouble and wants to send me back to my brother? This shit going on with our families has been a long-standing feud, Luca. The Russians and the Monaghans never had any problems as far as I know." She stops at the passenger door, and I open it for her before throwing my bag in the back seat and walking to the other side of the SUV.

She's right; my cousin's most pressing concern has always been the Cataldis. He's never mentioned the Russians, but after Alessia was taken and he found out they were willing to help Carlo and Farina take over Boston, his tune changed pretty damn quick.

"Finn has no problems taking out two birds with one stone. Trust me," I assure her as I start the engine.

"Am I supposed to be the stone? I already told you I won't be used as a pawn in this bullshit. I just want to be safe from whatever Carlo has planned for me."

"You will be, Giada. You'll be my wife, which will make you a Monaghan through marriage. Trust me, no one is going to take you from me."

"That's the thing, Luca, I don't trust you, but I'm desperate enough to go along with this."

It's not the answer I'd wish for, but it's not like I can be too bothered by the fact she's suspicious, especially when all she knows about the Monaghans has come from her father or brother.

Without saying anything further on the subject, I pull

out of the garage and begin the drive to Manchester. Giada is quiet on the car ride, and the silence is stifling. I want to know what she's thinking. Scratch that, I want her to be thinking that I'll take care of her, that she has nothing to worry about now that we're on the road, but I know she won't believe me. Every man in her life has used her as a pawn in their games for more power. That's what Carlo was going to do. Though it's not my intention, I'm sure she feels differently. At the very least, she's not ruling out the idea that, once again, she's somehow going to be used.

"Not exactly how you imagined your wedding day, I'll bet." Jesus, that's a stupid thing to say.

Giada lets out a chuckle that is completely devoid of humor. "The only thing I knew about my wedding day was I wasn't going to be happy about the groom I was going to be marrying." She looks over at me. "So, I suppose this is exactly how I imagined it."

Fucking ouch.

I want to tell her if she's going to be a brat about it we can call the whole thing off. But I know I won't, and I know she won't either. Right now, she's angry and scared. And hurt. If lashing out makes her feel better or makes her feel like she has some control over her life, I won't hold it against her. It's not like I handled being told everything I'd known about my life was a lie with any sort of grace. I lashed out a hell of a lot worse than she is. Does it make the drive any more comfortable? No. There's nothing I can say that'll make her believe me. The only way she'll be confident that she's safe and no one is going to use her or lie to her again is for her to actually see it. Anyone can tell you one thing and do the exact opposite. If I want Giada to trust me, it's going to take work and patience.

"So, is my last name going to be Bennetti or was that a lie too?"

I haven't thought about it. I used the same last name that I've had my entire life. If anyone had done any digging, all they'd find was a kid with a dead father and a chip on his shoulder. It didn't seem necessary to change everything about myself.

"My last name is Bennetti. At least that's what I've always gone by, but my dad, Frank, told me that my real father's name was Romano."

"And my father had him killed." This is the first time since I told her the truth about my parentage that she's brought it up.

"He did." My hands tighten around the steering wheel at the mention of Francesco. It's as though now that I don't have to pretend I don't hate the man, it's impossible to temper my reaction.

"Why though? Falling in love with someone doesn't seem like that big of an offense." I appreciate the curiosity, but damn, this is the last thing I want to talk about. I told her she could trust me though, and the first thing I do can't be to shut the conversation down just because I'm uncomfortable.

"My father, Elio, fell in love with Maeve Monaghan's

sister. It's no secret your father expects the utmost loyalty from his men. My father was his consigliere, and when he found out Elio was with my mother and they had a child together, he was convinced my father was betraying him and talking to the Irish."

"So he had him killed? Why not try to talk to him?"

"I don't know. You'd have to ask him. But from what I know of your father, he's the shoot first, ask questions later kind of boss."

"Can't argue that. And Frank. How does he fit into all this?"

"He was the hit man sent to kill my parents. When he found me in my crib, he couldn't finish what your father wanted him to. Said there was some spiritual woo-woo moment or some shit."

"Spiritual woo-woo?" she asks, looking confused at my description.

"He explained it better. But yeah. He knew he was sent there to protect me."

"So he just took off with you?"

"Kind of. He called your house and your mother answered. She told him to run and gave him some money."

"Wait. My mother knew about you?"

"Yeah. Frank said she was a good woman. A devout Catholic. He needed help and knew she wouldn't turn him away or turn him into Francesco. I don't know. I kind of think he needed a woman who believed in God but also knew what was expected of someone in this life to tell him he was doing the right thing. That's what she did."

Giada stares out the window at the passing scenery. It's spring in Massachusetts and the trees along the stretch of highway between Boston and Manchester are lined with budding green trees. New beginnings and all that.

"If you have any questions I'll answer with one-hundred-percent honesty, Giada. I don't want lies between us.

"I don't," she snaps.

It's a lot to take in, so I don't try to continue the conversation even though I'm sure there's more she's curious about. I kind of get the feeling that anything, including the sound of my voice, is liable to set her off. There's no denying our nerves are at an all-time high. We're running from her brother and the Petrovs. In about thirty minutes, she'll have a new last name, and after that, I'll have to call my cousin and explain why it's time I come out of hiding with my new wife.

Hell, it's definitely not how I saw today going when I opened my eyes this morning.

Chapter Twelve
Giada

How is this what my life has turned into? The entire drive, I was trying and failing to come up with a plan that would get me out of whatever insane deal my brother made with the Petrovs while continuously telling myself jumping out of a moving vehicle was not the way to escape this predicament. Yes, Luca took a huge risk in telling me who he really was. But to say the admission didn't spark some sense of buried family loyalty would be a lie. Not enough to make me want to run and tell someone that he was an impostor and has been working against our family since he arrived at the estate seven years ago, though. I feel completely betrayed that he played his role for seven years and I still wasn't sure of his true motivations for wanting to now be my knight in shining armor. The one he said he wasn't and never would be when I was younger.

Luca finds a parking spot on the street. We look out of the dirty window of his SUV and read the time on the giant clock on the city hall building in Manchester. Nearly eleven in the morning. Guess I was right about this being taken care of before lunch.

Luca and I stare at the building, neither of us moving or barely breathing at this point.

"You ready to do this?" he asks. If I didn't know better, I would swear there was a note of nervousness in his voice.

I turn to him in time to see him swallow roughly, staring at the building before his gaze flicks to mine and all traces of anxiety are gone.

"Promise me again you won't use me against my family, Luca. I need to know you're doing this only because neither of us can see another way out and not because this is part of some elaborate scheme to take down my family."

Luca's gaze softens as he stares into my pleading eyes. "Your brother will stop at nothing to take back control of Boston from my cousin and his father-in-law. I wish like hell it hadn't come down to this, Giada, I truly do, but he's using you to make an alliance with the Russians. I want to keep you safe. But you should know before we go in there your brother was involved with trying to hurt my cousin's wife."

Fucking Carlo. Using or hurting women has never been an issue for him. The fact he tried with Monaghan's wife isn't surprising, just incredibly stupid.

"Finn's been looking for him and not to have a coffee and a chat. The Russians want to use him to get to Boston, and he's willing to trade you for their help. This is the only way I can think of to keep them from making that alliance. I understand if you view that as using you, but this is also the only way I can think to keep you out of the Russians' hands for good. It's not like if Finn finds Carlo and the world is short another asshole, the Russians will let you go. Honestly, who knows what the hell they would do with you. But if you're with me, if you're my wife, my family will make damn sure no one touches you. You will have the backing of the entire Monaghan organization, regardless of who you're related to. From what my cousin told me, my aunt takes marriage quite seriously. All of them do. Family is what's most important to them."

The sad part about what he just said is I have no idea how that feels. To me, family has always felt like a chain around me. Sure, it was under the guise of loyalty, but it wasn't from a place of love for family; it was always about control.

I consider his statement and appreciate his honesty. But fuck, I'm still pissed as hell at him for lying to me, for springing this on me. I'm pissed I'm in this situation at all and that he's right. I can't run. Where the hell would I go? If my brother signed any sort of contract with the Russians, I'm as good as theirs. Not only will Carlo be searching for me, but I'll most likely have the Petrovs on my tail as well. There's no way in hell I'd make it more than a week on my own, not with all the people my brother and the Russians know.

But if I'm married, well, you can't be married to two people at the same time. Any contract signed by my brother would be null and void. He'll be pissed, but all

I can say about that is too fucking bad. He thought I was going to roll over and do his bidding. If Luca wasn't there with another plan, I most likely would have.

I open the car door. "No turning back now. They probably already know we're gone. I may be pissed as hell you lied, and I hate how you came into my life. I sure as hell don't trust the Monaghans, but I also don't have another choice. It's just another time where I don't have much of a say." The look on his face is remorseful that, once again, I'm put in a situation where everyone has control over my life. Everyone except me.

Luca jogs to catch up to me as I hastily make my way to the front door of city hall. As far as weddings go, I suppose it's better than the one my brother or my father would have planned for me. Between the two of them, they would have been like peacocks showing off their fancy feathers, or in this case, they'd each be wearing wide sharklike grins, knowing my union to the husband of their choice would ensure a powerful alliance. I would've been expected to play the part of an excited and deliriously happy bride. It would have been a lie then just as it's a lie now.

He opens the door, and a sign hangs overhead, directing us to where we need to get our marriage license. The sound of our footsteps echoes off the walls. I should feel as though each step I take is a step toward freedom, but I'm scared. Luca is a good liar. He'd have to be to have survived in this little undercover sting operation he was a part of. The thought crosses my mind for the hundredth time that this could be a ploy to get me under his control and use me against my family. It's not the thought of destroying Carlo or my father that scares me; it's what will happen to me when I'm no longer useful. But the thought of being given away to the Russians scares me more, and that's what propels me forward.

Before we get in line for the designated counter for marriage licenses, Luca gently grips my elbow and pulls me aside.

"When all of this is said and done," he says in a low voice, standing so close I have to tilt my chin up to look in his eyes. "I won't expect you to stay married to me. I know you want out of this life and out of Boston. I won't hold you prisoner, Giada."

I nod subtly, too overcome with nerves to give him much more of a reaction. I'm afraid if I open my mouth now, everything will come pouring out. About how much of a crush I had on him when I was younger, that I used to dream of marrying him and of him running away with me like some sappy romance movie. Or that the last few months of being around him again, seeing him every day, made me wish things were different. My feelings for Luca never completely disappeared. What was once a teenage crush turned into something else in the last few months, at least for me. And for a time, I thought maybe for him too. Now, I'm going through my memory with this new information about who he really is, and it puts a different slant on just about every interaction we've ever had. The times he would stop himself from speaking. Was it because he wanted to come clean? To be honest with me because he didn't want lies and buried truths between us? Or am I romanticizing a liar and a criminal because I'm desperate to have someone in my corner who actually cares about what happens to me?

I suppose his reasons don't matter. He's the lifeline I have to grab. We may not know what's in store after we say our vows, but I sure as hell know what's in store if I let Nikolai Petrov get his hands on me. I was right earlier in saying I'm choosing the lesser of two evils. If there's one thing I'm sure of, there are no white knights or saviors in this life. But maybe Luca will take pity on me and stay true to his word, letting me go after all is said and done. Regardless of how terrified I am that I could be putting my trust in someone who has done nothing but lie to me for years, I'm not left with much of a choice.

The people in the line start moving toward the counter with happy and excited smiles on their faces. I suppose none of them are being chased by their deranged brother, who's trying to trade her to another criminal organization for power and protection. This is probably one of the happiest days of their life, and under different circumstances or in a different life, it would have been mine, too.

"Come on, let's get in line. The quicker we get this done, the quicker we can go see your cousin."

Luca's face falls a bit when he realizes I'm not going to respond to his promise of letting me go. He probably assumes I don't believe him, and he's right. I don't. Not fully anyways. But his reaction is a step in the right direction because I want to trust him, naive as it may be. I want to believe his story is true and even though he's lied for years, he's at least being honest about this one thing. It's all I have at this point.

The line moves fairly quickly, and before long, he has the license in his hand. The clerk directs us to the justice of the peace, and it's another short wait for her to perform the ceremony. I can't help but look at the two couples before us; both of the women are wearing white dresses as they stand to wait for their turn.

"I'm sorry you don't have a dress," Luca says, looking down at the jeans and sweater I hastily put on before leaving the house. Of course, he's dressed in a pair of black slacks and a white dress shirt, which is the staple uniform of the guards at my house. Well, I suppose it isn't my house anymore.

I shrug. "Considering we're running from my brother and the Russians, I don't think it matters what I'm wearing in the grand scheme of things."

"Fair point. Maybe I would have liked to see you in white though."

"Maybe I would have liked to not have to marry you to save myself from a Russian psychopath and my brother, but here we are."

Luca's eyes drop to the floor and his jaw tics with

frustration. He's trying to make this better for me. I don't think he regrets the decision he made to come to Boston years ago to avenge his parents' murders, but I do believe he regrets my being pulled into this situation.

"I'm sorry. That was uncalled for," I say, feeling a pang of remorse at my harsh words. "You're risking your life to help me."

"I understand, Giada, more than you could imagine. I know what it's like to be lied to by someone you care about. I can't expect you to trust me yet, but I hope I can prove to you I'm not here to hurt you or use you."

"Maybe you can put that in your vows?" I joke quietly, lifting the corner of my mouth in a small grin.

Luca's eyes brighten with my joke, a touch of relief in his gaze. "That might get a strange look from her." He nods toward the woman standing behind the desk, watching as the couple in front of her share their first kiss as husband and wife.

There's one couple in front of us, and when they get to the part where they're exchanging rings, Luca looks at me with a sad smile. "I don't have a ring for you."

There's something about the dismay on his face that thaws a tiny part of me. It's such an inconsequential thing, considering I don't think either of us woke up this morning thinking this is where we would be. The disappointment he has because he can't give me some small sense of normalcy in the incredibly abnormal situation makes me feel...I don't know, less angry, less alone.

I reach into my pocket and pull out a small gold band, holding it between us. "This was my grandmother's. My uncle gave it to me on my last trip. Said my mother would have given it to me herself, but..." Everyone knows she died when I was a child.

"Giada, I don't want you to use that for this wedding. After all is said and done, what if you meet the man of your dreams and want him to slide that ring on your finger? Your mother would want you to wear that ring as a sign of love and commitment to the man you choose to be with, not me."

At one point I thought Luca was the man of my dreams, but I don't tell him that. "My mother would want me to marry someone who promises to protect me. That's what you're doing. I don't think she would have a problem with me using this ring, so you shouldn't either."

Luca nods and takes the ring before putting it in his pocket. "I do want to protect you, Giada. That's what I've always tried to do."

The last couple before us finish with their short ceremony and we get up to walk to the desk, handing the license to the woman's cheery-faced assistant. She smiles and signs the paper as the witness then the justice of the peace begins her speech. Luca and I stare at each other, and I barely make out what the woman is saying through the noise of rushing blood in my head. The urge to cry takes me by surprise. The man in front of me was the star of this little fantasy when I was younger, and now it's my reality. But this reality leaves so much to be desired it's almost laughable. In exactly none of my fantasies about this moment did I consider the only reason he would be marrying me was because my brother was about to hand me over to a ruthless organization. I imagined a look of love and devotion in his eyes, not the apologetic one I see now.

Luca slips the gold band on my finger and repeats the words he's supposed to. I do the same, minus the ring, and a moment later, we're pronounced husband and wife.

"You may kiss the bride," the justice of the peace says.

I stand in front of Luca, momentarily frozen, my heart galloping in my chest as he leans in, his soft lips brushing mine. A zap of electricity runs through me at the contact. His kiss is gentle. He doesn't try to deepen it in any way, but holy shit, I wish he would. That thought takes me by surprise as I back away from him and stare into his blue eyes. Confusion and surprise flick through his gaze, the same as mine, I'm sure. What the hell was that? I've kissed other men, hell, I've done more than that, but never have I felt tiny fireworks explode throughout my chest at the simple touch of a man's lips to mine.

Luca clears his throat and the trance is broken. He thanks the justice of the peace and her assistant before we turn and silently walk out of the building. I feel like I should say something. I don't know what, but the silence between us is weighing heavily on me as I still taste him on my lips.

Luca guides me back to the car and opens the passenger door. When he gets in on the other side, his body turns toward mine and he studies me for a moment. "That part's done. I need to call my cousin," he says after a few beats of crushing silence.

And there's the stab to the heart. I didn't necessarily think he was going to wax poetic about marriage and commitment or be overly joyous that I was now officially his wife. But to say absolutely nothing about what I know he felt in there when we sealed our marriage vows stings in a way I wasn't prepared for.

He pulls a phone from his pocket and brings it to his ear. "Hey. We need to talk about my leaving. And by talk, I mean I'm leaving with Giada. Today." Luca is silent for a few moments as he listens to his cousin on the other end. He looks at me and offers a small smile then steps out of the car, but I can still hear the muffled conversation.

"Listen, Finn. We've been doing it your way, and I understand, but Carlo hasn't been here in months, and Giada got word that she needed to pack her things and be ready for some Russian to pick her up later today. He was going to ship her off to marry a man who will do God knows what to her. I'm done fighting in the shadows, Finn. And I'm not going to stand back while he hurts an innocent. I'm getting out, and Giada is coming with me." Luca watches me through the dusty window and listens to his cousin before briefly closing his eyes.

"Too late," he says and opens his eyes again, looking at me with steely determination. "Well, she can't exactly marry the Pakhan's son if she's already married. I married her, Finn."

He gives Finn our location then it sounds like he tries to apologize. I can't lie to myself and say that doesn't scare me, especially considering Luca told me that Carlo went after Finn's wife. What if Finn decides that Luca's decision puts his family in too much danger? He's the head of the Irish mob. If he wants to send me back to my brother, he has the power to do it, and if he's anything like my brother, Luca doesn't stand a chance, which means neither do I.

Luca gets back in the car and blows out a breath. "We're going to Finn's penthouse in Boston. He's meeting us there."

"Is he upset?" Is he going to send me back?

"He was...surprised." Luca gives me a reassuring smile. "It'll be fine. We'll go to the penthouse, and Finn will help us figure it out from there. Carlo can't get to you now."

I appreciate that he has faith in his cousin.

I just wish I had the same.

Chapter Thirteen

Luca

G IADA IS GNAWING ON her bottom lip as we drive to Boston. The lip I kissed not even an hour ago. The kiss that had me questioning everything I thought I knew about myself. I was here to make sure Francesco Cataldi paid for what he did to my parents, to the Monaghans, and to the man who raised me. I wasn't meant to come to Boston and fall for his daughter. But there is no denying the heat that raced through me when her lips met mine after we said our vows.

"Hey," I say, taking my hand from the wheel and using my thumb to pull her abused lip from her teeth. "You don't have anything to worry about. Finn understands there was no way I was going to allow Carlo to trade you to the Russians."

"Carlo tried to hurt his wife. You don't think that's going to be playing through his mind when he looks at me?"

I let out a breath. "I think Finn is going to see a girl who needs help. My family doesn't view women the same as yours. He doesn't use them to make deals and gain power."

"That's not what I heard. He married an Amatto to do just that."

"Fair," I concede. "But Finn loves his wife, regardless of why they got married. He respects her and has her working in his casino. From what I hear, she runs the place and he doesn't allow anyone to utter one cross word about her. That's not a man who doesn't care about his woman."

"One woman. Fine. But me? That's a whole other story."

"I said I would protect you. In fact, I remember making that vow to you less than an hour ago. Do you think I'm going to go back on my word now? We haven't even been married a full day. Give me a little credit."

"That was so my brother couldn't marry me off. It wasn't real."

"Seemed pretty real to me." That kiss was sure as hell real.

Giada stares at her hands lying in her lap, her fingers twisting and pulling.

"What are you really worried about?" I ask. Her nerves are understandable and it's been a hell of a morning, but there's something else going on in her mind. I want more than anything for her to have the same courage she's always had with me and tell me what she's thinking.

"What if he sends me back?" she whispers, continuing to stare at her lap. "What if he doesn't want anything to do with me because I'm a Cataldi and he wants me gone and away from his family? I'm dangerous, Luca."

"First of all, you're not dangerous. That's your brother. Our marriage has all but incapacitated him as far as what moves he can make now. If you're married to me, the Russians won't help him. Even they don't have the power to override the state of New Hampshire, and as of eleven thirty this morning, they attested to the fact that you are now my wife. Second, you're no longer a Cataldi. You're a Bennetti, and by extension, a Monaghan. Even my cousin can't deny that. So, as far as I'm concerned, you're family, just as much as me."

Giada's stare bores into me as I continue to drive down the highway to the penthouse.

"What?" I ask, glancing at her.

"I'm your wife."

"That's what I just said."

A laugh bubbles from her, and I'll admit, I'm a little scared the day has caught up to her and she's cracking under the pressure. Not that I could blame her.

"I don't know why I find it funny. I'm still pissed you pulled the wool over my eyes for years, but it just hit me that we're married now."

"Giada, you know why I couldn't say anything. Even when you'd confided in me, I had to be careful—"

"I understand. What you did was incredibly dangerous, and I'm glad as hell you weren't caught. Otherwise, I'd be on my way to New York right now, and you'd be..." She pauses, the weight of what she was going to say suddenly heavy in the SUV.

"I'd be dead."

"As your wife, I think it's well within my rights to tell you never to do something like that again."

I smile at the no-nonsense tone in her voice. "I'll give you that."

The feeling in the car lightens as we make our way into the city, but as soon as we pull into the underground parking of Finn's penthouse and Giada gets a look at the three armed guards waiting for us to park, her jaw tenses along with every muscle in her body.

"Remember what I said. You're my wife, and that means you're family."

"Being related to someone by blood or marriage has never meant the same in my family as it has in yours."

"Exactly. It doesn't mean the same thing. So when I tell you you're safe, please believe I'm saying that as the man who married you to make sure you stay that way. I wouldn't bring you here if I didn't know for certain I can keep that promise." I reach over and cover her hand with mine. "Giada?" I prompt when she doesn't move a muscle.

When her eyes meet mine, there's still fear in them, but there's a flicker of certainty that she knows I'm telling her the truth. I can work with that.

"Okay," she breathes out. "Introduce me to your cousin."

I squeeze her clammy palm once more for a little extra reassurance, then step out of the car and walk to her side of the SUV to open the door for her. As soon as she stands, the elevator door opens, and Finn steps into the garage.

He walks to where we're standing and wraps me in a hug. "I'm glad to see you, cousin." Finn pats my back twice then releases me, turning his attention to Giada. "Finn Monaghan," he introduces, a smile playing on his lips as he holds his hand out for her to shake.

If the tension rolling off Giada wasn't breaking my heart, I would laugh at the surprise in her eyes at the warm greeting my cousin is giving her. So different from what thoughts I'm sure are swirling in that beautiful head of hers.

"Giada Cataldi."

I clear my throat and she gives me a small smile.

"I mean Giada Bennetti."

Finn looks between the two of us and smiles even wider while shaking his head. "You two really know how to make an exit," he says, humor in his voice.

"Have you heard anything yet?"

"No. Not that I expect to. You were my only line inside the family. With you gone, we're blind."

"I'd say I'm sorry about that—"

"Yeah, yeah." He waves a hand in front of him. "You did what you had to do. I'd have done the same if I were in your shoes. Come on." Finn tilts his head toward the elevator. "I'll have my guy update the keypad with your handprints so you can come and go as you please, though I wouldn't suggest leaving the penthouse anytime soon. Carlo and the Russians are sure to be on the lookout for this one," he says, pointing his thumb at Giada.

"Thank you," she tells Finn. "For letting me come here. I know this puts you in a dangerous situation."

He looks between my new wife and me before settling his gaze back on her. "You're family now," he replies as though it explains everything. To him, it does. For her, it's going to take a little time for that not to be a meaningless word.

We head into the elevator and Finn shows us into the spacious loft-style penthouse with exposed brick walls and huge windows letting in the natural sunlight of the early afternoon.

His wife, Alessia, is sitting on the couch, and when she turns, her face breaks into a wide smile. She stands and comes over to Giada. "So good to see you again," she says, holding out her hand. "I don't know if you remember me, but we met years ago. Gosh, you were maybe eight?"

Giada nods as relief washes over her. I'm sure she was nervous about seeing the woman in front of her after what her brother tried to do not that long ago. "I remember. It was at your family's Christmas party. I loved the tiara you had on, and you let me wear it for the night."

Alessia laughs at the memory, and I smirk. "So I wasn't far off in calling you princess."

Giada shoots me a narrow look. "I was eight, and it

was sparkly."

Finn's phone rings and he takes the call, his brow furrowed. When he hangs up Alessia's concerned look has me on edge.

"What is it?" she asks her husband.

"It was one of the guards."

"Is it my brother?" Giada asks, fear lacing her words.

"No," Finn replies. "It's mine." His eyes find mine. "And my mother."

I guess it's a good day for a wedding and a family reunion.

Moments later the front door swings open, and an older version of a woman that looks so much like my mother barges in, with a younger man who is obviously her son trailing behind.

"You have a lot of nerve, Finnegan Monaghan. How dare you keep such a secret from me?"

"Really, Eoghan?" Finn grits out at his brother. "Bet you couldn't wait to run to Mom with this little tidbit, could you?"

"Don't blame me, brother. Did you honestly think I was going to keep this from her? She has a right to know her nephew is alive and well."

"Yeah, he is, but I didn't know if that was going to stay the case. It's not like he was living his life, happy as a clam somewhere and I kept it from her. I didn't want her heart to break all over again if someone found out who he was and—"

"Do not make excuses for your poor judgment. You

should have told me the second you found out he was alive. If I thought it would do any good, I'd put you over my knee and spank some sense into you." She points a threatening finger at Finn.

Though Maeve is shooting fire at her eldest son with her eyes, the moment they land on me, tears douse the flames. Her hand goes to her mouth, and she stops in the middle of the room, staring at me.

"Oh my God," she whispers. "You look just like your mother." My aunt races to me and throws her arms around my shoulders, pulling me down to envelop me in a fierce embrace. "I prayed and wished this day would come. That you would find your way home to us," she cries into my shoulder.

I'm stunned to have this woman I've never met wrap me so tightly in her arms that it takes a moment for me to return the hug. When I do, she starts crying harder, and I feel my eyes get watery right along with hers. This is the closest I'll ever get to hugging my mother. The moment feels surreal to finally meet the woman my cousin has always spoken so highly of.

Maeve backs up a step but keeps a firm grasp on my upper arms. "My God. You have her eyes," she says in awe as she stares into them. "Oh, sweet boy." She starts to cry again and Finn walks up behind her, resting a hand on her back.

"Come on, Mom. Let's not overwhelm Luca. He's had a day as it is."

Maeve whirls on Finn. "I'm so damn angry at you right

now. You know what I went through. You know the years I searched for this boy in the face of every child his age on the street. But you don't know about the nights your father held me while I cried, so overcome with grief I could hardly breathe. And you knew he was alive for seven years."

Finn looks at his wife for help, but she gives him the look of *you're on your own here, pal.* I don't blame her. Maeve Monaghan is a force, but since I agreed to the plan of keeping my identity a secret, I feel a responsibility to shoulder at least some of the blame.

"It was my fault, too. When I found out who I really was and who my family was, I didn't want to put you through losing another family member all over again. I'd just lost my dad, and I didn't want anyone to go through that kind of pain."

Maeve takes a deep breath and releases it through her nose. "I can't imagine what it was like for you growing up. I'm so sorry I wasn't there for you. I wish I could have been."

"Frank was a good man. He raised me right and I never wanted for anything," I say, suddenly feeling defensive over my childhood. Then, I remember Frank also murdered her sister. Yeah, I don't think she's going to want to hear anything remotely good about the man.

"How did this happen? Where have you been the last twenty-eight years?" she asks.

I'm nervous about telling her my story. To tell her that after I found out who Frank really was, I still stayed, still took care of him until he died. I've often wondered if he hadn't been sick, would I have stayed? Or would I have left California and gone straight to the Monaghans with what I knew and let them sort it out? On the one hand, Frank was responsible for the death of my parents, but he saved me. Francesco Cataldi is a monster. One who didn't care that he sent someone to kill an innocent baby. The man who raised me and the man who is a murderer are two different people in my mind. Or maybe that's what I need to tell myself in order to justify my decision to take care of him in his last days.

"It's a long story, Mom," Finn interjects, seeing the nerves and anxiety written all over my face. "Let's let Giada and Luca settle in. There's plenty of time for him to tell you his story."

I can tell it's taking everything for Maeve not to bulldoze her way into the situation and get every detail from me this very second, but she nods at her oldest son and a sense of relief flows through me. I've never had to explain why I stayed with Frank or why, after what he did to my real parents, I'll always love the man who raised me. I'm still coming to terms with it even after all these years.

Maeve turns to Giada who has been standing silently next to Alessia. "You must be Giada," she greets with a warm smile. She walks over to my wife and wraps her in a hug. Giada stiffens for a moment then returns the embrace with a look of surprise and relief etched across her face.

"Nice to meet you, Mrs. Monaghan."

My aunt pulls away and still holds Giada's arms like she did mine, as though she wants my wife to really hear her. "Call me Aunt Maeve. You're family now. Though I'm not sure how comforting that is considering you married into a family where sons lie to their mothers for years." She shoots Finn a pointed look.

"Mom," Finn groans out. "I had my reasons."

"Yes, son. I'm well aware. You always do." Her tone tells me and everyone else that she wholeheartedly disagrees with his reasons.

An hour later, Maeve and the rest of the Monaghans are still at the penthouse. The tension has cooled between Maeve and Finn. Finn is still annoyed with his brother for dragging their mother into this without warning him first so we could discuss how best to explain the situation to everyone. Then Finn receives another call from his guard, letting him know that Cormac Monaghan has arrived. If I thought Giada was nervous about meeting my aunt, it's nothing compared to the fear in her eyes when Cormac walks through the door. Her father hated the man. I can only imagine all the things she must have heard about him through the years, considering my wife has always had a knack for eavesdropping on conversations she shouldn't have been privy to.

He walks to his wife, who's sitting on the couch next to Alessia first and kisses her. They stare at each other for a moment, communicating with just a look before

Maeve nods and smiles. Then he stands and looks at his son, who is sitting on the opposite sofa. "You and I will discuss this later," he tells Finn, pointing a finger at him. I don't miss the smirk on Eoghan's face. When his father turns to him, he points the same finger in his direction. "And I'll be talking to you as well."

Eoghan's face falls and he looks around the room. "What the hell did I do?"

"Language," Maeve admonishes.

Cormac pays him no mind when he turns to me and Giada sitting in the two club chairs we pulled to form a circle with the rest of the living room furniture.

I stand and hold out my hand. "Luca Bennetti," I introduce. "And this is my wife, Giada Bennetti."

Cormac smiles, picking up on the fact that she is no longer a Cataldi and now has my last name and is under my protection.

"I'm glad to meet you, Luca," he says, shaking my hand. I'm grateful he doesn't pepper me with questions like my aunt did, though I'm sure he wants the answers just as much as she does.

Giada nervously stands next to me, and Cormac turns his eyes on her then holds out his hand. "Welcome to the family," he tells her with a kind smile. She returns it, and he leans in, kissing both of her cheeks.

"I already said that," Maeve tells him.

"Well, dear wife, it doesn't hurt for the girl to hear it from me." He winks and smiles wide at Giada. And just like that, I watch the tension fall away from her as she smiles back at my uncle.

"Thank you," she replies, and I take her hand, squeezing it as if to say *see, I told you they were different from what you've always known.*

Early afternoon turns into evening as Giada and I spend the day getting to know my family. Maeve and Eoghan do most of the talking, keeping the conversation light, mostly reminiscing about family trips and funny moments they had together growing up. No one asks me about my life before coming to Boston, and I'm thankful for it. I know it's not because they don't want to know. Finn asked them to hold off on questioning me, understanding that all of this can be a little overwhelming and our day already started out on shaky ground, to put it mildly.

When Eoghan's stomach lets out a loud growl, we realize that it's well past dinnertime. Giada and I haven't eaten today, but until now, I didn't notice how hungry I am. It's been a hell of a day and my nerves are shot, as I'm sure Giada's are.

"Finn, do you have anything to eat here?" Maeve asks.

"I brought a few things with me," Alessia answers before standing.

"Please, let me help," Giada offers as Alessia walks past her into the open kitchen.

Alessia nods and the women begin opening cupboards and the refrigerator, pulling out all kinds of ingredients.

"You're lucky your wife volunteers to cook," Finn says.

"Mine barely makes me a sandwich if I ask."

"Finnegan Monaghan, you have two hands and are perfectly capable of making your own damn food. Not to mention, we're hardly ever home for me to cook dinner, so you can shove it," Alessia calls from behind the large counter that separates the kitchen from the living room. "And don't act like I never cook. I wrestled that damn tiramisu recipe from my mother's cook and made it for you last week, and what did you say?"

"I said it was delicious," he replies.

"No, you said it was delicious, but my mother's cook was still better and that I should practice more."

Maeve gasps. "Finn!"

My cousin holds up his palms. "In my defense, I only said that because Alessia is as stubborn as they come, and I thought if I challenged her to be even better than her parents' cook, I'd be swimming in tiramisu."

I bark out a laugh. "How did that work out for you?" I ask.

Finn shakes his head and blows out a breath. "Not well."

Cormac laughs, and we fall back into easy conversation. My uncle imparts his wisdom of staying married for the last thirty-five years and it basically boils down to happy wife, happy life. As I watch Giada and Alessia cook together, I wonder if I'll be sitting with her in thirty-five years or if, once all is said and done, she'll take me up on the offer I made her today before we said our vows. That as soon as she's safe and her brother is taken care of, she's free to move on and get out of this life that has brought her nothing but pain and heartache.

After eating a delicious meal of pasta with a light tomato sauce and garlic bread, the Monaghans say their goodbyes, Finn telling us he'll be back in the morning and we'll discuss our plans now that shit is sure to have hit the fan. Maeve hugs me long and tight before getting into the elevator with the rest of her family, a teary smile on her face as the door shuts.

Giada is cleaning up the plates from dinner when I walk back into the kitchen.

"Here, let me help." She looks at me with surprise in her eyes. "You cooked, I can clean."

Giada shakes her head, clearing her thoughts. "Sorry, I'm not used to a man doing 'woman's work.'"

I roll my eyes because that's something I'm sure her father and brother said countless times about various things. "That's some antiquated bullshit, Giada. We've both had a long fucking day, and there's no reason any of this"—I sweep my hand over the pile of dishes in the sink—"should fall on you just because you're a woman."

She smiles and steps back, taking her glass of wine and sitting on the couch while I roll up my sleeves and get to work.

When I've finished, Giada is practically falling asleep where she sits.

"Come on," I say. "Let's go to bed."

Her gaze darts to me and she looks at the loft on the

other side of the open space where the only bedroom is.

"I'll take the couch," I offer, and she nods. If I'm not mistaken, there's a hint of disappointment in her gaze, but she doesn't argue with me as she trudges up the stairs.

An hour later, I'm wide awake, lying on the couch with nothing but a throw blanket and decorative pillow to rest my head on. I'm sure I could go in search of something more comfortable, but I don't want to disturb Giada. She's had a hell of a day, and she's probably fast asleep by now, seeing as her eyes were half-closed when she walked up the wrought iron staircase to the loft bedroom. It's not until I hear muffled sobs that I realize I'm not the only one who can't seem to calm my racing mind.

The sounds coming from the room tug at my chest. There's no way I can keep myself on this couch while Giada is up there crying, probably completely overwhelmed by everything that's happened in the last twelve hours. My god, was it just this morning I drove her away from that house in the trunk of my car to escape her brother and the Russians?

I make my way up the stairs and see a lump curled up under the blankets of the California king bed facing away from me.

"Giada," I say gently as I lie down next to her and turn on my side, facing the crying girl. "Talk to me."

She turns over, and I can scarcely make out her face

in the darkness of the room, but I catch the glistening of tears on her cheeks.

"Being here, with the Monaghans, it's so different than I expected. I don't remember my father ever looking at my mother the way I saw Cormac look at Maeve. I've never felt the love Cormac so obviously has for his sons and the way he was kind and respectful to Alessia. I've never had that, Luca. My house was so cold. I had nannies and housekeepers make sure my needs were met, but no one showed me the love I saw tonight. I guess…I guess I'm just sad that I missed out on that. I thought that's how all fathers in this life were—cold and distant. It never occurred to me it's not this life that made him that way, that's who my father is to the core. The Monaghans are proof of that. It made me realize if he wanted to give a shit about me, there was nothing stopping him. Caring about his family wouldn't have made him sacrifice his business or his power. He could have had both. But he didn't. Why couldn't he have just been a father to me? Why couldn't he have loved me like he should have?"

Her broken sobs break my fucking heart because I don't have the answer. Except that Francesco is a heartless bastard, but Giada knows that. She's just now seeing it didn't have to be that way because he was head of a Mafia family, and that's what's hurting her. If he wanted to, if it was important to him, he could have been the father she deserves, but he never was.

"I don't know, sweetheart. I wish like hell I did. I

wish you could have grown up in a house where you were told how special you are and how incredible you are. That they're so damn lucky you're their daughter. Because he is, Giada. He was blessed to have a daughter like you, and he never appreciated it like he should have."

"You're lucky, Luca. To have the Monaghans. I saw how much they love each other and how strong their bonds are. I'm so glad you get to have that."

"They're your family now too. You have the family you always deserved; it just took a little longer to find them."

Giada hums but doesn't say anything further on the subject. That's okay. Today is a lot to process, and she needs some time to work out her thoughts.

With nothing but silence between us, I move to get up and go back downstairs.

"Don't," Giada whispers. "Stay here."

I pause and slowly lie back down next to her, sinking into the plush mattress.

"Thank you," she says when she feels me settle. "I just...I don't want to be alone."

"Neither do I," I reply and cover her hand resting between us before closing my eyes, letting exhaustion pull me into a dreamless sleep.

Chapter Fourteen
Giada

I WAKE TO AN unfamiliar room with what feels like a furnace pressed to my back and a heavy arm banded around my waist. *Luca.* He stayed all night. The thought brings a smile to my lips. Yesterday was beyond hard. I think I ran through every emotion possible. From nearly paralyzing fear to anger to relief, then a soul-deep sadness that Luca tried to ease by simply staying with me all night like I asked. There's still so much to deal with—to process—but having him with me lightens the load just a bit, and I'm so grateful. Finally, I feel like I'm not completely alone, that someone is in my corner and we're going to figure it out together. Scratch that, several *someones*. We have the support of the Monaghans now, which is something I never thought I'd say or find comfort in.

When Luca's phone rings, he stirs behind me and peels himself from my back, grabbing it and answering with a soft hello.

"She's sleeping. I'll wake her and let her know."

He says goodbye to whoever he's talking to, and I turn to face him. I've never seen Luca first thing in the morning before he's showered and dressed for the day. Well, except for yesterday, but I don't think that counts, considering the frantic way I barged into his room. But this morning, looking at him with sleep-mussed hair, his eyes still tired after just opening them, a little flutter of...something makes itself known in my chest.

"Sorry, did I wake you?" he asks as we lie facing each other in the same position we fell asleep in last night.

"No, I was awake."

His eyes search mine before he uses his finger to swipe away the hair covering half my face and tuck it behind my ear.

Okay, that little flutter is turning into a riot.

"How are you feeling this morning?" he asks.

I exhale a breath through my nose, conscientious of my morning breath. "Honestly, I'm not sure. I'm feeling a little of everything right now. Scared, relieved, pissed, acceptance. It's all tangled inside at the moment." Giddy with excitement that I'm waking up next to you. That one is definitely mixed in there too.

"That was Finn on the phone. Alessia is on her way with some breakfast and coffee from her favorite café. I think she wants to have a little time with you. Make sure you're really okay since she's the only one you kind of knew when you walked in here yesterday."

I smile, grateful that she'd take it upon herself to reach out, especially after my brother nearly kidnapping her.

"Finn is going to meet us here in a bit, too. He just has

to take care of a couple things this morning."

"I like Finn. Actually, I like all the Monaghans."

"And you thought you had something to be worried about." Luca sits up and extends his arms above himself then tilts his head from side to side, stretching the muscles in his neck. Is this how he starts every morning when he wakes? Am I going to spend another night in his arms and find out for myself?

Throwing the blanket off me, I realize I'm only in a thin tank and sleep shorts. I turn and see Luca's eyes flare when he sees my next-to-nothing pajamas before he turns his head to give me a bit of privacy, a light blush covering his cheeks.

"I'll hop in the shower," I say.

"Take your time, I'll wait for Alessia downstairs."

I head into the bathroom, and just before I close the door, I catch Luca shaking his head like he's arguing with himself about something. Seems I'm not the only one with errant thoughts running through their head this morning.

When I come down fresh from the shower and dressed in an oversized sweater and yoga pants, Alessia smiles wide from the kitchen, where she's laying out an array of bagels and other breakfast pastries.

"I didn't know what you like, so I grabbed a few of everything. And, of course, coffee." She holds up a bag of grounds. "Don't worry, I already made some," she says, nodding to the state-of-the-art coffee machine on the counter.

"Thank you," I reply and walk over to fill my cup.

"You can make espresso, too. I have one at home and loved it so much I bought one for this place."

"I'm going to head upstairs and take a shower," Luca says from the couch.

He stands and gives me a look, asking if I'm okay. I smile back at him and nod slightly. When did we become the couple that talks without words? When did we become a couple at all? Oh right, maybe when we said I *do* yesterday.

"You look well rested," Alessia says. "I'm sure yesterday was a lot to deal with."

"Oh, you mean nearly being traded to a Russian by my brother, going on the run with my bodyguard, marrying said bodyguard, then coming to the home of my family's sworn enemy for protection?"

Alessia chokes on her coffee and then laughs as she wipes her mouth. "Yeah, that's a lot."

I shrug and send her an apologetic smile. "Sorry, it's all mixed up in my head right now. I certainly didn't wake up yesterday expecting to end up here," I say, looking around the spacious penthouse.

"You don't have to talk to me about everything if you don't want to or if you don't know where to start. But I'm an ear if you need one. I know all about men like your father and brother, though mine was vastly different. But I was raised in the life, too."

"Thank you." I sip the delicious coffee and shake my head. "I don't even know where to begin."

"Let's start small. Do you have any hobbies? What did you do in your spare time?"

"I kind of had nothing but spare time. My dad didn't see the point in me going to college since I'd never be allowed to work." I know Alessia worked for her father and now with her husband, but that was definitely not something most women were able to do. "When I graduated high school, I traveled to Italy and stayed with my mother's family as much as I could." It was the one place I felt loved for just being me. "And I started dancing again. I took ballet when I was little but quit when I was in high school. The last few months, I started taking classes to get out of the house and do something rather than sit around waiting for my father to go to prison." That would have driven me crazy. "What about you?"

"I like to shoot to relieve stress. And box. I enjoy mixed martial arts."

It's my turn to nearly choke on my coffee. "Wow. That's not what I expected."

She shrugs a slim shoulder, and her green eyes sparkle. "My dad taught me how to handle a gun after...some things happened to me. It helped me work through my shit and not feel so powerless. I could teach you if you want?"

I mull her offer over for a moment. "I've never shot a gun before," I tell her.

"Neither had I the first time I went to the range. But I've found it helps me work through things when it all gets too heavy."

That's exactly how I feel right now. Everything is too heavy.

"Okay, I'd really appreciate it."

"Great," she says. "Grab a Danish."

Alessia walks to a door I noticed yesterday at the far end of the penthouse and opens it, placing her hand on a scanner on the other side before the narrow elevator door opens.

"Now?" I ask, grabbing a pastry and folding it into a napkin.

"No time like the present," she says, shooting me a broad smile.

I follow her inside and we travel down a couple levels before the door opens into a brightly lit room with more guns hanging on the walls than I've ever seen in my life.

"Holy shit," I say and take a bite of the Danish in my hand.

"That was my first reaction, too. Finn has a room like this in all of his homes. Some aren't quite as well stocked as this one, but the man likes variety."

I shoot her a wide-eyed look.

"With guns only. He's not getting any variety anywhere else. Trust me."

I can't help the laugh that escapes. It's more common than not to be married and step out on your wife whenever the mood strikes. I've overheard how plenty of married men speak about other women and their side pieces. It's so common in this life I'm surprised

Alessia is as confident as she is. But I suppose if any of those men were married to a woman who looks like Alessia when she takes a gun off the wall and loads it with practiced efficiency, they wouldn't be so inclined to disrespect their wives or marriage vows.

"This one is a little lighter. I think it would be a good one for you to start with. Now, the first thing you do when you pick up a gun is keep it pointed in a safe direction. No accidentally shooting the person with you. Then check to see if it's loaded." She shows me how to do that even though I watched her load it.

She flips a switch on the wall and the rest of the room illuminates, revealing a long range with a paper target at the end. Alessia presses a button and the target moves toward her so she can unclip it and replace it with a fresh one.

"I'll go first then you can give it a try."

She hands me ear protection, and when she fires, the noise is muffled but still distinct. Not that I've been around much gunfire in my life. Though, I guess that could change at any time now.

She brings the target back to her, and I see where the three shots she fired hit their mark. Two in the chest and one through the forehead.

"Impressive," I say as she takes the target off the clips and replaces it.

"Practice makes perfect," she says with a smile and hands me the gun. "Your turn."

Thirty minutes later, we head back to the penthouse.

Though now I know how to fire a weapon, I'd say I'm a long way off from being comfortable with a gun in my hand or being anywhere near as efficient with the weapon like Alessia is.

When the elevator doors slide open, Finn is there talking with Luca on one of the sofas.

"I understand your hesitance in involving your wife, Luca. Trust me, I fucking get it, but it's the fastest way to put an end to this, and you know it. I'm just asking you to consider."

"What are you talking about, Finn?" Alessia asks as she comes to sit next to her husband on the leather sofa.

Finn looks between Luca and me. "Ways to get that snake out of hiding."

"And I told him there's no way in hell I'm asking Giada to put herself in danger. Who the hell knows what he'll do if he gets his hands on her?"

"Nothing pleasant, I'm sure," I mumble, sitting next to Luca on the other couch across from one of the most powerful couples in all of Boston.

Luca turns his body toward me. "I promised you I wouldn't use you to bring down your family. You're more than someone we can use to our advantage. I don't want you to feel like you're stuck in the middle. Or that by not helping us, we'll send you back to that monster, Giada. That would never happen."

"Of course it wouldn't," Finn confirms. "I was just suggesting that she can draw him out."

"Which is using her," Luca shoots back at his cousin,

obviously tired of explaining himself.

"I don't like it, Finn," Alessia says, looking her husband dead in the eye. "It's dangerous as hell and Giada has no way to defend herself. Hell, today is the first day she shot a gun for chrissake." I've never met a woman who would contradict her husband in front of other people. That was certainly never tolerated in my house.

"We would be with her the entire time. I'd make sure to have our guys placed around her so Carlo wouldn't get even close to taking her."

"No. There're too many variables that could fuck that plan up," Luca says.

"What do you have in mind?" I ask Finn, curious about his idea.

"Giada—" Luca starts.

"No, I want to hear." My gaze turns to Luca. "I understand what you're saying, Luca. Yes, anything having to do with my brother is dangerous. But that's because my brother is dangerous. Look what he tried to do to Alessia. Look what he tried to do to me. Hell, look what he's been doing with other women. I hold no loyalty to him."

When I made Luca promise he wouldn't use me, it was under the assumption that it was the only reason he was marrying me. That once he'd accomplished whatever plan he was concocting with the Monaghans, he would throw me away like some useless thing he no longer needed or had an interest in. Yesterday, especially last night, showed me something else. Maybe

I'm just seeing what I want and have dreamed of since I was younger. Someone who cared about me for me and not the advantages I can offer them. Someone who's more interested in protecting me than feeding me to the wolves for their own benefit. My long-buried feelings for Luca may make me naive to have me wishing with everything in me that person's him. But seeing the way he took care of me yesterday and the way he's willing to stand up to his cousin in my defense makes me believe he's that man for me, at least for now.

"I was thinking you could call him and set up a meeting. Tell him you made a mistake in trusting Luca, that you were just scared. You want to come home, and you're ready to sign a marriage contract because you're loyal to your family."

"That plan has more holes in it than Swiss cheese," Alessia comments, rolling her eyes.

"To you, yes," Finn says, turning to his wife. "But Carlo is running scared and desperate. Trying to take you is proof he isn't thinking clearly and is basically throwing spaghetti at the wall to see what sticks. Plus, he doesn't think things through like you and me. That's something his capos have been complaining about for years."

Luca nods in confirmation. "That's true. They've always thought he was more of a liability than a leader."

"Exactly. That's why he's desperate. He isn't getting the support he needs within his own organization. I always knew the Cataldi family would crumble with Francesco gone. Now, with Giada gone, he has nowhere to turn. It sounded like the deal with the Russians was contingent on her marriage to Nikolai. With her out of the picture, he doesn't have anything," Finn says.

"Right. Which is why I say we wait for him to poke his head out then go after him with everything we have," Luca argues.

"That could take months, and who knows who he tries to work with or what he offers them in the meantime. Carlo is out for blood. It needs to be handled right away." Finn is trying to get Luca to see his point, but he continues to shake his head in disagreement.

"Finn's right, Luca. Carlo won't stop." I turn back to Finn. "But I don't know that he'd be willing to meet with me. Carlo doesn't find women particularly useful, even if he thinks trading me to the Russians is going to work in his favor. Especially now that I'm missing. Plus, I'm not entirely sure my father's capos won't work with him again. If he can guarantee that following him will make them money, there's definitely a few who will be more than willing to go along with him until they can get rid of him themselves." I take a deep breath. "I'll do whatever you need."

"I'm not risking your safety," Luca says firmly.

"And I'm not asking for your permission. I need this over as much as you do, Luca."

I notice a small smile on Alessia's face, but she smothers it before Luca can notice.

Finn is silent for a few moments. "So we need to make sure the other Cataldi capos know what working with Carlo will bring them. I'll reach out and set up a meeting. Luca, you'll come with me. We'll make it clear that working with Carlo means death for them, and Giada is now your wife, which means she's under our protection. I'll let them know we'll go to war with anyone who supports Carlo from this day forward."

"There's still the Russian problem," Alessia points out.

"One thing at a time, wife," Finn says. "Giada is safe from the Russians for the time being since she's married to Luca. Their beef over Carlo not being able to hold up his end of the bargain is with him."

"One can hope," Alessia mumbles.

After lunch, Finn and Alessia head back to their house since they have to work at the casino tonight. It's still a little surprising to me that Finn allows her to work in his casino, but it's just another testament to how different the Monaghans are compared to every other organization I've ever seen.

"I don't like that you're so willing to put yourself in harm's way for Finn," Luca says while we're washing the dishes from lunch.

"Seriously?" I ask irritably. "We've been over this. Carlo isn't going to stop until he gets what he wants and that's the Monaghans cut off at the knees. He already tried when he tried to take Alessia. I refuse to look over my shoulder at every turn. None of us will have any peace until Carlo is gone."

"It's dangerous. I hate the idea of you being used as bait. There are a million things that can go wrong between now and when we finally have Carlo. Don't you see? I'm trying to protect you. Finn's plan is half-baked at best, just like Alessia said."

"Then come up with a better one. Try going to the capos. Hell, try whatever you want, but if it fails, we're going to try it Finn's way. There isn't another choice."

"There's always another choice, Giada," Luca says, his irritation matching mine. "I'm willing to do just about anything to keep you safe. Even if it means from my cousin."

"I know, I know," I mock. "It's your job." I scrub the bowl I'm holding that much harder. "In case you haven't noticed, Luca, you aren't my bodyguard anymore."

Luca sets the plate he was drying down and turns to me, leaning his hip against the counter with his arms crossed over his broad chest. Damn, have his arms always been that big? *Knock it off, Giada. He's being insufferable and that does not turn you on.*

"It's been more than just because it's my job for a long while. Honestly, since you came back from Italy with a tan and an attitude. I never allowed myself to see you as more than Carlo's little sister or Francesco's daughter. I knew what would happen if Carlo or your father thought I was going to make a play for you. But when I saw you walking down the stairs, so sure of yourself, ready to put me in my place." He quirks his brow and gives me a look that says he knew exactly what I was doing that night. "There was this challenge in you to make me see you as more than that. As the women you'd grown into while I was away. And I saw it, Giada. God, it was so hard watching you give that asshole attention, knowing what a piece of shit he was. But I couldn't claim to be any better. I had to play my part. It was the first time I wanted to say fuck it and prove to you I'm not the man I made you believe I was." Luca pauses and takes a deep breath, collecting his thoughts. "You have no idea how hard I had to work after that to keep myself in line. But I couldn't dare show my cards. If I had, it meant I would've had to leave you alone in that house with no one looking out for you, and I wasn't willing to risk it. Just like I'm not now. Which is what pisses me the hell off. You're too damn willing to run headfirst into danger."

"No. I'm willing to do what it takes to finish this. Are you?" The challenge is clear in my voice. "The time for sitting back and waiting for something to fall into our laps is over. If we don't do what needs to be done now, Carlo is going to get away with everything. I refuse to let that happen just because you have reservations."

"God, you're so fucking stubborn," he says, the volume of his voice increasing with every word.

"Yes. I am," I yell back. "You should know that by now. You should also know you can't protect me forever."

"The hell I can't. You're my wife."

"In name only."

His eyes are hard as he stares at me, and before he says another word, his lips crash to mine. I drop the bowl in the sink and let out a gasp, allowing Luca to invade my mouth with his demanding tongue.

He pulls away and stares into my confused gaze. "Not in name only."

Before I can think better about what a monumental mistake this could potentially be, I do what any rational person in my position would do and throw my arms around his neck, fusing my lips to his.

Teeth clanking and tongues tangling, I let out a deep moan, which makes Luca tighten his grip around my waist, pressing me so tightly into him it's as though he's trying to meld our bodies into one. He spins me around and my back crashes into the counter of the island separating the kitchen from the living room, and I let out a grunt of discomfort.

"Shit, sorry," Luca says, breaking the kiss.

"It's fine. Don't stop." I slam my mouth to his again, tangling my fingers in the short strands of his dark hair.

His strong hand cradles my lower back to keep it away from the edge of the counter as his other moves to my waist under my sweater. His fingers glide up my waist and around to the front of my shirt and over my ribs, his thumb rubbing the skin just under the cup of my bra.

Luca breaks the kiss, and his gaze bores into me, his touch so close to where I want it but not quite there.

"This is probably a bad idea," he says but doesn't make a move to pull away.

"It could be."

"I know you don't see this marriage as real, and I unders—"

"Luca," I interrupt. "Can we please talk about this later when your hand isn't up my shirt?" I quirk a brow. "If you stop now, I will fucking scream. We can figure it out later, but right now, I need you to please shut the hell up."

"You're very demanding," he says roughly as the tension between us threatens to explode. "I thought Italian wives were supposed to be sweet to their husbands."

"Um, have we met? What part of me do you think is sweet?"

The feral grin that widens his mouth sends shivers down my spine. "I'm not sure. But I'm going to find out."

Luca's lips travel down the column of my neck, licking and sucking the heated flesh as he goes. "That's pretty sweet." His hands find the bottom of my sweater, and he tears the material over my head before grasping my waist in his large hands. His lips continue their descent over the hollow of my throat to the tops of my lace-covered breasts. "Still sweet," he says, trailing his palms up my sides, landing just below my breasts as he swipes his thumbs over my hardened nipples. I stare at him, my breaths coming in hard pants as I watch him lower himself to his knees. My hands grip the edge of the counter to keep myself upright as my legs threaten to give out from the sight before me—Luca on his knees, his blue eyes darkened with a look I've never seen from him. Lust, pure and unadulterated and finally able to be acted upon.

His hands move to the waistband of my pants, and he pulls just a touch, his brows lifting as if asking permission.

"Please," I say in a whisper. "Don't stop."

His eyes hold mine as he kisses my skin right above the elastic waist of my pants then slowly pulls the material down past my hips and over my thighs—holding my gaze with every inch of skin he exposes. When my pants are completely off, his eyes move to my center, surely seeing my panties soaked through. If I could form thoughts, I might be embarrassed to have him on his knees staring at the wet spot on the front of my panties, but the only thing I feel is an intense ache in my core that I need him to fucking do something about. But apparently my husband loves to torture me.

His thumb glides right over the wet spot, and I gasp. He lets out a low growl deep in his throat before pulling the lace down my legs then using the tip of his tongue to part my lower lips. I jerk my hips at the slight contact and thank the fucking heavens he's done teasing me in the next breath. His tongue runs over my clit in quick, precise movements before my fingers grab hold of his hair, holding his head at my center as he devours my pussy with his hot mouth. Luca slips a finger inside me, then two, stretching me and pumping his hand in and out

"Oh fuck, oh fuck. Right there," I moan as my legs begin to shake. He groans and between the vibrations, his expert tongue and his finger, I come undone, screaming out his name as waves of bliss wash through me. He removes his fingers from my core, but his tongue still moves in circles around and over my clit as he follows me down, wringing every last bit of pleasure from me.

When he pulls away, he looks up at me, a wide, wet smile taking over his face. "Very sweet."

"Holy shit...that was..." I can't seem to form words as he stands to his full height.

"That was the first one," he says, quirking his mouth in a satisfied smirk.

Holy. Shit.

Chapter Fifteen
Luca

I THINK THIS IS the first time I've ever seen Giada speechless. Hell, if I knew this would have done the trick, I would have eaten her sweet cunt months ago. And fuck, my wife tastes fucking delicious.

"You're a little overdressed," Giada says, nodding at my shirt and jeans I'm still wearing.

I grab the back of my shirt and pull it over my head, discarding it on the floor next to her yoga pants. Her hand travels over the scar on my side. The one I got just before I came to work for her father.

"What happened?" she asks.

"Knife," I reply.

"And here?" She runs her fingers over the scar from when my cousin shot me at the warehouse so her brother wouldn't be suspicious that I walked away scot-free.

"Bullet grazed me."

"Is this all because of my family?"

"No," I reply honestly. "Because of mine." I've been stabbed and shot for my family. For the decisions I made to put myself here.

"I don't want to talk about my scars." There're too many she can't see anyways.

"What do you want to talk about?" Her lips tip in a half smile and my palms skate up her arms and over her shoulders until I'm holding her flushed cheeks in my hands.

"Absolutely nothing."

I swipe my lips over hers and she wastes no time opening her mouth to allow me entrance. The kiss turns heated within seconds as Giada's small hands come to the button of my pants and she pulls the zipper down, freeing me from the confines of my too-tight jeans.

When she reaches her hand in and pulls my hard cock free, I hiss. "Fuck, that feels good." Her grip tightens around my cock, slowly moving her palm base to tip.

Our foreheads are pressed together as we watch her pump me a few times before I pull away. "If you keep doing that, this is going to be over before it starts." I'm not some two-pump chump, but her tight fist around me feels too damn good, and I'm way too worked up.

"You tasted me, I think it's only fair you let me have my turn," she says in a throaty voice.

"We have plenty of time for that. I need to feel your sweet pussy squeezing me the first time I come anywhere in your body."

I grab her by the back of the neck and yank her face to mine, delving my tongue deep into her mouth. Giada returns the kiss with the same fire. My hands skirt down her naked ass to the back of her strong thighs that have been conditioned from her hours at the dance studio. Her legs wrap around me, and I begin walking to the spiral staircase to the bedroom, each step making my cock brush against her wet entrance.

When we make it to the bedroom, I lay Giada on the bed and shuck my jeans off, standing before her completely naked.

"Now who's overdressed?" I ask, pointing to the bra she's still wearing. The material is nearly see-through, but as soon as she removes it from her body, my breath whooshes out of me. My wife is fucking perfection. Her round breasts fall from the material with her dusty-pink nipples hardened into points, begging for my mouth. I don't waste any time and sit on the edge of the bed, grabbing her by the waist and hauling her to my lap so I can have her tits in my face. Giada lets out a squeal, but as soon as my mouth attaches to her breast, she throws her head back on a moan, grabbing tightly to the hair on the back of my head. Her hips move over my cock that's aching to be inside of her as I give each breast the equal amount of attention they deserve.

I've been too scared to imagine being here with Giada. Certain if I did, I wouldn't be able to resist kissing her like I finally allowed myself to do in the kitchen. I worked so hard to keep walls up, even in my own mind, because I knew once I allowed those thoughts in my head, I wouldn't be able to concentrate on anything else. Now, though, all bets are off. My mind is filled with images of her riding me, bringing us both to orgasm.

Me pumping inside of her while her hair is splayed on the pillow below me. My face buried in her sweet fucking pussy over and over and so much more. It's like the floodgates have opened, and I don't have to hide anym ore.

I remove her nipple from my mouth with a pop and stare into her amber eyes through a haze of desire. She's absolutely stunning, and I have to give myself a little mental pat on the back for being able to keep myself together being around her these past months. If I had known she would be every fantasy come to life like she is now, with her rosy cheeks and eyes that stare at me with unabashed desire, I don't know that I wouldn't have risked it all for a taste of her.

I grab the side of her neck and pull her mouth to mine, invading it with my tongue as it tangles with hers. God, I don't think I'll ever get enough of her.

When she breaks the kiss, her hand finds my cock and she lifts her hips, slowly sliding me into her heat. Our eyes stay locked as we connect in the most intimate and primal way two people can for the first time.

"Oh my God," she says, lifting slightly then sliding back down.

My hand grips her neck harder and her pulse thumps wildly against my palm. "Fuck, you feel so good," I grind out, my other hand moving to her hip and clutching it while she rides me, grabbing my shoulders to steady herself. My hand that was around her neck moves to her hip and I dig my fingers into her flesh, pulling her harder down onto me to grind into her clit.

"Fuck," she cries out as she reaches behind her to clutch my knees as I lift her then slam her down, over and over. I'm so deep inside of her like this, and it doesn't take more than a few minutes for the telltale sign of my impending orgasm to make itself known.

"I need you there, baby." My finger finds her clit and I begin rubbing furiously, desperate to feel her come on my cock.

"Oh God, oh God," she chants over and over. "I'm going to come. Don't stop."

Like I could.

Her entire body tightens and the orgasm explodes through her, her pussy clamping down and pulsing around me, the feeling setting off my own as I come deep inside my wife for the first time.

"Fuck," I bellow, the pleasure so intense my vision blinks in and out as I fall from the peak, taking Giada with me.

Giada is still seated on my lap as our breaths and heartbeats slow to a normal rate. Her fingertips lightly run up and down my arms as I languidly kiss her mouth, her neck, her shoulder. We aren't in the frenzied rush we were a few minutes ago, instead taking our time to touch each other, to gently reassure each other that this is happening, we're here and alive and together.

"I'm going to get a washcloth, then when I come back to bed, I'll lie on my back and you're going to ride my face until I make you scream again. Sound good?"

Her mouth tilts up in a half smile as I feel her pussy ripple with anticipation.

"Yeah, I can tell you like the idea."

The afternoon falls into evening, and Giada and I only leave the bed for dinner and to refill our water glasses. I've barely scratched the surface of all the ways I want my wife, coming up with new ones as we bring each other to unimaginable highs. My favorite was when she used the overripe bananas on the counter to make bread, and after putting it in the oven, she dropped to her knees and took my hard cock in her mouth, bringing me to orgasm while she played with her clit and made herself come with me.

Now that we've admitted the attraction we've had for each other, it's as though the barriers between us have fallen away and we can't keep our hands off one another. That's one of the reasons I'm finding it hard to leave the penthouse this morning when Finn comes to pick me up for the meeting with the capos he'd set up yesterday.

I'm upstairs and Giada is sitting cross-legged on the bed wearing one of my oversized T-shirts as I attempt to knot my tie, but I am too damn distracted by her long legs as she rubs lotion into her skin after our shower.

Her eyes meet my heated stare and she smirks,

watching me undo the mess I've made.

"Come here," she says, kneeling at the edge of the bed.

I stand in front of her, and she takes the tie at each end and begins crossing and looping the silk material together.

"There," she says, and I lean down to kiss her soft lips, my hands grazing her hips and moving under the cotton material so I can feel her skin.

"Do me a favor," she says, her lips a hairsbreadth from mine. "Come back in one piece."

I pull back and look into Giada's worried eyes. Lifting my hand to cup her cheek, I stare into her amber eyes so she can see and feel the weight of my words. "There is no scenario where I wouldn't come back here to you, Giada. Finn and I are going to be fine." I smile and kiss the tip of her nose. "Now, do me a favor and be in nothing but my shirt when I get back." I shoot her a wink and my heart leaps at her tinkling giggle.

"You're something else, Luca Benetti."

"Right back at you, Mrs. Benetti."

I head down the stairs and meet my cousin in the hallway. "Let's get this over with. I have a honeymoon to get back to."

The meeting is being held at a bar outside of Boston

just before Amatto territory. This is one of the few places that stays neutral, but the owner has no problem burying a body for the right price if things go sideways. Mario met us here, and the six living capos of the Cataldi organization are seated in the large private space in the back of the bar that usually houses backroom card games.

Tensions are high when we walk in and the Cataldi men see me standing next to my cousin.

"Can't say I saw this coming," Dario, one of the Cataldi capos, says when I sit, Finn to my right and Mario on the other side of him.

"I won't keep you long, gentleman," Finn starts. "It's no secret my family and the Cataldis haven't exactly coexisted peacefully the last several years."

"Or ever," another capo, Leandro, mumbles. Both he and Dario are on the younger side, maybe midforties, while the other four sitting at the table have been around since the beginning of Francesco's reign.

"That's fair. But a lot of the high tensions, shall we say, were the result of your former boss, Francesco, pinning several murders on my father when, in fact, it was Francesco who ordered the hits on his men."

The six men narrow their eyes at Finn. "Why the hell would Francesco kill his own men? We would have known about it." The question comes from a man with Salvatore, one of the capos who's been in the organization the longest.

"He had a man years ago, another capo who doubled

as his personal assassin when he wanted to deal with things quietly. Constantine Barelli."

"How the hell do you know that name? Constantine died years ago," Salvatore says.

"Actually, he didn't." I decide now's as good a time as any to speak up. "Francesco ordered him to kill my parents and me when I was a baby, but he couldn't finish the job. He took me and ran, staying hidden until he died just over eight years ago. Raised me as his own. Before he passed, he told me the whole story and who my parents really were."

"And who were your parents, kid?" Dario asks.

"My father was Elio Romano, and my mother was Ciara, Maeve Monaghan's sister."

Salvatore scoffs and waves his hand at me. "You really believe this, Amatto? That's not how our world works. Maybe the Irish have no problem killing their own, but the Italians don't go around murdering their own capos."

"I'm well aware of what the Italians do and don't do, Sal. So yes, I believe my son-in-law and his cousin." Mario gives Salvatore a hard stare and the older capo returns it before another man speaks.

Tomasso's gravelly voice shuts everyone up. "It's true. Constantine killed Elio. When he disappeared, Francesco confided in me, and I was the bearer of many of his secrets for years after. I helped him stage Elio and Ciara's body in his car to make it look like an Irish hit. That's the story we wanted everyone to believe anyway."

"My father knew Cataldi was responsible for his sister-in-law's death but couldn't prove it. No one knew what happened to Luca until he reached out after Constantine's death," Finn explains.

It's strange hearing Frank being referred to as Constantine. Constantine was the man who murdered my parents, Frank was my father. Yet they're the same person.

"Francesco has been responsible for too many deaths within the organization. I didn't know just how many until Constantine was gone and he needed someone else to help with his dirty work. That person was me," Tomasso informs the room. The other capos look on in astonishment, especially Salvatore, as Tomasso continues. "Francesco was a paranoid dictator. He preached unity and collaboration in the organization, but it was all talk. If he suspected another man of scheming against him in any way, he took him out without any sort of discussion. He suspected his wife was going to leave him and had her killed as well. Paid off the investigator to say it was her brakes. There was an accident, but what killed her was the bullet to the h ead."

Holy. Shit.

Giada's father killed her mother.

I look around the room. Some of the men are horrified with the news and others don't seem to care. Guess they subscribe to the belief that what a man does to his wife is his business and no one else's.

"How the hell did you come to work for Francesco then?" Leandro asks me.

"Francesco killed my parents. I wanted revenge. Simple as that. Finn wanted power over Boston, and together, we planned to take Francesco out."

Leandro looks at me with disgust pouring from his gaze. "Jesus Christ. You were a mole for the Irish this whole time."

"You can call my cousin names and detest him all you want. But it doesn't change the situation we're in now." Finn gives every capo in the room a hard stare. "Carlo was going to use his sister to gain power since he couldn't find the support he needed." To my recollection, Dario was the only capo who agreed to meet with Carlo. "He offered her in marriage to the Russians. They want a foothold in Massachusetts and Carlo wants to regain control of Boston. That's who you're dealing with, gentlemen. A man who would gladly allow those Russian bastards into your territory and give them a piece of your pie."

The jaw of every capo clenches when they realize what Carlo is really up to.

"That's who's been helping him?" Salvatore asks.

"Yes, but I've seen to it that there's no longer a reason for the Russians to help Carlo."

"How's that?" Leandro asks.

A small grin spreads across my mouth. "I married Giada instead."

Shocked silence fills the room, but Finn doesn't allow

it to linger. "Giada is protected by my family now. The Russians can't get to her, and Carlo doesn't have another ace up his sleeve."

"What about Farina? He knows what you did to his son. He probably hates you more than Carlo at this point."

"Orlando got what was coming to him and his father knows that. If he tries to help Carlo, he knows exactly what I'm capable of. Orlando already tried and failed. I doubt his father is going to risk it." Finn looks around the room. "Same goes for any man sitting here. If you try to give Carlo any assistance in any way, Orlando won't be the only Italian I put to ground in this war. My issue is with Carlo and Carlo alone. I'll make this offer one time only. You can keep your territory and your businesses. Instead of paying dues to Carlo, they'll be paid to me and Mario. The Cataldi organization will be absorbed by our family. And if anyone thinks Farina is going to help them, think again. Partnering with him means you're signing your death warrant. There will be no second chances."

"You got a lot of fucking nerve coming in here and threatening us," Salvatore grits out.

"I do. And I have the means to back it up. Do you?" The challenging glare Finn sends Salvatore doesn't waver for a second. It's the first time I've seen my cousin as the Irish mob boss. Makes me fucking glad as hell we're on the same side.

Dario and Salvatore glance at each other, obviously not taking kindly to being challenged by Finn. Leandro and Tomasso are less angry, resignation playing over their features.

"I'm too old for a war. I want to enjoy what I have while I'm still alive and not fight for scraps. And I sure as hell won't work under Carlo. I accept your offer, Finn," Tomasso says.

Leandro agrees, and the other two capos, Donny and Cesare, who've stayed pretty quiet during the meeting, nod their heads. There's only Dario and Salvatore left.

Seeing as there's no support from the rest of the men, they begrudgingly agree as well.

Finn and Mario shake hands with the men, but they aren't particularly thrilled with my presence. It's no surprise. I was a mole for their enemy up until two days ago. When the men leave, it's me, Finn and Mario left in the room.

"You good, cousin?"

I nod and blow out a breath. "Yeah. Shocked as hell that Francesco killed his wife, though."

Mario shakes his head. "That man is a piece of shit." From what Finn has told me about Mario Amatto, he holds his wife and daughter's safety and well-being in the highest regard. Not common whatsoever in this life.

"Giada is going to be devastated," I say.

"You don't have to tell her," Finn offers. "If that's what you decide, no one here will say a word to her."

"Would you keep something like that from Alessia?"

Finn chuckles. "No. I value my dick where it is."

Mario clears his throat and shoots Finn a look who

doesn't look the least bit contrite. "Sorry. But it's not like you don't know exactly what your daughter is capable of."

"Oh, I know," Mario replies. "I raised her that way." A proud smile covers his face and Finn laughs.

"Come on. Let's get you home," Finn says, turning to me.

It's still early afternoon when we emerge from the bar. A sense of dread fills me, thinking about telling Giada what I learned. When she came to my room the morning we got married with tears on her face, it gutted me. And that was before I married her and spent the night showing her how I felt about her. Now it's different. This news might destroy her. We both know her father is a monster and I hate him for everything he put her through, but no one is prepared for news like this. But I also swore I wouldn't lie to her. And I'll be damned if I break a single promise to her now.

Chapter Sixteen
Giada

I'VE SPENT THE LAST three hours worried about Luca coming home safely. There isn't much else for me to do alone in the penthouse apartment. Alessia brought me a couple books yesterday in case I was a reader, which I am. Unfortunately, even those can't keep my attention as the clock hanging on the wall ticks loudly through the silent penthouse. It's maddening. I never cared when Carlo or my father had to leave the house for some meeting, but Luca is a different story. I actually want him to come back.

Instead of driving myself crazy with the silence, I move the couches to the side of the room and start warming up my deliciously sore muscles to run through some dance routines. I figure it will keep my body moving and hopefully focus my mind on something other than waiting for my husband to return.

I'm halfway through the routine I was working on before everything...well, blew up. When the front door opens and Luca walks in, I stop and face him, the relief visible on his face.

"Hey," I greet. "How'd it go?" I'm not used to asking

such questions considering any other man I know in this life would tell me it was none of my business.

He jerks his head. "Keep going. I want to watch."

"You're not going to talk to me about it?" I ask, slightly offended I'm getting the brush-off.

"I'll tell you all about it, but right now, I want to watch you do something you love. The way your face lights up when you dance...I just need to watch, yeah?"

I nod and continue moving to the sultry beat of the music. Having Luca watch me adds something to the mix I don't generally feel while I'm in class. Desire. Having his eyes on me while he stands just inside the doorway watching me is making my skin hot and tight everywhere. My breath is picking up and it's not from exertion, though this particular routine has me bending my body in all kinds of interesting and strenuous ways.

When I finish, I'm panting hard and Luca claps. "Not exactly the drunk hip-shaking I saw at the bar, but I'll take it."

I laugh, remembering the day that feels like a lifetime ago. It was the first time I started opening myself to the man standing before me. The first time I shared my mother's records with anyone. Though the day started like absolute shit, remembering he was the one who put me to bed and made sure I was taken care of warms me. Even then he was showing me how much he cared when he couldn't say it.

Luca walks into the apartment and sits on the couch I've moved in front of the window, staring at the skyline outside. He holds out his arm in invitation for me to sit next to him. Naturally, I don't deny him and curl myself into his side, his arm draping over me almost possessively even though we're the only two in the room. He leans down and kisses me softly on the mouth, his lips lingering, simply tasting me.

He pulls away but keeps me in his hold, and I lean my head on his chest, listening to the thrum of his heartbeat.

"I came here so angry, ready to take down your father. I never thought in a million years I would stay in the organization for as long as I did, or that we'd find ourselves here. He took so much from me. Even before I was old enough to realize it. I knew Francesco was responsible for so much heartache and misery, but I never realized how close it was to his family. To you."

I look into Luca's eyes, my gaze questioning. He knows how I felt growing up, never being cared for by my father, shoved to the side and only being deemed useful once I was old enough to be married off. So I'm curious what's bringing this up now. "What are you talking about?"

Luca lets out a breath. "At the meeting today. One of the capos there, Tomasso, he kind of took over Frank's role after he left. He knew Frank had run and your father needed someone else he trusted to do the same work. The hits that Francesco didn't want anyone to know about."

"Okay...It makes sense my father would use someone

else."

"It's what he used him for."

"Spit it out, Luca. You don't have to tiptoe around me."

"Giada, your mother didn't die in a car accident. Your father killed her, and Tomasso helped make it look like an accident so no one would question Francesco."

The breath stalls in my chest. "Tomasso has to be lying. My mother died when she hit black ice and lost control of her car. The police report and medical examiner all said so."

"Your father paid them to say that."

I sit up and tears fill my eyes. "My father...killed my mother?" I choke out in a broken whisper.

"I'm so sorry. I think your mother was trying to leave him, and he found out."

I was so young when she died. I don't remember them fighting or her being scared. I do remember thinking she acted differently around him, but to a five-year-old, what does that really mean?

"He killed my mother." The words play on repeat in my mind. "He took my mother from me. The one person who cared about me in that godforsaken house. He ripped her from me because he's a monster and she knew. She knew!"

I jump from my seat with rage like I've never known coursing through me. Would my life have turned out differently had she been around? I don't know. It certainly would have been a hell of a lot better. Especially if she'd succeeded in running away from him.

But he couldn't have the smallest shred of humanity. No. If he wasn't going to have his way, he'd mow down anyone in it, including his own wife.

"How could he possibly murder the woman he married? Who gave birth to his children? How could he do that?" I can't stop asking how. It's screaming over and over in my head. *How? How? How?* "Does my brother know? Does he know the man he idolized his entire life is the kind of monster who could do that to his family? A man who could tear apart his children's lives because he's a horrible human being?"

"I don't know what your brother knows, Giada. He never mentioned it to me."

I don't suppose he would have even if he did know. If a man is okay with his father murdering his own mother, what kind of loyalty would that inspire from his men?

"I need to call Carlo."

"Why? How is that going to help you?" Luca asks.

"I don't know," I reply, pacing the floor in front of him. "I just need to know if he knew. If he knows about the man he's spent his miserable life being loyal to." My brother is a monster like our father, there's no doubt in my mind, but what made him that way? I grew up in the same house, and I sure as hell didn't turn out like Carlo.

Luca studies me a few moments before pulling his phone from his pocket. "This goes against every bone in my body, Giada. When I said I'd do anything to protect you, I meant it, but I also said I wouldn't lie to you again."

"He can't hurt me. He doesn't even know where I am."

"He doesn't need to be in front of you to hurt you."

I consider his statement, but it doesn't deter me. Grabbing the phone from Luca's hand, I dial the number I've unfortunately had memorized for years.

"Hello?" Carlo answers.

"It's Giada."

"Where the hell are you? I've been looking everywhere for you."

"I'm not telling you that."

"You little bitch. Do you know what your disappearing act cost me?" he yells into the phone.

"I do. And you know exactly what it would have cost me if I'd stayed."

Luca is looking on with pride in his eyes that I'm standing up to my brother. It's not the first time he's seen it, but it is the first time he's been able to show me how he feels about it.

"I need to know something, Carlo. For once in your life, I need you to be straight with me."

"You don't get to make demands. Just wait until I find you, Giada."

"Shut up and listen. I found something out today and I need to know if you know about it."

"Jesus Christ. What?" Carlo sounds annoyed with the conversation, but that's par for the course with the two of us.

"Did you know our father killed our mother?"

The icy laugh that comes across the line sends chills racing down my spine. "I see you've been talking to

Tomasso."

My gaze clashes with Luca's and I put the phone on speaker so he can hear everything Carlo is about to tell me. Do I think it will help him or Finn with their plan? No. But I need someone else to hear this because I can barely believe what I'm hearing myself.

"What do you know, Carlo?"

"Well, since you've already fucked me over with the Russians, I'll let you in on a little secret. Good luck running to any of our father's associates now once you find out who you really are. They'll throw you on your ass like yesterday's trash. Yes, my father killed our mother. She was going to leave him and take us with her. Maybe she thought running to Italy with her family would save her, but Father wouldn't hear of it. He wanted to raise me to take over, and she wasn't going to take my birthright from me. He caught up to her and killed her, then staged it as a car accident."

"How could you still want anything to do with him after learning that, Carlo? She was our mother!" I'm shaking with volatile rage at the way he so flippantly tells me that he's known this for God knows how long.

"What happens between a man and his wife is his business. He had every right as her husband to deal with her as he saw fit. I'm not going to question his decision. She would have taken me from what I was born to be."

I scoff. "Yeah, that turned out really well for you, didn't it?"

"I may be down, Giada, but I'm far from out." He

pauses, and I stare at Luca, whose face is a mask of unreadable emotion. But if I had to guess, I'd say underneath, he's as angry as I am. "Here's the kicker, though. He found out you weren't his daughter. That she fucked some bodyguard of hers and he promised to save her from the life she was completely ungrateful f or."

My eyes widen and Luca's mirror my shocked expression. It also doesn't pass my notice that I'm a lot more like my mother than I would have ever thought, considering I'm standing in front of my former bodyguard turned husband.

"What do you mean? Who's my father?"

"I don't know his name. Doesn't matter. He was killed the same night as our mother."

"Why the hell did he keep me? Why not give me away when he found out?" It's not as though my father, or rather Francesco, has an altruistic bone in his body or had some sort of attack of conscience.

"To punish his dead wife who betrayed him. He told her that he would tie you to this life forever. That he would use you and your future marriage for his gain. He had a son who would take over and a daughter who could facilitate an alliance with a powerful family. And if you didn't fulfill your end of the bargain, he would make sure you joined her in the afterlife sooner rather than later. And wouldn't you know? You've decided to run off and shirk your responsibilities."

"Are you out of your mind?" I yell into the phone. "I'm

not going to live out some asshole's vendetta against our mother. I don't give a shit if it's for the man who I called father for the last twenty-two years."

"Then I will find you and you'll join our mother," Carlo threatens.

"You aren't going to get anywhere near her, you sick son of a bitch," Luca growls, grabbing the phone from my grip.

"I should have fucking known," Carlo says, and I can imagine the sneer on his face so clearly. "Luca Bennetti. I've been looking for you. I see Giada convinced you to forfeit your life to help her with her little plan. Is her pussy really that good?"

If Luca grips the phone any tighter, he's likely to break it. "You will not talk about my wife. You don't think about her or speak of her," he growls through a clenched jaw. "I'll be seeing you real soon, Carlo." Luca disconnects the call and looks at the phone, taking several deep breaths to calm himself down. "Fucking scumbag," he mutters before pocketing the device. Well, at least he didn't smash it into a million pieces like I would've expected.

When his angry blue gaze finds mine, his eyes soften, seeing the look of devastation that I'm sure is written all over my face.

"Sweetheart," he whispers and opens his arms. I don't waste a second and fall into them, allowing the tears to run freely down my face, soaking his white button-down shirt.

"How could he know what Francesco did and still blindly follow him? How could he possibly be okay with even being in the same room with him?" I tilt my chin up and look into Luca's sympathetic eyes. "Everything I thought I knew about myself, Luca, who I thought I was…gone. Francesco isn't my father. Oh my God. He killed my real father and mother." Tears pour from my eyes. He knows exactly what I'm feeling, doesn't he? Who I thought was my father sentenced him to the same fate years ago as well.

Luca pulls me closer, rubbing small circles over my back. This is so screwed up. Everything is just…fucked.

Luca walks us over to the sofa and sits, placing me across his lap and cradling me in his strong arms as I cling to him.

"There you go, sweetheart, cry it out."

And I do. I cry harder than I ever have in my life, probably harder than I did when I found out my mother had died. Back then, it was a nanny comforting me because that's what she was paid to do. Now, it's my husband, the one person in the world I know I can rely on, take comfort in. Someone who knows exactly what I'm going through because he's been through it himself.

"He's a monster. Francesco and Carlo. They're both monsters." That doesn't even seem like a strong enough word to describe the horrible humans that've put both of us in this situation.

"They are. But I promise you, Giada, They won't get away with it."

I wake in the bed Luca and I have been sharing for the last two nights. God, has it only been two nights since my world imploded? First, escaping the only life I knew, then marrying Luca, and today, finding out who I thought my family was...isn't. I don't know how to process any of this. My mind is like a battlefield warring with itself. Anger at being lied to, rage at what Francesco did to my mother and real father, and gratitude that I have Luca next to me.

I turn and face my husband, whose eyes are open, his soft gaze wary with worry.

"You carried me up here?" I rasp out.

"Yeah, figured it would be more comfortable for both of us here instead of the couch."

Always taking care of me.

I lean in and brush my lips against his, seeking a comfort only he can give me. When I try to deepen the kiss, he pulls away.

"Giada, I don't think—"

"I don't want to think, Luca. I need to feel something good, something that will take away the horrible thoughts swirling around my head. Something true." And something that's mine.

Luca studies me and then leans in for a kiss, allowing my tongue to delve into his mouth. When I pull away, he brushes the side of my face, which I'm sure is covered in dried tears. "Anything you need, sweetheart. I've got you."

My mouth crashes to his and when I rub my center against him, I find him ready to do just that. I quickly slip out of the tank and yoga pants I was wearing when he came home, and he looks at me with his molten blue eyes. It's exactly what I need. Not pity in his gaze but the burning desire we've just begun exploring. I lift his undershirt from his body and press myself into him, needing his skin against mine before finding his mouth again. The kiss is desperate and slightly unhinged, but Luca doesn't stop and doesn't question me again. My hands find his belt, then his zipper, and I lower it, reaching in and grasping his hard length in my palm. His hand yanks down his pants and he shimmies them off his legs before grabbing one of mine and wrapping it around his hips, opening me up to him. When he guides himself into me, I let out a moan into our kiss. His hand grasps my hip as he begins to move slowly and so fucking deep. He never breaks the kiss; he just gives me what I desperately need from him right now—an escape.

"Oh, God," I cry, breaking the kiss. "I'm almost there."

His hand comes to where we're connected and his expert finger begins strumming my clit. "That's it, Giada. Strangle my cock. God, you feel so good."

It's all so much, nearly too much. His finger and the angle he's hitting so deep inside break me, and I fall into an abyss of sensation as I come apart in his arms. Luca's groan fills the room and I feel his cock jerk as he comes, still thrusting so deep inside of me. He takes my mouth in a ravenous kiss before stilling and eventually pulling out.

When he breaks our connection, his eyes find mine, and I trace my finger along the sweat lining his brow.

"Thank you," I whisper. "For being here, for being who you are. I..." *I want you. I need you. I think I love you.* "I couldn't do this without you."

Luca looks in my eyes, surely seeing the unspoken words I'm too afraid to say.

"Always," is all he says before wrapping me in his arms and tucking me into his chest. I let out a contented sigh, feeling safe and protected before sleep claims me.

Chapter Seventeen
Luca

THE LAST THREE DAYS haven't brought us any new information about Carlo's whereabouts. Finn has his people actively looking for him, along with his father-in-law's men. That bastard is damn good at hiding, I'll give him that.

Alessia has stopped by every day and worked with Giada on her target practice. Of course I offered, I'm not too shabby myself, but Giada enjoys Alessia's company, finding an almost big sister in her. Personally, I think forming a bond with Alessia is the best thing for her after the hell she grew up around. She needs all the support and care she can get right now.

My wife hasn't talked too much about what she found out the day I came home from the meeting with the other capos in the Cataldi organization. I also haven't pushed. When I found out who Frank was and what he'd done, it took a full three weeks before I could look him in the eye without wanting to scream and rage at him. And that was after years of love and support from him. Honestly, had he not been dying, I don't know if I would have been able to forgive him or, at the very least, give him any sort of compassion during the last nineteen months of his life. Death is permanent. Feelings are not. Though I can't say I've fully forgiven Frank for what he did and the lies through the years, I was able to be the son he raised when he needed it, and I can live with that.

I'm finishing up a workout in the living room, having moved the furniture again like I've been doing for Giada so she can lose herself in dance. It's one of the things that helps keep her mind from spinning with the new reality she's found herself in. When she dances, there's always a smile on her face. She told me it's one of the ways she feels closer to her mom since they shared a love for it.

The elevator doors that lead to the underground gun range open, and Giada and Alessia come walking into the penthouse with smiles on their faces. Giada stops when she sees I'm shirtless and sweaty after having worked out. The instant flare of desire in her eyes doesn't make me stand a bit taller, nor does it send a small amount of pride through me that my wife appreciates the physical shape I've worked through the years to keep myself in. Nope. Not at all.

Alessia chuckles next to her, seeing the brief exchange and recognizing it for what it is. I don't think the woman misses a thing, just like her husband.

"Thanks for coming over again," Giada says to Alessia. "I think I'm getting better."

Alessia smiles proudly at my wife and nods. "I think so too. It won't be long until you're as good as me."

Giada shakes her head. "Let's not get ahead of ourselves. I only just started hitting the actual target and not the space around it."

"No one is perfect their first time out. Trust me. When I started practicing with my dad and Enzo, I was a shaking mess. They probably shouldn't have even let me hold a gun, let alone fire one."

Giada told me a few things about Alessia's past that I already knew from Finn and why she takes learning any and all self-defense methods for women so seriously. There was a reason Orlando Farina is dead and it's not just for helping Carlo try to kidnap Alessia and shooting her guard in the back. He would have died regardless, but there was a brutality in the way Finn handled the situation that was very personal. I can't help but wish I'd been there to see that piece of shit take his last breath.

Giada lets out a loud yawn then shakes her head. "Sorry," she tells Alessia. "I haven't been sleeping great."

That's putting it mildly. No more than a couple hours pass before Giada jerks awake every night. Then, when she eventually succumbs to sleep, she tosses and turns. Neither of us has been sleeping well because of it, but it's understandable. The three weeks I spent away from Frank I was barely functioning off a few hours of sleep a night, instead lying awake thinking about everything he told me on a loop over and over. Imagining what it must have been like for my parents to know they were taking their last breaths, that they were being ripped away from each other and their baby.

Alessia waves off her concerns. "Don't worry about it. Go take a nap. I'll come by tomorrow, and we'll practice some more. If you want, I can invite my best friend over and we can start some hand-to-hand self-defense lessons."

"That sounds great." Giada gives Alessia a sleepy smile. "See you tomorrow."

Giada walks up the stairs to our bedroom and my eyes trail her the entire time, watching the sway of her hips that I love grabbing hold of as she takes each step.

Turning back around, I catch Alessia's perceptive stare, along with the little smirk playing on her lips.

"Let me walk you out," I say as Alessia grabs her purse from the counter and opens the front door.

"Things have changed between you two," she comments as I close the door behind me.

I don't give her any sort of explanation. It's not as though she's asking, just voicing her observations.

"I'm worried about her."

She nods in understanding. "A lot has changed for her. She told me about the conversation with her brother. It shouldn't, but it never ceases to amaze me the cruelty in this world, in this life. I had no idea Francesco wasn't her real father."

The memory of that phone call still sends molten heat through my veins. How cold he was to her, how amused he was to be crushing her world more than he and his father already had. Knowing it was for nothing more than to torture her mother into her afterlife.

"She isn't…handling it well. Barely sleeps, has nightmares. She doesn't talk to me much about it. I don't know, maybe she thinks I won't care or something."

"No, I don't think that's it at all. She's most likely worried about it bringing up pieces of your past that were painful to deal with. You two are kind of in the same boat. Being lied to about who your real parents are, being kept from the truth for years. Your dad may have had different reasons, but it doesn't take away the sting of betrayal."

"It's different for me, though. I had a happy childhood, and Frank genuinely loved me. Francesco never cared about Giada, only wanted to send his wife to her death with the knowledge that he was going to use her for his own gain. This life is the opposite of what Frank wanted for me."

"Did you feel that way when you first found out? Did it matter to you that he kept you safe and loved you?"

I blow out a breath and shake my head. "No."

"Talk to her about it. I think the two of you trying to spare each other's feelings isn't helping either one of you. Communication is key."

"Is this marriage advice?"

"Sure as shit is. I'm an old pro now." Alessia laughs and presses the button to call the elevator. "Maeve and Cormac are having a little birthday dinner for me next week. Maeve wants you and Giada there. I think Finn is making her back off a little to give you two some space, but she told him times up. My parents will be there, too."

I think about Giada being there among the people her father trained her to fear and despise.

"Is it weird for your parents to spend time with the Monaghans even though your father pretty much hated them his entire life?"

The elevator doors open as Alessia considers my question. "I thought it would be, but I think they were more business rivals than anything else. Nothing like how the Monaghans or my father views the Cataldis. My father used to cuss up a storm when Finn poached deals. But he always respected him, even though he never admitted it. I'll just say I'm glad we're all on the same side now and leave it at that." She steps into the elevator and holds my gaze before the doors close. "Talk to your wife, Luca."

I smile and give her a little wave before she's closed off from view and I head back into the penthouse.

Walking up the stairs, I find Giada curled under the blankets, still awake and facing me. She lifts the comforter, inviting me to lie down with her, and I notice she's in one of my T-shirts. God, I love seeing her in my clothes. It sets off some primal instinct that screams *mine.*

I crawl in next to her and lie on my back, hauling her body so she's draped over me, her cheek resting on my bare chest.

"How was shooting with Alessia?"

I feel her smile. "It was good. I never really got to know her even though we grew up in the same circles.

The other families didn't socialize much after a big trial sent a bunch of capos to prison about fifteen years ago. Only special occasions like weddings or funerals. Well, not Alessia and Finn's wedding, obviously. But it's nice having someone around who understands the traditions of the Italian Mafia compared to the Irish. My family was still different though." She pauses and I feel the tension in her body. "Well, I guess they aren't my family. Never really were."

My hand lightly trails up and down her back in what I hope is a comforting gesture. "Yeah, I know a little something about that."

"I feel like I was raised to be this person that doesn't really exist. Like my entire life was a lie. I was never the daughter of Francesco Cataldi. It's not like he showed me fatherly affection, either. But I was still loyal because I had to be, because no matter what, he was my father, and even though he was a shit dad, that meant something to me. Finding out that was all a lie, I don't know...it makes me feel like that loyalty was stolen somehow. Does that make sense?"

"More than you know, sweetheart. When Frank told me who he really was and what he'd done, it was like this switch flipped in me. Suddenly, he went from being this great dad who did everything he could to raise me right to a monster who took everything from me. I suppose, in a way, he did. His lies are the reason I love him. Hell, I practically worshiped the ground he walked on. Honestly, if he hadn't been sick, I don't know that

I would have ever spoken to him again." I kiss the top of her head. "But we also had years of love between us. Nothing like what happened with your father."

I've spent nearly a decade shoving those feelings in a box and keeping it locked tight. Being here, being at that meeting a few days ago, it's another reminder of the person Frank was when he was a capo in the Cataldi organization. It's so different from who he was when we lived in California. Constantine and Frank really were two different people. The same way I had to be when I came to Boston. I can tell myself I did the things I did because the end goal was justified, but I spent years having to stand by and watch innocent people get hurt. In a way, it made me understand my dad more and why he wanted me far from this world. I felt myself getting sucked deeper and deeper into the role I was playing. I felt the rot taking root in my soul. The same rot that consumed Francesco and Carlo. Had Giada not been there needing my help, needing me to be the man I was raised to be, I don't know what would have happened to me.

"I'm mad at my mom, too," she says softly, almost as though she's ashamed to admit it. "She could have told the Monaghans what happened. She should have. What was she thinking leaving you with a criminal who killed your parents? It makes no sense to me."

I spent a lot of time wondering about that, too. But I always go back to why Frank didn't leave me on the Monaghans' doorstep and disappear. "It was a bloody time for our families. When Frank told me he left with me because he didn't want me growing up in this life, that the baby he saved was more valuable than being another soldier in this fight, it made sense to me. Now I know the Monaghans are different from what he thought, but at the time, he didn't. Maybe your mom thought the same thing. Maybe that's why she wanted to take you and Carlo and run. She didn't want her kids growing up in a world that was trying to kill them."

Giada hums. "Maybe." She's silent for a few moments. "Do you believe in fate, Luca?"

"I never gave it much thought. Why?"

"Maybe the reason Frank felt compelled to take you and leave Boston was so you would be here when I needed you. If you'd grown up with the Monaghans, you would've grown up hating my family. If you hadn't wanted revenge and come back to Boston, I would be in the hands of the Russians. Maybe this was the universe's way of righting the wrongs of our parents." She tilts her head so she can look me in the eye. "You saved me, Luca."

I kiss her soft lips because I can't help myself. Giada grounds me, reminds me why I'm here and why those bastards won't win.

"You saved me too, sweetheart."

CHAPTER EIGHTEEN
GIADA

"Y OU'RE DOING GREAT. YUP. Like that," Gemma, Alessia's best friend, comments as Alessia and I spar on the mat she brought over four days ago. We're set up in the living room again while Luca and Finn are downstairs in the gun range doing a little target practice.

Being a dancer has helped me learn the moves the two women have spent their afternoons teaching me. I'm already accustomed to bending my body in ways that don't feel natural and picking up on different moves after only a couple of demonstrations. Learning all of this is similar, except for the force I have to put into it. I'm not trying to hurt anyone in dance, quite the opposite, so I struggle with using the strength in my body to do so.

"Let's take a break," Alessia says before grabbing her water and taking a long pull from the bottle. "I have to say, I'm rather impressed at how well you're picking up on everything."

I preen a bit at her compliment. Alessia has stopped by nearly every day to work with me on either target practice or with Gemma to work on self-defense moves. I've never had someone care so much about me being able to take care of myself—or care about me at all, really. My brother, and who I thought was my father, sure as hell never wanted me to learn how to defend myself. They wanted to turn me into the perfect little Mafia wife. It's astounding that a man as powerful as Mario Amatto was the one to teach his daughter how to handle a gun and support her training in boxing and all different kinds of martial arts. She was raised in the same world as me but so different. It makes me wonder about my real father, the one Francesco killed alongside my mother. Would he have made sure I knew how to handle a weapon? Would he have taught me the things Alessia knows now? There are so many things I'll never know about him. I don't even know what he looks like and it's not as though I can go searching through my mother's things. Everything was thrown out except her records that were in an old forgotten box when she died, as though Francesco didn't want me to have anything of hers that would bring me comfort.

"Gemma, you're coming tonight, right?" I ask. Tonight is Alessia's birthday dinner at the Monaghans. It will be the first time we're leaving the penthouse in over a week. I'm a little nervous about it if I'm being honest. Not about being outside of these walls; I'm excited for that, but about spending time with the Amattos and the Monaghans. We haven't seen Maeve and Cormac since the first day we were here. I think Luca is a bit nervous as well. His family wants to get to know him, but there's so much about his past he's afraid to share. Like the fact he doesn't hate the man who raised him. Luca has been struggling with merging the two men in his mind, the one who killed his parents and the one who cared for him and didn't want him to have anything to do with this life.

Gemma rolls her eyes. "Of course I'll be there. It's Alessia's birthday party."

"Ugh," Alessia groans. "Don't remind me. I'm sure there will be plenty of talk about how I'm not getting any younger, and Finn and I should start thinking about having a family. We haven't even been married for six months and my mother and Maeve are already salivating over the thought of grandchildren."

Gemma gives her a sympathetic look. "I'm sorry, sweetie. I know that's a tough subject for you."

I'm curious about why she says that, but I don't pry.

"Well, you'll have me to steer the conversation," Gemma says brightly. "And as long as Eoghan stays out of my way, there won't be any bloodshed." Her wide smile is in stark contrast to her violent words.

"You don't like Eoghan?" I ask, curious about the dynamics I'll be walking into tonight.

"Oh, come on. Finn told you he was playing a joke on his brother at our wedding. Eoghan had no idea who that girl was," Alessia says.

"Fair. But it's not as though that makes Eoghan a saint. I swear, every time he's around, it's like he's undressing me with his eyes."

"Does he make you uncomfortable?" I ask. The idea that the goofy little brother could cause a woman to feel discomfort in any way surprises me. It doesn't mean it's not true, but it's hard to imagine from what I know about him.

"She's uncomfortable because he's the exact kind of guy who she usually drools over." Alessia laughs and Gemma sends her a scathing look.

"Exactly," Gemma says. "I'm done with fuckboys. He's all about the chase and getting what he wants."

"I think you both want it," Alessia mumbles.

"Shut it, lady. What I want and what's good for me are two very different things, and it's time I started focusing on finding serious relationships, not spending my time chasing losers."

"Eoghan is pretty far from a loser," Alessia comments.

"He's also pretty far from being the type to settle down and take a relationship seriously," Gemma retorts.

I watch the women banter back and forth lightheartedly, and a pang of sadness hits me. They remind me of me and my cousin back in Italy. God, I miss her and my family there.

"Let's try to keep the claws sheathed. I love my mother-in-law and would hate for her to have to clean blood out of the carpets. It's such a pain in the ass."

Gemma grins. "Okay. I'll do it for Maeve."

The elevator doors open and Luca and Finn step out. My husband wears a smile I've been seeing more and more lately. As though he's finally able to be happy now that he can be around his family and not have to hide behind the mask he wore at my house. It makes me regret that he had to hide himself for so long when he worked for my father. I know he doesn't see it like that, though. He was doing what needed to be done for his cousin and himself.

Of course, there's still this living, breathing tension with not knowing where my brother is. But in these moments when we're surrounded by family and friends, or it's just us, the tension eases, and Luca is allowed a few moments of peace.

Although when he notices me in a tight tank and workout shorts Alessia bought for me, his gaze is anything but peaceful. His hungry eyes sweep over me while his tongue wets his full bottom lip like he's imagining what I taste like on it.

"I had a car sent over for you and Giada. Figured you didn't want to drive that old jalopy you came here with," Finn says, breaking Luca out of wherever his thoughts went.

"Sounds good," my husband replies, his eyes moving to his cousin.

Luca and Finn move the mat to the far wall of the penthouse and set the living room back to rights before Finn grabs his wife's and Gemma's bag and they say their goodbyes.

After the door closes, Luca's eyes find me and the heat he doused when his cousin spoke to him is back in full force as he stalks toward me, grabbing me around the waist and pressing my body into his body. "Fucking hell, sweetheart. It's a good thing I'm not the one working out with you. I don't think I'd be able to keep my hands off you."

"That's kinda the point," I say, leaning up to kiss him. "You grab me, and I try to get away."

"Wanna try now?" he whispers against my lips before gently grazing them over the damp column of my neck.

"Not even a little," I reply, sliding my hands under his shirt. "But right now, I need to take a shower."

"Mmm, You wanna know what I need?" His hands travel to the waist of my shorts and he dips his fingers just inside the elastic band.

"What?" I ask, having a very strong feeling of what it is.

"I need to taste you coming on my tongue."

Luca's lips travel from my neck to my chest as one of his hands comes to the neckline of my tank, yanking it down to expose my breasts to his waiting mouth. He wastes no time in wrapping his lips around my nipple and sucking hard, his other hand delving inside my shorts, two of his fingers spreading me as he rubs my clit between them.

"God, that feels so good," I moan and clutch the skin of his neck, digging my nails into the heated flesh.

Luca backs me up to the backside of the couch and releases my nipple with a pop before lowering to his knees, kissing and licking my chest, stomach and hips on his way down, needing to taste every inch of me.

I've discovered a side to my husband that I never would have guessed was there. He's filled with passion and a drive to make me come every which way he can. This particular position is one of his favorites, him on his knees, desperate to eat me out.

He pulls my shorts down and helps me step out of them before his mouth attaches to my center. I'm immediately overwhelmed by the feel of his hot mouth on my delicate flesh.

"Mmm, baby. Just like that. Ride my face."

My hands clutch the back of the couch as my hips writhe over his tongue, grinding myself into his face.

The two fingers rubbing my clit slip inside of me as his tongue starts flicking over and over, first with just the tip, then he takes a long lick up and down, the change in tempo keeping me on the edge of orgasm.

"Luca, please," I cry out, throwing my head back, desperate for him to make me come.

His chuckle vibrates against my flesh and he's working hard to bring me to the peak as fast as possible, which for me isn't long at all. His skillful tongue is licking right where I need him. Then he curves the two fingers inside my wet channel and rubs over the bundle of nerves inside of me.

"Ahh," I scream out as my orgasm tumbles through me, making my belly clench and my thighs shake as each wave crashes through me.

Luca rips his mouth from me. "Fuck, I need to be

inside of you." He stands and whips his shirt over his head before he roughly spins me so I'm facing the back of the couch and places my hands back on the top. "Hold on, baby."

In one thrust, he's buried himself so deep. The sudden intrusion takes my breath away. Actually everything about my husband has a tendency to make me breathless.

His movements are rough and possessive, unlike the times he's taken me gently while we've both been coming to terms with the maelstrom of emotions threatening us in every silent moment. Now he's taking what he needs and giving me the same. I need him unbidden and unafraid to remove the kid gloves and fuck me like our sanity depends on it. I need the brutality because it tells me he knows I can handle every part of him.

"God, I'm so close," I cry into the room as his damp chest curls over my back, hearing the slap of wet flesh.

His fingers reach around to where we're connected and he feels where his hard cock is moving deliciously inside of me, collecting the wetness there before strumming my clit. The touch is all it takes to set me off again, and I scream as another orgasm rushes through me, lighting my entire body on fire.

"Fuuuck," he yells when his cock jerks inside of me, and he empties himself on a roar.

The sound of Luca's panting breath is loud in my ear in the otherwise silent space. It's in moments like these where the outside world feels so far off, and the only thing that matters is this little slice of happiness Luca and I have created for ourselves. The place where we can lose ourselves in each other like any normal newly married couple. You know, the ones that didn't run from their psychotic brother and had their bodyguard marry them so they didn't have to marry the son of a powerful criminal, only to find out that their new husband is part of a criminal family that hates theirs and has been working for years to bring them down. Jesus, this is all such a mess.

"I'm still buried inside of you, wife, and I can practically hear you overthinking." Luca pulls out and kisses the back of my neck before standing straight and pulling my back to his front, wrapping a comforting arm around my middle.

"I'm a little nervous about spending time with your family, to be honest." I turn my head toward him and look at his flushed face.

"I know, sweetheart."

The first time we met, everyone seemed friendly, but I'd be lying if I said the years I was programmed to hate the Irish didn't leave me with lingering doubts. And I fucking hate that. I have to remind myself nearly every day that I was lied to my entire life by a man who wasn't my father, who basically stole me for his own gain. Nothing he told me was true.

The Irish aren't the monsters I've always been led to believe. I lived with the real monsters.

"Come on," I say after standing in the living room for a few moments while Luca rubs small circles with his thumb over my belly. "Let's get cleaned up."

When we pull up to the Monaghan's large two-story house painted white with black shutters, several cars are already in the drive.

"Full house," I mumble.

"Think of it this way; it takes the pressure off us a bit."

"I don't think that's possible. I'm the daughter of the Monaghans and the Amattos' number one enemy, and you're the long-lost cousin who's secretly been trying to take down my family. But sure, we can go with that."

"Look at me, Giada."

I turn my body toward Luca, who I'm sure is facing the same nerves as me, and here I am, thinking about how I'm being affected and not my husband. I'm really killing it with this whole wife thing.

"We're Luca and Giada Bennetti. None of what you said defines us. It may be our circumstances, but it's not who we are."

"Who are we?" I whisper.

"We're figuring it out." He leans over the console and places a soft kiss on my lips. "Come on, sweetheart. I got you."

When we knock on the door, Maeve opens it with a

wide smile on her face. Looking into her blue gaze, I see what everyone says about the Monaghan eyes. Luca, Eoghan, and Finn all share the same blue eyes.

"Come in, come in," Maeve says, leaning in to give Luca a hug, then me.

"They would if you gave them a chance to step through the door, love," Cormac comments, stepping behind his wife.

Maeve playfully smacks him in the arm. "I'm excited. Sue me."

Cormac laughs and gently pulls his wife out of the way before stepping to the side to allow us entrance.

Walking into the large family room, I spot Alessia and Finn on the couch, with Gemma sitting across from them next to Lilliana Amatto and her husband, Mario. Eoghan is perched on the arm of the couch next to Gemma, who seems to be leaning away from him and doing her best to ignore his presence. The group sees us in the doorway, and everyone stands, welcoming Luca and me with kind smiles. When Lilliana and Mario greet us, their expressions are open and warm.

Lilliana leans in and kisses both of my cheeks. "Congratulations on your marriage, Giada," she says in her light Italian accent. "Mario and I were thrilled when we heard the news."

I smile in her direction, not really knowing what to say and wondering if she's aware of the circumstances surrounding our union.

Mario leans in next, kissing both cheeks like the

Italians do. "It's good to see you again, Giada. Happy to have you here."

"I'm going to check in with the cook. Dinner should be just about ready," Maeve announces and walks out of the room.

"Drink?" Eoghan offers, walking to the small bar against the wall.

"I'll have a glass of red wine if you have it," I reply, and Luca asks for whiskey.

Small talk ensues, mostly about sports. Turns out Alessia and Mario are huge Red Sox fans and Finn is a die-hard Yankees fan.

"I'm sorry, Papa. You have no idea how hard I've tried to convert him. Please don't hold it against him. I'm sure in time he'll see the light," Alessia jokes with her dad.

"I just don't understand how you can be born and raised in Boston and like"—Mario fake coughs—"the Yankees."

"He's a disgrace to the family," Eoghan interjects. "See, Alessia? You chose the wrong brother."

Finn shoots his brother a glare that would make most men wither, but Eoghan just lets out a bark of laughter.

Maeve comes back into the room and announces dinner is ready. We all gather in their large dining room to see a beautifully set table with a large arrangement of red calla lilies as the centerpiece. Finn and Alessia share a knowing smile before she mouths, "I love you." His finger gently swipes across her red lips, then he leans in to kiss her softly before pulling her chair out for her.

Once we're all seated, everyone begins passing trays of food around the table. It's so different from the dinners I'd had growing up. Everyone here is family, made evident by the comfortable conversations taking place around me. I don't know why I was ever nervous about coming tonight. This isn't some formal, stuffy affair. It's a family eating together, celebrating one of their own on her birthday.

"This veal is amazing," Alessia tells Maeve.

"Finn said it was one of your favorites," she replies.

It's amazing to me he knows that and his mother made her favorite for her birthday. The most I remember is one of my nannies baking me a cake when I was little.

Tears threaten to prick my eyes when I think about how I've missed out on having a family like this my entire life. I clear my throat, trying to dislodge the lump that suddenly appeared. Luca's hand finds my thigh, and he squeezes gently. When I meet his gaze, he smiles slightly and gives me a wink. Yeah, he knows what I'm feeling. It's unexpected and overwhelming but in the best way.

After everyone has finished eating, I offer to help with clearing the plates, but Maeve waves me off. "The cook will take care of it. I actually wanted a minute to talk with you, if you don't mind."

Unsure of what she has to say, I nod and follow her into another room next to what looks to be Cormac's office.

Maeve leads me into a room with bookshelves lining the walls. There's a small desk in one corner and a pale-gray overstuffed chair in the other that looks like the perfect spot to curl up with a book.

"Cormac set this space up for me. We went to dinner at the Amattos' one night not too long ago and I fell in love with their library. I'd been hounding my husband to build me one, and I think seeing Mario's lit a fire under his ass." Maeve chuckles. "Never let it be said my husband will stand by and be outdone by an Italian."

"Our families certainly enjoy showing off our wealth." I think about the difference in our estate and the Monaghan's. Granted, I haven't seen where Finn lives, but Maeve and Cormac's house, even though it's huge, has that comfortable, lived-in feel, not the cold museum I grew up in.

Maeve walks to the other side of her desk, pulls out an envelope and stares at it for a few moments before shutting the drawer and walking toward me.

"I met your mother once," she starts, and I can tell whatever she's about to tell me is going to be hard for her. "She found me at church one day after I attended a Wednesday mass. When she introduced herself, I had no idea what to expect. Our husbands were not business associates; quite the opposite. Your mom was so...nervous but determined for me to hear her out. She gave me a letter to give to you when I had a chance. To say I was surprised she came to me is putting it mildly. I told her I may never get the opportunity to speak to you and she said she knew it would find its way to you when the time was right. From one mother to another, she asked me to keep this for you. She was worried that she wouldn't be around to explain things to you. I asked if I could help her, but she said she had everything handled. This was a just-in-case situation. Quite the long shot, if you ask me. But she had this knowing look in her eye like she had faith that one day I would meet you and be able to talk to you."

Surprise and shock have my head spinning as I listen to her. She met my mother before she died?

Maeve lets out a huff of air. "Cormac absolutely forbade me from approaching you. Said it would do nothing but cause problems, and we already had enough of those with your father." She hands me the letter. "I know what she did the night Luca disappeared. I can't say I forgive her for telling Frank to leave with my nephew, but part of me understands. To raise children in this life...is a decision not everyone is comfortable with. I'm sure there're plenty of people who think we raise murderers and thieves. That we were having kids to churn out more criminals. But that's not what this life ever meant to me. It's not only my husband and our boys that live by their own code. I do too." Maeve gives me a sad smile. "I'll never fully understand what was going through your mom's mind that night, but I won't keep this from you. Our mistakes are ours, and you and Luca don't deserve to pay for anyone else's sins."

I take the letter from her hand and immediately

recognize my mother's handwriting. I don't move, don't breathe, just stare. I haven't seen her handwriting since she died.

"I'll give you a minute," Maeve says, squeezing my arm on the way out.

I nod absentmindedly, still staring at the envelope in my hand. She leaves, and I sit on the edge of the overstuffed chair and open the envelope. When I unfold the note inside, there's a picture tucked in the paper. It's me when I was probably barely one and a man holding my arms up like he's helping me stand. He's smiling into the camera. It matches the wide, toothy grin on my young face. He's dressed in the usual uniform of one of the guards, white shirt, black pants, and a gun holster around his shoulders. It's his smile that captivates me. It's not just wide like mine is in the picture—it looks exactly like mine. My hands shake as I start reading the l etter.

Dearest Giada,

Oh sweet girl, how I hope you never read this letter. If you do, it means I'm not there with you, living a happy life far away from Francesco. It will mean that he found out about my plan to leave him and this life. I can only pray that he kept you safe as best as he could and he never discovered what I have spent the last six years hiding from him. Francesco isn't your real father. Your real father is the man in the picture with you. His name is Marco Talesio. He's my personal guard, and we didn't mean to, but we fell in love. He doesn't know you're his.

I was too afraid if he knew, he wouldn't be able to hide the truth. It kills me every day to not be able to be honest with him. But if I am and Francesco finds out, it will mean death for us all. Although if this letter finds you, it means I'm gone.

Marco already loves you so much, my sweet baby girl. This is the only picture I have of him and it's my favorite of you. You have his smile and his big heart. I can see it in you now and you're only five. I'm so sorry I won't see you turn into the woman you're going to become. I've made so many mistakes, Giada, but falling in love with Marco isn't one of them. Having you will never be one of them. He was the only man I felt truly happy with, and I hope one day you can find the same. If you never read this letter, then it means you have a shot at it. If you do read this letter, then I'm not sure what your future will hold. But know I will always love you and your brother, even if I'm only able to watch over you from heaven.

I love you so much,

Mama

Tears are pouring down my face as I read her words. Carlo told me all of this over the phone, well, most of it. But seeing it in her words—in her handwriting—there's none of the disdain that was in Carlo's voice when he explained Francesco wasn't my real father. My mother loved my real father and wanted a life where we would be safe away from the clutches of this world and Francesco.

A knock sounds at the door, and Luca peeks his head

in.

As soon as he sees the tears dripping down my cheeks, he rushes over and kneels in front of me. "What's going on?" he asks, cupping my cheeks in his strong palms. "Did someone say something to you?"

I shake my head and hand him the picture. "This was in a letter my mom asked Maeve to give me."

Luca's eyes scan the letter. "Why would she ask Maeve?"

"I don't know. She was probably the only person my mom didn't have to worry about reporting back to my father."

He looks at the picture, then to me. "This is your father." It's not a question.

"His name was Marco."

Luca gathers me in his sturdy arms and holds me, letting me cry. Is this how he felt when Frank showed him a picture of his dead parents that he never had the chance to know? Completely devastated and missing something to the very marrow of your bones that you never really had? Because, it turns out, not only do I have more in common with my husband than I could have thought, I have more in common with my mother.

I've fallen wholly and completely in love with my bodyguard.

Chapter Nineteen
Luca

WHEN MAEVE TOLD ME my wife needed me and where to find her, I was worried the woman had said something to upset her. Finn explained the situation I grew up in to my aunt, and to say she took it well would be a gross overstatement. I appreciated the fact he took it upon himself to tell her my story. I still have so many mixed emotions about Frank. I don't know how I would have handled that conversation.

After walking into Maeve's library and seeing Giada crying on the chair with a picture and a letter in her hand, I had no idea what to expect. Never in a million years did I think she'd be reading a note from her dead mother given to her by the wife of her father's enemy. I can't begin to know what her mother was thinking or why she thought Maeve would ever have the opportunity to give this to Giada. But desperate people do desperate things. If she was ready to risk her life and run with her daughter and son, I'd imagine that's as desperate as it gets.

"This is crazy, right? It's not just me?" Giada asks.

"What, sweetheart?"

"That my mother went to your aunt, knowing what she did about your disappearance when you were a baby. Why wouldn't she have told your aunt about you? She felt comfortable enough to give her a letter like this, but she was never honest with her."

"I think your mother hated what this life did to people, and maybe in some part of her mind, she thought she'd done the right thing. She knew Frank would keep me away from this world. Her trying to take you and Carlo proves she wanted no part in it. I didn't know her, so I can't say what was going through her mind when she delivered this to my aunt."

I wish to hell I did though. But if Cormac and Maeve had found out that Frank had taken me to California, would they have come to take me back? The answer to that question is a resounding yes, and Cormac would have killed Frank in the process. Of that, I'm one one-hundred-percent sure.

"The truth is, we'll never know," Giada says, calmer than she was when I walked into the room. "I'm not going to allow the sins of our parents to affect me at this point. I've spent my entire life doing that. You're right; we're never going to know what my mother was thinking when she went to your aunt." Giada holds up the picture of Marco and her. "I vaguely remember him," she says with a small grin. "My mom was always happy when he was around."

"You look a lot like him. I see him in your smile."

"I wonder if he ever suspected he was my real father."

I shake my head. "We'll have to chalk it up to one of the things we'll never know."

That list seems to be getting longer and longer.

"I feel bad for saying this, but I'm glad she had him. At least for a little while, she had someone who loved her and made her happy." Giada looks at me with an unsure smile mixed with a touch of guilt.

"You should never feel bad for being glad your mom had some happiness. It's okay to separate the people we love from the mistakes they made, especially if they aren't here to defend themselves."

"You're awfully calm about this. I would think, of anyone, you'd be the most upset about what my mother did, then her having the audacity to approach your aunt to ask her to give me this." She holds the paper between us.

I lift my shoulder and blow out a breath. "I love my dad. Not Elio, but Frank. Do you think I should hate him or completely disregard the years spent thinking he was my father and loved me because I found out the truth?" She shakes her head. "I've just had more time than you to come to terms with people we love not always doing the right thing. Or at least the right thing in our eyes." I kiss the top of her head. "I'm not saying it's easy or that I got here overnight. There are days I still struggle, still feel like it's a betrayal to my family that I love the man who stole me and lied to me. But I stopped letting it consume me a long time ago. I found peace with it, even if I don't understand it."

Giada gives me a watery smile. "You're pretty amazing, Luca Bennetti."

I kiss her sweet lips. "Right back at you, Mrs. Bennetti."

The celebration continues with a birthday cake and more wine for my wife. When we came out of the room, Alessia looked between Giada and me and gave me a knowing smile. Who would have thought her advice about communication would be all it takes to find a deeper understanding and acceptance of both our pasts? It's not like there's some sort of guide for how to work through all this shit.

Giada is talking animatedly with Gemma and Alessia about some story involving her cousin and a trip they took to Spain a few years ago. I love how comfortable she's become in the short time she's known Alessia and Gemma. Though I rarely saw the charming side of my wife when she was a bratty teenager in high school, she's shining tonight. Although, I suppose it could be the wine.

It strikes me that we've never talked about what's going to happen after her brother is dealt with. The only time I mentioned anything about her being free after this was handled was the day of our wedding. So much has changed between us since then, but the fact still remains that Giada doesn't want any part of this life. I don't know exactly what's in store for me within the Monaghan organization after all is said and done, but it's not like I have many options for future employment. I don't think mole for the Irish mob is something you can put on a resumé.

While Finn and Eoghan discuss something or other about the next bar they want to organize a fight night at, I think about my future. Honestly, I never gave anything much thought as far as *after*. I wasn't sure I'd make it out alive, so the idea of planning a future seemed a little far-fetched at the time. Will Finn want to put me on a crew? Where will I live? Will Giada be living with me? We haven't discussed any of this.

"You ever thought about getting in the ring?" Eoghan asks. "I bet after a bit of training, you would be a hell of a fighter."

I shoot him a half smile. "I'm more a lover than a fighter," I reply as Giada walks up to me, and I wrap my arm around her shoulder.

"Tell that to the guy whose nose you broke a few months ago at the club," she says.

Finn chuckles and Eoghan laughs along.

"Are you about ready to go home?" I ask Giada, her glazed eyes finding mine. My wife is a bit tipsy, it seems.

"Sure," she replies.

"We're going to head out, too," Finn says before catching his wife's eye. "It's a rare night where neither of us are expected at the casino and I'd like to take my wife home and…"

"Please don't finish that sentence, Finnegan Monaghan," Maeve says, walking up behind her son.

"What? I was going to say give her the present I left at the house."

"Oh, present?" Alessia asks, walking up to the group.

"Mmhmm," Finn hums. "You're going to love it."

"I didn't tell you what I wanted," Alessia says.

Finn rolls his eyes dramatically. "Haven't you learned by now, wife? I know what makes that heart inside of you tick. You think I need you to tell me what to get you?"

Alessia smiles and kisses Finn on the mouth. "Fair."

We say our goodbyes and head out the door. I tuck Giada into her seat and start the car, pulling out to the main road behind Finn. We aren't driving for more than five minutes before I notice the car behind us coming up way too fast. Before I have time to warn Giada, the dark sedan rams us from behind. I swerve but am able to keep our car on the road.

"Holy shit, Luca!" Giada yells, twisting in her seat.

"Turn around," I tell her, speeding up, trying to get the hell away from whoever is in the car behind us.

I grab my phone and call Finn. "We have a tail. They just tried to run me off the road."

Just then, the car behind us rams into us again, but this time, I'm not so lucky. Our car goes off the side of the highway, flipping down the embankment as Giada screams before landing on its side against a tree.

I'm jarred from the impact but manage to get my seat belt off. "Giada," I call, my hands cupping her cheeks while my frantic eyes look into hers.

She's dazed but doesn't appear injured. "I'm okay, I'm okay."

As the words leave her lips, I hear the sound of heavy boots coming toward us. I look out the window as the masked man raises his gun and opens fire into the car. My body covers Giada as best as I can while she's still belted into her seat, and I pray my cousin is already out there.

When the shooting stops, Finn shouts, "Luca. Talk to me."

Other than the broken glass that rained over me, I don't think I was hit. "I'm okay." I remove myself from Giada's front, and to my horror, I come away with blood covering my light-gray shirt. I look at Giada, and her eyes are wide with terror. "Luca?" she asks before we both look down and see the blood pumping from her shoulder.

"Oh God. Finn, Giada's been hit," I yell and look into my wife's eyes. "You're going to be okay, baby. We'll get out of here and get you stitched up." Before I finish my sentence, her eyes close and her body goes limp, only being held in place by the belt around her chest. "Finn, hurry up."

He rushes to the front window that's been shot out by our would-be assassin's bullets and looks inside. "Shit," he hisses as Alessia comes up behind him, a look of shock and fear marring her features.

"Okay, Luca, I need you to hold her while you undo the belt. I'm going to reach in and have you hand her to me through the window. Alessia, call the doctor and let him know we're on our way. His contact information is in my phone in the car." Alessia nods and turns, running toward the car parked on the side of the street.

As gently as I can, I release Giada from the seat belt and pass her to Finn, doing my damndest not to jostle her. Once she's safely in his arms, I crawl out of the window myself and look at my wife's pale face. Ripping the shirt from my body, I put it over the wound on Giada's chest. We hurry up the embankment, Finn with Giada in his arms and me applying pressure to where she's shot. Alessia opens the back door of the sedan, and I quickly climb in before he passes my wife to me. I continue holding the shirt to her chest as Finn rushes around the car and hops in the driver's seat.

He grabs his phone and dials a number. "Eoghan. I'm sending you my location. Luca's car was run off the road, and Giada was shot. The shooter and the car are on the east side of the street. I need a cleanup. We're headed to the doc's house now." Finn hangs up and sends our location to his brother before he speeds away on the quiet highway.

Alessia turns in her seat and looks from me to Giada with tears in her eyes. "She's going to be okay. Our doctor saved my bodyguard. She'll be fine."

I don't respond. My gaze is focused on my wife's face

as I pray she opens her amber eyes again.

It takes Finn seven minutes to get to the doctor's house. Seven of the longest and most excruciating minutes of my life. The doctor meets us in the back driveway and takes one look at Giada before a flurry of activity begins. The doc shouts orders at his staff waiting outside of the operating room as they wheel my wife behind the door.

I try to go in, but the doctor stops me. "You need to stay out here. One of the nurses will come by with something for you to change into."

"I need to be with my wife," I growl at the man in my way.

"I need to be with your wife, and I can't do that if I'm out here arguing with you," the doctor tells me.

"Come on, Luca. He needs to get in there," Finn says, grabbing my shoulder and tugging me back. The doctor spins and goes through the doors where they took Giada.

"It's going to be okay. She's in the best hands money can buy."

I allow him to lead me to a couch set up just outside the doors. He has a seat next to me and Alessia sits on the couch opposite us. When I glance at her, I see the worried look on her face. That was a lot of blood, and Giada was so fucking pale, as though it all had leaked from her. Alessia tries to offer me a reassuring smile, but it's useless. Everyone in this room knows how fragile life is, and Giada may not have one after tonight.

A nurse brings me a change of clothes and leads me into the bathroom. As I wash the blood from my hands and neck with a damp cloth, my eyes stay fixed on my reflection. Why wasn't I faster? If I would have covered her faster, the bullet would have gone into me instead of her. I'm the one with the stains on my soul, not her. She doesn't deserve being shot and fighting for her life.

Staring at myself, rage like I've never known overtakes every cell in my body and explodes through my fist into the mirror. I keep punching until my knuckles are broken and bloody. Until Giada's blood mixes with mine on my cut palms.

The pounding on the door breaks me from my violent haze. "Luca," Finn says through the door.

I open the door and find him standing there. He looks from the mirror to my knuckles, then meets my gaze. "Come on. I'll find someone to stitch your hand."

The same nurse who handed me the change of clothes is now cleaning glass from my skin.

"I'm sorry about the mess," I say robotically since that's what a rational person would do in this situation, even though I feel like anything but.

She raises her shoulder, shrugging off my apology. "Don't worry about it. I've been working with the doc for nearly ten years. You're not the first person to break something around here." She smiles, but I don't return it. The sum of everything that is good in my life is lying on an operating table, and I don't have it in me to feel anything other than anger that she's there at all.

When the nurse finishes cleaning the wound, she applies a few stitches to the deepest of the cuts then covers them with gauze. "I'll see if I can get an update on your wife. It may be too soon right now, though. Okay?"

I nod and Finn shoves off the wall he was leaning against while the nurse patched me up.

"No speeches about how I should control my temper better than that?" I ask my cousin when he sits next to me, his expression giving nothing away.

Finn shakes his head and releases a huff of breath. "Are you serious? If I were in your shoes, I would've probably done the same thing. I think you forget the kind of man I am."

"Yeah, what kind is that?"

"The kind who would move heaven and hell to protect his wife and cut through any motherfucker who stood in his way. If busting a mirror and your hands make the pain in your chest lessen for even a second, who the hell am I to judge?" Finn looks at me. "A guy I know once told me it changes when you have someone who carries your heart in their body."

"It sure as fuck does."

Finn smiles. "Yeah, that's what I said, too."

Three grueling hours later, the doctor meets me in the waiting room. "She's going to be fine," he says. "The bullet went straight through. It tore up some muscles but missed the major arteries, which is always a concern with gunshot wounds like this. She's going into recovery now, and you can see her once she's settled. She's asleep and heavily medicated for pain, so when she wakes up, she won't be fully cognitive."

I nod and thank the doctor, apologizing again for the mirror.

"It's fine. I'll bill your cousin."

When he walks away, Alessia looks in the direction he went then back to her husband. "Holy shit, did the doc just crack a joke?"

"Doubtful. I fully expect an invoice by morning," Finn replies.

Alessia lets out a small laugh then turns to me and smiles.

This time, I return it.

CHAPTER TWENTY
GIADA

WAKING IN THE HOSPITAL, or rather the doctor's house, was a surprise, to say the least. When people say they don't remember their accident, I don't understand how. I remembered every second of it. The fear in my husband's eyes when he saw me bleeding in the car will forever be ingrained in my memory. As soon as I realized what happened in that car, I was terrified. I was certain that when my eyes closed, they would never open again. And I couldn't stop it from happening. When I did eventually wake up to Luca sitting beside me, I was so damn thankful. I don't know how I would've possibly handled him lying unconscious in a hospital be d.

The doctor kept me for a few days for observation. Thankfully, the bullet went all the way through, and no major damage was done. He said the shot was one in a million. I'd be good with not testing those odds ever again.

Instead of heading back to the penthouse, Luca and Finn decided to have us stay at Finn's estate outside of Boston, where we've been for the last two weeks. They aren't sure how the shooter knew where we were, but best guess is they were watching Maeve and Cormac's house for any signs of us. At least, we're assuming they were after me and Luca since Eoghan found pictures of the two of us in the hit man's car.

The one thing I know for certain, deep in my bones, is my brother ordered it. Though no one from the Cataldi organization will touch him with a ten-foot pole now, it's not as though he couldn't go out and hire any asshole off the street. Any reservations about what Finn and Luca plan to do to my brother when they find him were wiped away with that bullet. Not that I have any. We all know what being in this life means. My loyalty to my brother ended the day he was willing to give me away to our enemy. Before that, if I really think about it. My allegiance to the Monaghans was solidified the moment Luca told me what Carlo did to Alessia. I had a choice to make in that moment, and I chose my husband and his family. And I don't regret it for a single second.

Since it's been nearly three weeks since the shooting, the doctor has cleared me for light duty, not that I have anything to do in the house. Today, I decided to try my hand at baking. I called Isabella, and her mom sent me some of my grandmother's old recipes. I'm assuming they were the ones my mother used to make with me in the kitchen when I was younger, but I really have no way of knowing. There are so many things I'll never know about my mother, but Luca was right when he said we can separate the person from their mistakes and love them regardless. Today, the urge to somehow be closer to the woman who died with so many secrets is strong.

While I'm putting the finishing touches on the fiocco di neve, Finn and Alessia come back from their morning run.

"Oh my God," Finn groans, walking up to the counter as I sprinkle the powdered sugar on the pastries. "Is this what it's like being married to a proper Italian woman who actually cooks?"

I laugh and shake my head. I swear this man loves to goad his wife into an argument any chance he gets.

"Keep it up, husband, and I'll be sure to have Giada bake these for your funeral next week." Alessia shoots Finn a sharktooth smile while her eyes stare daggers into him.

"You love me too much to ever kill me," Finn replies, walking over to give his wife a smacking kiss on her cheek. I'm honestly surprised he has the balls to stand so close to her.

"Whatever helps you sleep at night, dear."

Luca enters the kitchen in a pair of gym shorts with a tight workout shirt stretched across his broad chest. God, he looks edible. It's been weeks since we've been able to have any more intimate moments together. Luca sleeps next to me every night, but he hasn't *touched* me since the shooting. Yes, there're sweet kisses every day and lingering looks, but other than that...nothing. I realize I was just given the okay, but he's been treating me like a fragile glass figurine, as though if you knock into me, I'll fall and shatter.

"Hey, sweetheart," he says, coming up and giving me another *sweet* kiss on the mouth. He pops one of the bite-sized pastries in his mouth and lets out a nearly indecent moan. God, what I wouldn't do to feel that moan on my body. He licks the sugar from his lip, and I'm staring at his mouth so hard Alessia clears her throat and sends me a knowing look.

"What do you say to some target practice?" she asks.

"That sounds like a great idea." That's what she does when she's stressed or is trying to work something out in her head. Seems like I could use some of that.

"Are you sure that's okay with the doctor?" Luca asks.

I swear, the first time I attempted to brush my damn teeth, he asked if it was "doctor-approved." I told him yes, that five out of five dentists recommend it. He didn't find it amusing.

"I spoke with Dr. Simmons two days ago. He said I was fine for light work. I told you that." Irritation is evident in my tone, but he's acting like a mother hen at this point.

"Is shooting considered 'light?'"

"If it aggravates my shoulder too badly, I'll stop. Deal?"

"I don't know abo—"

Before he can finish his sentence, I shove a fiocco di neve in his mouth. "I said I'll be fine." I turn to Alessia. "Come on. I want to see your present from Finn."

When we get downstairs to the range that doubles as a safe room, Alessia pulls out the custom 9mm Finn had made for her birthday.

"Isn't she pretty?" Alessia says when she hands me the gun. I make sure it's pointed at the ground when I take it from her grip and promptly check if it's loaded.

"Good girl," she says with a wide smile.

"I don't know much about guns." I look at the engraving. "My heart, my loyalty, and my life," I read out loud. "That's sweet."

Alessia smiles. "My husband can be quite the poet when he wants."

Handing the gun back to Alessia, I stare at the wall of firearms.

She grabs a .22 and hands it to me. "I think this one is good enough for now. Less kickback."

I load the gun and grab ear protection while she loads a paper target for me. As soon as I begin firing and my sole focus is on hitting the target, my worries begin to melt away. The only thing I'm focused on is keeping my arm steady and my aim true. Well, as true as it can be for someone who's only had about a week's worth of practice. When I press the button to bring the target back to me, I see I hit the paper seven out of ten times.

"You're getting better. I think that's the most you've hit in one go."

"I have a good teacher," I say, smiling at Alessia.

"So, what's really going on? I sensed a little tension upstairs." She nods toward the floor above us.

Letting out a sigh, I set the gun on the counter and turn to her. "Luca's just being overprotective, and it's starting to wear on me." She offers me a sympathetic smile as I continue. "We're safe, but he's acting like Carlo is going to jump out of the shadows at any second and finish the job himself. Or I'm going to start bleeding out if I move wrong. I mean, I appreciate having someone worried about me, but I want a partner, not an overprotective father."

"I can understand how that would be frustrating."

"Was Finn like that with you after everything that happened with my brother?"

"Not to the same extent, no. But Luca isn't Finn, and I wasn't the one lying in a hospital bed. You didn't see him when we brought you in, honey. I've never seen a man more scared that the woman he loves is going to die before he's had a chance to live a life with her."

"He's never said he loves me."

Alessia laughs. "That doesn't mean shit.," she says, waving her hand. "I knew I loved Finn way before I told him. I knew I wanted a future with him, not because I was tied to him for our business's sake, but because I couldn't imagine another man on the planet making me feel the way he does. Physically and emotionally."

I groan in frustration. "That's another thing that's bugging me. The doctor told me three days ago I was fine to resume *normal activities*, and Luca acts like we never had that conversation."

"Ahh, I see."

"See what?"

"You're horny."

"Oh my God, Alessia!" I exclaim with wide eyes. "That's not what I said."

Her laughter booms off the steel-reinforced walls. "You didn't have to. Listen, talk to him about it. Maybe he's taking his cues from you and he doesn't think you're ready."

"Talk to my husband? What a novel concept."

When we've finished with target practice for the day, we head back upstairs in search of our husbands. My shoulder is a little sore, but that's to be expected for a few more weeks yet. Not that I'll tell Luca. He'll just fuss over me some more.

Alessia knocks on the door to Finn's office and opens it to find him and Luca.

"Fuck. I feel like we're missing something. The asshole's out there somewhere," Finn says to Luca.

"What are you guys doing?" Alessia asks, rounding the corner of her husband's desk to have a seat on his lap.

"Trying to figure out where the hell Carlo is hiding," Luca answers as I have a seat on the leather club chair next to his.

"Me and Mario have had guys on all his known associates, even the other capos, to make sure they weren't blowing smoke up our asses at the meeting, and we haven't seen any sign of him. We've been searching every known Cataldi property and still nothing," Finn says, frustration lacing his words.

"Can I see the list of properties?" I ask.

"Sure." Finn hands me a piece of paper with all the businesses, houses and any other piece of land my family owns. I look through every listing, most of them I don't recognize since I was never privy to the daily operations of the business, but I notice one missing.

"There's a lake house we own that isn't on here. My mom used to take Carlo and me there..." A memory I'd long since buried surfaces; it's of the last time we were there. "We were there right before my mom died." I look at Luca. "Marco was with us. I remember walking into the kitchen late one night because I wanted a drink. They were standing there, and he was holding her. I didn't see them kiss or anything, but when she saw me, she pushed away from him and rushed over to me. I remember being a little freaked out from her over-the-top reaction, worried I was in trouble for being out of my bed. But Marco was staring at me with this big grin on his face." My hand comes to my mouth. "Do you think she told him I was his daughter that night?"

Luca reaches over and grabs my other hand, kissing it softly. "She could have. Her letter made it sound like she was going to."

"I remember my dad coming the next day with three of his men. He was so angry, not in a yelling kind of way, but with that quiet rage that used to scare me. He put Carlo, me, and my mom in the car, and on the drive home, I remember my mom crying silently in the front seat. I was so mad at my dad for not comforting her, but I was too scared to say anything. When I saw my mom later, I asked where Marco was and she told me he got another job. She died in a car accident two days later. Or what I thought was a car accident."

"Why are there no property records for the house?" Finn asks.

"I have no idea. I don't even remember exactly where it is. I know we passed through a little town called Shine to get there though. I thought that was a neat name for a town when I was little. That's where we'd stop and grab groceries. The house was maybe another half hour from there."

"I'll call Ozzy," Finn says. "He might know where you're talking about. Fuck, he's gonna be pissed. If that's where Carlo is, he was right under their noses the whole time."

While Finn is on the phone, I turn to Luca. "Who's Ozzy?"

"Remember the MC president your brother pissed off?"

I nod. "Why he went on the run?"

"Yeah. Ozzy's president of the MC and the woman your brother tried to sell into the skin trade is his woman."

Holy shit. It's a small freaking world.

Finn disconnects the call and rubs a hand over his face. "Lake Masqak. He said that's where a bunch of rich assholes own vacation houses, and it's about twenty-five miles north of Shine with nothing in between."

"That has to be it," I say, looking between Finn and Luca.

"Would Carlo be that fucking brazen to stay so close to Shine?" Finn asks.

Luca and I answer with a resounding yes.

"He probably knows there's no record of my family owning the place, and it's not like we ever went back after my mom died. Plus, if he's there, he's getting some sick satisfaction knowing he's so close and we have no idea." Disgust laces my words with the knowledge Carlo could be there, that his presence is tainting a place that holds memories with our mother. He doesn't deserve to be there. Not after...everything.

"Don't suppose you remember the address?" Finn asks, already knowing I don't.

"I was five the last time I was there, so no. But I'd definitely recognize it if I saw it."

"There's no way in hell you're going up there with us, Giada. I won't allow it."

I turn to my husband, who has obviously forgotten who he's speaking to.

"You don't order me around, Luca Bennetti. This is the first lead we've had. If he's there, we'll finally be able to end this bullshit once and for all. What would your plan be? To go up there and drive around calling his name to see if he comes out of the house? Get real. You need me to find the house."

"I'm not putting you in danger again, *Mrs. Benneti.*"

"My last name was Cataldi first, and it's going to take a Cataldi to catch one. If you think you're going to stop me, then you have another thing coming. You can't keep me here locked up and hope Carlo what? Turns himself over to you? We're in danger every time we leave this property until we find him. I'm not going to be a prisoner in this house." I turn to Finn. "No offense."

"None taken," he replies, looking between me and my pigheaded husband. "She's right, though." Luca looks ready to murder his cousin where he sits. "Look, I don't like the idea of putting her in danger, but we need this over. *I* need this over. I can't watch anyone else I care about be hurt by that piece of shit. I'll call Ozzy. I'm sure we can stay at the clubhouse for a couple nights. Plus, I know he wants his pound of flesh. It's a win-win."

"Easy for you to say; it's not your wife who's going to be putting her life in danger," Luca spits out.

"Hey," Alessia barks. "My life *was* in danger *in this very house.* He came in here and shot my friend and almost took me to God knows where to do God knows what. And if you think I'm going to let the three of you go without me, then you're fucking crazy. If Giada's going, then I'm going."

"I don't want either of you going. That's what you're not getting," Luca says, looking between me and Alessia.

"You don't have a choice. So you can stay here and sulk, or we can go and finish this. But either way, I'm going to Shine, with or without you," I say firmly, getting up from my chair and walking out of the room.

Later that night after Luca and I have done a fantastic job of avoiding each other, I'm brushing my hair in the en suite bathroom when Luca walks into the room. He sits on the mattress, his elbows on his spread knees with his head hanging low.

"You don't know what it was like for me in that car," he starts, his voice low and full of pain. "When I saw the blood, your blood, soaking into my shirt." He looks up and meets my eyes in the mirror. "I didn't get to you in time. He got a shot off before I covered you, and I wasn't fast enough."

I set the brush on the counter and turn to my husband, who has guilt swimming through his blue eyes.

"It wasn't your fault, Luca. You tried to get control of the car. You threw yourself over my body to protect me. It could have easily been you instead of me lying in that hospital bed."

"But it wasn't."

I walk over to him and step between his knees. Luca's hands grip my waist and rests his forehead against my stomach.

"I can't lose you, not like that. I can't have your life snuffed out because you were born into a life you never asked for. I promised I'd protect you, and I failed."

My hands tunnel through his dark hair, that's gotten longer than I've seen it in years since being confined to the house with me.

"You have done everything you can to keep me safe, including marrying me to keep me out of the Russians' hands. Don't you understand? It's my turn to protect you and everyone else we care about. If Carlo isn't stopped, who knows who he'll go after next. Are you willing to risk Alessia or Finn? What about Eoghan or your aunt? This is our best shot. *I'm* your best shot."

His deep breath is full of resignation as he grips me tighter. "I'm not going to be able to talk you out of coming, am I?"

"No," I answer simply. "There's no use fighting about this. It's not going to change anything."

This has to end before anyone else I love dies.

Chapter Twenty-One
Luca

NEVER IN MY LIFE did I think I'd be taking my wife to a clubhouse full of bikers. Finn assured me they are aware of who I am and why I was in the Cataldi organization. He also made sure to let me know again that these guys may participate in illegal activities to make their money, but they hold the same values as our family, especially when it comes to the women in their lives. It does little to ease the tension I have as we drive through the gates, though.

Parking the car in the gravel lot, the four of us step out of the vehicle next to the row of motorcycles in a line off to the right. A large man with a neatly trimmed beard with a little gray around the edges of his otherwise dark hair walks over to us with two other men all wearing the same cut. The man in front has a president patch on his, and the other two are wearing enforcer patches.

"Ozzy," Finn calls, "Thank you for having us." He walks up to the MC president with his hand outstretched.

Ozzy grips it in his large palm and claps Finn on the shoulder. "I told you to call if you needed assistance. Glad you did."

Finn nods. "Let me introduce you to my wife." Alessia walks from the other side of the car and shakes Ozzy's hand then greets the other two men, Linc and Jude. "And this is my cousin Luca and his wife, Giada."

Ozzy walks up to me and takes my hand in the same firm grip as he did with Finn. "You saved two of our women, Luca. If there's anything you ever need, know we're in your debt."

"Appreciate it," I reply before he introduces me to Jude and Linc, whose old lady was the girl from the warehouse who Alberto was about to buy.

"Good to finally meet you, man," Linc says, shaking my hand.

Giada is standing silently next to me with a practiced smile on her face. I wrap my arm around her shoulders to offer her some comfort, but I think the drive here has brought up a lot of memories for her. When we drove through the little town of Shine, her head was on a swivel, looking at every building and shop we passed. She pointed out a candy store her mom used to take them to before they made it to the house. The memory brought a smile to her face, but a few moments later, it dropped, and she was back to being quiet. Giada is still coming to terms with loving her mom and being angry that she participated in the lies from both of our childhoods.

"Eoghan didn't make the trip?" Jude asks as we grab our bags and walk toward the front door.

"He and Cillian will be up later," Finn says.

"Good, he can finally meet my old lady. I can't wait for her to beat his ass at pool." The affectionate smile on the otherwise tough biker's face when he speaks of his woman eases my tension further. It's obvious these men love and respect the women in their lives, just as Finn assured me.

When we walk into the clubhouse, it's not as I would've expected a biker hangout. There are no half-naked women lying around or a bunch of drunk assholes leering at Alessia and Giada when we walk in. A couple of the members are playing pool to the left, another man is sitting at the bar sipping coffee and reading a newspaper, and there's a woman is sitting with a laptop in front of her and papers spread across a table.

"Pretty girl, come here a minute. I want to introduce you to some people," Ozzy says.

When she looks up from her work, her eyes meet his then she finds mine. A wide smile stretches across her face as she approaches us. "You must be Luca," she says, shaking my hand. "If it wasn't for you, God knows what would have happened to us."

"I was in the right place at the right time. Glad to help."

When Ozzy and Freya were kidnapped by Carlo, I overheard the two goons who worked for Carlo talking about the lawyer bitch and the MC president at one of the Cataldi warehouses, waiting for Carlo to get there to take care of them. I took a chance and called Finn from my phone, warning him that something was going down. Though Carlo got away that day, Roberto and Ernesto weren't so lucky. Good fucking riddance.

Two women come out through a swinging door on the right side of the room, and I recognize one of them immediately. The girl that Alberto was going to buy. She looks a hell of a lot better than the first time I laid eyes on her.

She walks up to Linc, and he wraps his arm around her shoulders, kissing the top of her head. I can only imagine how she feels seeing me again. The first time she met me, I was playing the part of human trafficker. And I played it well. She was out of the warehouse before we took out the men inside.

Charlie offers me a small smile. "I never thought I'd be thanking you if I ever saw you again. You play a convincing bad guy."

I nod and return her smile. "I'm glad you made it out."

Not all the women Alberto bought through the years were as lucky, and that guilt still eats away at me.

"I'm Lucy," a short woman standing next to Jude says, shaking hands with Giada and Alessia. "I heard you're a bit of a gun expert," she says to Alessia.

Alessia laughs. "I heard you're the only person here who has a shot at beating my brother-in-law at pool."

"Hey," Jude exclaims. "Eoghan doesn't win every game."

The women share a laugh at Jude's expense before we're shown to our rooms.

"We don't usually stay here," Lucy explains as we walk down the hallway. "But with the idea of Carlo being so close, Ozzy called everyone in. At least until we find out if he's really at your old lake house." She looks at Giada. "I know a little something about fucked-up families."

"I'm sorry," my wife says, giving Lucy a small smile. "I hope they got what they deserved."

The tilt of Lucy's lips makes me a little nervous if I'm being honest. "They definitely did. Oh, hey, Cece," she says, turning her attention to the tall, willowy blonde woman stepping out from the door we're in front of. "This is Finn, Luca, Giada and Alessia."

Cece smiles and says a quiet hello before scurrying off. Lucy looks after her as she rounds the corner. "That's my sister. She's still a little skittish around people she doesn't know. You're most likely only going to see her if you go in the kitchen. Baking is her happy place. Especially around all these assholes," she says loudly, and I turn to see Jude walking up to her.

"Were you talking about me again, Lucifer?"

Lucy rolls her eyes. "How come every time I refer to someone as an asshole, you assume I'm talking about you?"

"Because you usually are," he replies, giving her a smacking kiss on the cheek before turning his attention to me and Finn. "Once you get settled, come outside. We have a car that will blend in a little better around here for you to take to the lake."

Finn and Alessia head into the room next to ours to

change and get ready to go before I shut the door to mine and Giada's room.

"You okay?" I ask as she unzips her bag and pulls out a sweatshirt and a hat. When we decided to go on this little hunt for Carlo, we knew we needed to try to disguise ourselves the best we could without looking like we were trying too hard.

Giada removes the sweater she's wearing, and I catch sight of her bullet wound. Every time I see it, that rage bubbles back to the surface. That motherfucker needs to die.

"A little overwhelmed, honestly. Being back here, well, in Shine, I've never been to an MC clubhouse before. I don't know; it's bringing up a lot of old memories I haven't thought of in years."

"Like what?" I ask as she slips into the hoodie and twists her hair up to put under the cap.

"My mom being happy. Of feeling like we didn't have to walk on eggshells like we did at our house. Of Marco here with her. It's like this town has unlocked so many good memories, but they're all tainted with everything I know now." She shrugs. "It's just a lot right now."

I pull her into my arms and tip the bill of the hat up so I can kiss her mouth. "There's nothing I can say except it'll take time to come to terms with everything. But know your mom loved you and wanted you to be happy. That's all I want, too."

She gives me a shaky smile and blows out a long breath. "Let's get going."

The drive to the lake is quiet as Giada looks out the window like she did when we drove through town. She made this drive with her mother and brother countless times, probably excited for a vacation. Now she's here to see if the boy who grew up to be an evil psychopath is hiding in the house that held so many happy memories for her.

When we pull off the highway into the neighborhood with several large houses dotting the lake, my nerves ratchet up about a thousand notches.

"If there's even a hint that he spots us, call Ozzy and have him haul ass here. I don't want this fucker getting away again," I tell my cousin, who's driving the midrange SUV owned by one of the club's friends. Definitely a smart move to have us bring this out instead of the luxury sedan that Finn drives. "And no matter what, you stay in the car. You're only here to point out the house," I tell my wife.

"We're armed to the teeth," Finn tells me. "Including Alessia."

Though this is a simple recon mission, Finn's made sure to come prepared on the off chance something happens. Neither of us are willing to be caught unaware when we're carrying precious cargo with us.

"Go down to the houses right along the shore. I remember being able to walk out the back door and having a dock in our backyard."

Finn does as instructed and we drive around the lake, not too slowly, so it doesn't appear like we're looking for something.

When we get to the other side, Giada gasps. "That's it," she says, trying not to crane her neck at the house on her right. "And there's a light on downstairs."

Finn passes the house without slowing and takes a left to get back to the highway.

"He's there," Giada says. "It has to be him, right?"

"I saw the street address. I'll have Cillian check the property records and see who owns it."

"It's him," Giada whispers and stares out the window as we head back to the clubhouse.

Three hours later, Cillian and Eoghan walk in with duffel bags in each of their hands.

"We made a trip to the warehouse. Brought a few extras just in case," Cillian says, setting the bags on the floor next to the bar. "I looked into the property records for the address you sent me," he tells Finn. "It's had the same owner since the sixties. Antonio Russo. Giada's grandfather."

I release a heavy breath. "It's Carlo then. You're sure it was never sold?"

Cillian looks at me like I asked the stupidest question he's heard all day. "Of course. The taxes on the property have been paid every year from a shell account that ended in the Caymans. If I recall, the Cataldis are particularly fond of using shell companies to hide their money."

"We go tonight. Before dawn breaks, I want that fucker six feet under," Finn says. We all nod in agreement as Ozzy, Linc and Jude walk over to greet Cillian and Eoghan.

"We have a plan?" Ozzy asks.

"To go in and kill Carlo and anyone else we find," I reply.

"Sounds solid," Jude says, his lip turning up in a little smirk. He looks down at the bags Eoghan and Cillian brought in. "And look. You brought more toys."

After going over the schematics for the home Cillian was able to bring up on his computer and getting a feel for the house we'll be heading to later, we have dinner with the club. Giada and Alessia sit with the other ladies, and Lucy regales them with stories about God knows what, but they're laughing and having a good time, which I'm grateful for. It's keeping Giada distracted, at least from what I can tell, and that's what she needs right now.

My family sits with Ozzy, Jude and Linc, who are going with us tonight, while Knox, the club's VP and Cash cover the only road leading to the highway just in case Carlo manages to slip out of our grasp.

"I think we're set, gentlemen," Ozzy says, getting up from his chair. "I'm going to spend some time with my fiancée before we head out." He walks over to Freya and whispers something in her ear before she gets up and follows him down the hallway.

"I'm going to take that as my cue to take my wife to our room," my cousin says and heads toward Alessia.

"Thank you for going with us," I tell Linc and Jude. "Taking care of Carlo is our responsibility, so I appreciate your willingness to put yourselves in the line of fire to help us."

"The Italians have been a problem for both of our families for far too long. I have a personal stake in this, too," Linc says.

"Yeah, and there's no way in hell I'm letting my prez or my best friend walk in there without me," Jude says, standing from his seat. "Now, if you two will excuse me, I'm going to go piss off my old lady."

After he turns, I shoot Linc a questioning look.

"It's their foreplay. It's fucking weird, but it works for them."

I chuckle and rise from my chair. "See you in a few hours."

When I reach Giada, she looks up at me with a sleepy smile.

"Come on, sweetheart. Let me take you to bed." That earns me a different kind of smile from my wife.

When I shut the door, Giada is standing at the foot of the bed, looking at me anxiously. "You haven't touched me since the shooting," she blurts out. "This is probably the worst time to bring it up, and there're so many other things to be worried about right now, but there it is."

I walk up to her and take her soft cheeks in the palm of my hand as she looks up at me, biting her lip. I pull it from her teeth and kiss her mouth. "I'm sorry. Seeing you hurt, almost losing you." I shake my head. "It made me go into overprotective mode. I didn't want you to overdo it and hurt yourself, or worse, have me be responsible for hurting you." I kiss her again. "But it was never because I didn't want you, sweetheart"

She leans up on her toes and kisses me back, wrapping her arms around my waist. "Then show me," she whispers, her hands grabbing the bottom of my T-shirt and lifting it up and over my head.

I don't waste a second, taking the soft material of her sweater in my hand and gently sliding it up her body. She no longer has to wear a bandage, but the wound from the bullet is still pink around the scar that's going to be with her for the rest of her life.

"The doctor said I could take the bandage off. The stitches have probably dissolved by now anyways. Now, I'm just left with this ugly scar."

I look into her eyes and bring my lips to the scar. "Nothing about you is ugly, wife. Least of all proof that you survived."

Giada grabs my face and crashes her mouth to mine. "We still have to take it easy. At least for a few more weeks."

"Were you planning on performing acrobatics?" I ask, quirking a brow.

She laughs lightly, the sound warming all the cold parts of my heart. "Not today."

I bend and leisurely taste her lips as though we have all the time in the world before guiding her onto the bed and bringing my body over hers but keeping my weight balanced on my arms.

My lips trail down the smooth column of her neck, over her breasts still encased in a sexy as fuck lace bra, licking my way over her stomach to the top of the pants she has on.

Looking up at her as she stares at me through half-lidded eyes, I press my lips to the skin at the edge of her pants. "I don't know how I got to be the lucky son of a bitch you let into your body, but fuck Giada, I'm so damn grateful I am." Her long fingers brush through the strands at the top of my head. "Now take your tits out of your bra and let me watch you play with your nipples while I taste you."

She smirks then brings the cups of her bra down, releasing her breasts from the material, moving her fingers to her nipples and twisting.

"Good fucking girl." The words come out in a rough growl as I slide her pants and panties down her legs and throw them behind me.

Guiding her to the edge of the bed, she sits and leans back, her arms behind her so she can clearly watch me eat her sweet cunt. I drape both of her legs over my shoulders, opening her up to my waiting mouth. The first lick I take through her wet pussy causes her to let out a hiss, the second has her grabbing the hair on the top of my head in her fist, and the third has her moaning, "Jesus Christ."

A smile tips my lips, but I don't stop. My eyes travel to her hand while she twists and pulls at her peaked nipple. I'm transfixed by the blissed-out expression on her face while I worship her delicious cunt that I've spent far too much time away from.

"Fuck, right there," she moans before biting her lip, trying to contain the screams that threaten to erupt in a clubhouse full of people.

I press two fingers into her tight heat and curl them, finding the bundle of nerves inside of her. That sets off a ripple through her pussy and a breathy, drawn-out moan as she comes undone, her body jerking with the intensity of her orgasm.

I slow my fingers and tongue, following her down from her peak of pleasure and kiss my way back up her body, taking her nipple in my mouth and sucking hard before releasing it with a pop then standing to my full height. The needy expression in her eyes as she stares at my hands undoing the button of my pants makes my cock jerk to attention. Dragging the zipper down before I pull them off my body sends excitement through me, and another emotion I'm not ready to put a name to. I've been so worried about hurting Giada I haven't even let myself think about fucking her, too worried that I'd let my dick do the thinking for me, and I'd say to hell with the doctor's orders.

"Move up the bed, sweetheart." Usually I would take her small waist in my hands and toss her up myself, but I have to stay mindful of the wound on her right shoulder.

I kiss my way up her smooth skin and settle my hips in the cradle of her thighs, keeping my weight on my elbows. Low enough to her that we're touching skin to skin, but she isn't taking any of my weight. I guide myself into her, feeling her for the first time in weeks. Her nails dig into the skin on my back as we slowly move together. My hips rock into her, and I get lost in the feel of her wrapped around my cock. Our eyes are locked, our breaths mingling with the words I haven't told her, coming out in heated pants. *I love you, I need you, don't leave me when this is over.*

It takes monumental effort not to slam into her over and over, but it's worth it just being inside of her again, connecting her to me in the way I've come to crave in our short marriage.

"You feel so good, Giada. I fucking love the way your pussy takes me. God, I never want to leave." Sweat drips down my forehead, tickling the side of my face. "I can't hold back," I say as I continue to bury myself inside her over and over.

"Don't. I want to feel you. God, I'm right there with you."

Her walls tighten and pulse around me as her second orgasm rushes through her, setting off my own. I crash my lips to hers and swallow her moans as we both lose ourselves in each other.

When her orgasm has ebbed, and she stills beneath me, I pull myself from her body and lie next to her, gathering her in my arms. Her head rests on my chest for a few moments before she speaks.

"When are you leaving?" she asks in a soft whisper.

"In a couple hours," My fingers glide up and down her damp back. "I'll be back before the sun rises."

"As long as you come back to me, Luca Bennetti."

"Always, Mrs. Bennetti."

CHAPTER TWENTY-TWO
LUCA

L EAVING GIADA IN THE bed is no small feat. She isn't asleep. I doubt she'll be getting any until we all make it back from the lake house. And we will all make it back. Too many times in both of our lives, the monsters have walked away free from having to answer for their crimes. Not tonight.

My wife watches me silently from the bed while I dress in a dark pair of jeans and a black Henley top.

"I would make a decent-looking biker, don't you think?" This seems to be the staple uniform for most of the men around here.

"I never thought I'd say this, but I think I prefer you in suits. But if you want to trade the Mafia for the MC, I suppose I wouldn't make a terrible old lady," she replies with a smile, trying to play along and let me lighten the heavy mood in the room. It doesn't last for more than a second before the tension on her face returns and worry swims through her tired amber eyes.

Once I'm dressed and have my shoulder holsters in place, I walk to the edge of the bed, bending to kiss Giada. My hand cups the side of her face and I press my forehead to hers, staring into her fearful eyes. Trying to come up with something to reassure her is useless. There's nothing I can say that will make her believe that all of this will be over soon. But I *will* be walking back through that door in a few hours, ready to start our lives free from the chains of worry, whatever that future looks like.

The sound of a knock on the door breaks our connection. "Yeah," I call to whoever is on the other side.

Finn pokes his head in. "We're about ready, just need to load up." His gaze turns to Giada. "The ladies are in the main room if you want some company."

I nod. "Thanks. We'll be out in a minute."

Finn shuts the door and Giada gets out of the bed in just my T-shirt and pulls on a pair of jeans before slipping her feet into a pair of sandals.

"Come on," I say, holding out my hand. Her warm palm slides into mine, and I have the strongest sensation of never wanting to let it go.

Walking out into the main area of the clubhouse, I notice the bar covered in all types of weapons, from guns to knives, a rolled-up rope, and a few pairs of handcuffs.

I kiss Giada on her temple and tilt my head to Alessia and the group of women sitting at a table with coffee cups in front of them.

She walks over and has a seat next to Lucy, who offers her a reassuring smile and hands her a cup. "There's a little whiskey in it," Lucy tells her as Giada takes a sip. "Helps calm the nerves." Giada nods in thanks.

Turning toward the bar, I spot Jude strapping several knives to his vest, and he gives me a wink.

"Jude has a certain affinity for knives," Linc says, walking up next to me.

"What about you?" I ask.

He pats the double holster strapped across his chest. "I prefer guns, but I'm not a showboat like some people," he says loud enough for Jude to take notice.

"Fuck off," Jude tells his friend. "There's a certain creativity involved in using knives that you, my friend, simply don't possess."

Linc chuckles. "I'll take the quick kill any day."

Jude shrugs. "That's exactly what I'm talking about. No imagination."

I have a feeling in another life, Jude could have been a serial killer. Good thing he's on our side.

After strapping myself with four 9mms courtesy of the Black Roses and loading up on magazines, it's time to head out. Five of us walk to the table where our women are sitting. I bend to taste Giada's coffee and whiskey-flavored lips and feel the small hiccup in her throat. When I meet her gaze, there are tears gathering there.

"I'll see you in a couple hours. Do me a favor?"

"What?" she whispers, trying so hard not to let the tears fall from her eyes.

"Be wearing my shirt when I get back. I fucking love

seeing you in my clothes."

Her small smile doesn't reach her eyes, but I can't expect it to. I wish I had more time to reassure her. Hell, I wish I had more time with her period.

I stand and follow the rest of the men outside.

"Let's finish this," Finn says to me, clasping me on the shoulder.

It all comes to an end tonight.

The truck we're in is quiet as Ozzy drives us to the lake house. Knox and Cash stop at the entrance and wave us off as we continue into the dark neighborhood. It's just after one o'clock in the morning. Anyone who lives here is most likely fast asleep, safely tucked into their bed. There's a narrow access road to reach a dock at the lake between two properties that we pull the truck into to keep it out of sight. The back of the house is visible from where we park, and thankfully, there are no lights on, signaling that Carlo and anyone else he happens to have inside are sleeping.

As silently as possible, we make our way through the large backyard and when we get to the back door of the house, Eoghan pulls out a lock-picking set from his pocket. Handy to have in situations where breaking down the door isn't a viable option.

When he opens the door, we all stand still, waiting

silently for any sign of an alarm. None are heard and the seven of us make our way into the house. Finn and I are at the front, Eoghan and Cillian right behind us, followed by Ozzy, Linc and Jude.

From the plans, we know there are four bedrooms. One downstairs off the side of the kitchen and three large bedrooms on the second level. Finn checks the one downstairs first and comes out a moment later, shaking his head. We didn't have time to set up any surveillance of the house before we made our way here, so we don't know how many guys, if any, Carlo has with hi m.

Ozzy points to Linc and Jude, then signals with his hands to have them wait down here as the five of us advance up the stairs to the top three bedrooms. There are four doors, two on the right and two on the left. The first door on the right leads to the bathroom.

When Cillian opens the second door on the right, he nods inside. There's a man sleeping on his back, but it isn't Carlo. At least he wasn't stupid enough to be here by himself. Cillian creeps in, pulls a .22 with a suppressor attached from his holster and shoots the man in the head where he sleeps. We wait for any noise indicating the small pop from the weapon roused anyone from sleep. Cillian walks out of the room and quietly pulls the door closed. One down, and who knows how many more to go.

Opening the door of the first room on the left, Ozzy shakes his head. One bedroom left. With Finn on one side of the doorframe and me on the other, I carefully turn the doorknob and allow the door to silently swing open. From the opening, I find Carlo sleeping on his back, not realizing there are seven men in the house waiting for the life to drain from him. Finn and I step in, me walking quietly to one side of the bed as Finn walks to the other. I raise my gun and train it on the man in front of me, the man responsible for nearly ending my wife's life.

Before I have a chance to fire, his eyes shoot open and lock with mine. "Hello, Carlo."

In a flash of movement, he spins to his side to grab the gun from his nightstand, but he's too late. He's staring down the suppressor of Finn's 9mm. "Not so fast, asshole," Finn growls at the man.

Carlo slowly rolls back over to his back and sits up with his hands on either side of him.

"You think this is over, Luca? You really think with me out of the way, you've won? You're nothing more than a street punk who married my half sister. You think the Irish are your saving grace? That what, you were going to be the new head of the Cataldi empire with my slut sister by your side? These Irish assholes aren't going to allow that." Carlo laughs. "You played right into their hands. They aren't going to protect you now that they've captured the big bad wolf."

"Jesus Christ, Carlo. You're fucking delusional," Finn says to the man. "The big bad wolf? You're nothing more than a sniveling asshole who was riding daddy's coattails. You could have walked away with your life, but you decided you wanted to play Mafia don. Too bad for you no one wanted to play with you. You really should have left well enough alone, but you made a grave error in judgment when you decided targeting women was going to give you the upper hand. All it did was make me and my cousin hungrier for your blood."

Carlo's eyes widen when he hears the word cousin and he turns to me. "You fucking rat."

I smile. "Surprise, motherfucker."

Rage takes over Carlo's features before his hand dives under the pillow next to him and he raises a .38 Special in my direction, firing off a shot. I duck to the side and he misses before I hear the familiar sound of a muffled pop coming from Finn's gun. Carlo howls in pain, bleeding profusely from his right arm that he was holding the gun with. It drops from his grasp and Finn swipes it from the bed. Carlo grabs his shoulder, his breath coming out in harsh pants between clenched teeth.

"You think killing me is going to somehow save your sorry ass?" I ask, raising my gun to his forehead.

"No. But if I'm going to hell, I'm taking you with me, you fucking rat bastard." The defiant sneer on his face makes me want to laugh.

"Actually, no. You're not."

Ozzy steps into the room, and Carlo's head tilts back, a pained *fuck* falling from his lips.

"Now, now, boys. Don't kill him too fast," Ozzy says,

walking up to the bed with an eerie smile on his face. "I haven't had my fun with him yet." The MC president digs his gloved finger into the bullet wound Finn gave Carlo, and it takes every bit of strength in the soon-to-be-dead man to not scream out in agony.

"You fucked up, Carlo. You went after what's mine. Twice."

Before Carlo can utter a word, Ozzy pulls a mean-as-hell-looking knife from the sheath at his waist and plunges it into Carlo's stomach, staring into his eyes as he twists it.

"Hurts like a bitch, don't it? Funny thing about stab wounds to the stomach. It takes a few minutes for them to kill you, but it'll be the most painful last minutes of your life. I bet if I keep the knife inside you, it'll buy me and my friends some extra time."

"You all have no idea what's coming for you," Carlo says, his wild eyes darting between the three of us as sweat pours down his face. "You think you've won? I'll see you all in hell before long."

"Maybe, but it won't be today," I tell him, raising my gun to his forehead once again.

I fire the shot, and he falls back on the pillow, brain matter and blood scattered across the headboard behind him.

My eyes stay fixed on his prone body, lying lifeless on the bed. He was the sum of all of our nightmares, all of Giada's fear and pain. There isn't a living man in this house who his evil hasn't touched. And it's over. We're free from the nightmare he held us all in. We're free. And so is my wife.

"You okay, cousin?" Finn asks.

"Yeah," I say, thoughts running through my head about what this means for my future with Giada. She's free to live however she wants. *Wherever she wants.* "Let's get this cleaned up."

Ozzy calls Cash and Knox and instructs the men to park behind our truck on the side of the property. The nine of us load everything that could contain any blood evidence in the back of Ozzy and Knox's trucks, including two dead bodies.

"What about Carlo and the other guy?" I ask Ozzy.

"We know a farmer who likes to keep his pigs well fed. For a certain fee, the bodies will be gone by daybreak."

That leaves me with disgusted images running through my mind as we drive back to the clubhouse. Knox, Cash, Cillian and Eoghan drive past the turnoff, heading to the farm Ozzy mentioned while we continue on the road that leads back to my wife. Apparently, Cillian is keen to meet this pig farmer to see if he'd be interested in potentially working with the family if the need were to arise.

Finn and the rest of the Black Roses head into the clubhouse, but I stand outside and stare into the night sky. Dawn will be breaking soon and with it, the start of a new life for Giada and me. We're truly free now. There is no more Cataldi organization. There is no more looking over our shoulders, wondering when Carlo is going to make his next move and if we'll be in time to stop him. He can't hunt Giada down if she decides to leave. She's free to do anything she wants, and I'm free to do the same.

Neither of us has ever been faced with a choice to live however we like. I've spent the last seven years trapped in a role I hated to the depths of my soul, but I did it to bring down the man responsible for my parents' death and his entire organization. I finished what I set out to do. Francesco is sitting alone in prison with mere months left to live, his empire in ruins. He holds no power, putting all of it in the hands of his son, who is on his way to being pig food. My purpose for being in Boston is over. I can start a life with my family out from behind the shadows of my time with the Cataldis. It's a heady feeling, one that I've never really let myself think about, and now I'm not sure what the hell to do.

"Luca Bennetti," I hear Giada call from behind me. "You scared the absolute shit out of me."

I turn and find my wife stomping toward me with her hands clutched into tight fists and an angry scowl across her mouth. When she gets closer, I see that she's been crying.

"Why are you crying, sweetheart?" I ask when she stops less than a foot from me. I want to reach out and touch her beautiful face, to pull her into me and feel her pressed against me. However, the look on her face tells me I may not want to let her that close to any vulnerable appendages.

"Well," she says, cocking her head to the side. "Finn thought you were right behind him when he walked through the door. He beelined straight for Alessia and started making out with her like a damn teenager." I chuckle at her indignant tone but quickly school my expression, noting the fire in her eyes *and not the good kind.* "Everyone was inside, too wrapped up in their women to realize you hadn't come in. When I didn't see you, I thought you were fucking dead!" she yells. "I stood there crying for a solid minute before Finn realized what was going on and told me you must be outside. You scared me half to death, Luca." Tears of anger and relief spill from her eyes and I close the gap between us, not being able to hold myself back.

"Shh. I'm sorry, sweetheart," I coo into her ear as sobs rack her body. "I'm here. I'm safe. We're safe."

My palms rub up and down her back in a calming caress until Giada quiets and looks up at me. I move my hands to the side of her face and wipe the tears from under her eyes.

"What are you doing out here?" she asks, her anger replaced with concern.

"I was thinking about what life is going to look like for us now without the threat of your brother hanging over our heads. We're free. You're free."

"And?"

"And you can go anywhere you want. You don't have to stay in Boston. You can move to Italy like you wanted and live with your family. You're finally free from this life." It would kill me to let her go, but I promised her on our wedding day she could leave when this was over. She doesn't have to be tied to the violence she grew up with. She finally has a choice.

Her eyes narrow, and I get the distinct impression I said the wrong thing.

"Are you stupid? Did you get hit over the head tonight or something?" The way she's looking at me tells me she could very well be the one with a blunt object in her hand if I don't tread lightly. "The only place I want to go is home with you. Wherever *we* decide that is. In case you're too dense to realize, I love you, Luca. Though I'm questioning your common fucking sense right now."

A choked laugh leaves my throat before my mouth crashes to hers. Though she's angry with me, she opens and allows me to deepen the kiss. When I pull away, we're both panting hard.

My forehead presses to hers. "I love you too, Giada. That's why I want you to have whatever you want. If that was moving to Italy and getting away from here, I wouldn't have stopped you. It would have torn me apart, but I wouldn't have gotten in your way. I wouldn't have broken my promise."

Giada tilts her head back so she can look me straight in the eyes. "Listen, we have a lot to figure out, but there's no chance in hell I'm leaving you. My decision was made the first time I kissed you, the first time you held me in your arms and promised to always protect me. There is no future I want that doesn't include you."

"Thank fuck, because to be honest, I may have shown up in Italy and begged you to stay with me. I can't imagine not seeing you dance or listening to those old records with you ever again. God, I love you."

I dive in for another breath-stealing kiss. Giada falls into me and I slide my hands around her thighs, picking her up so she can wrap her legs around my waist.

"I need a shower and to sink deep inside you before we fall asleep tonight. Then, tomorrow, we can go home and figure out what the hell we're going to do with the rest of our lives. Sound good, Mrs. Bennetti?"

"It's the smartest idea you've had all night, husband."

Epilogue

Luca

One Week Later

THE LAST WEEK SINCE coming home from Shine has been busy as hell. Giada and I have decided to take a proper honeymoon now that we aren't hiding from her psychotic brother. We're going to Italy to meet her family and travel to all of her favorite places. I still haven't figured out what I'm going to do with the rest of my life, but apparently, Finn has been setting aside money for me for the time I worked undercover in the Cataldi organization. After over seven years, I have a more than decent nest egg to live off until we figure out where we want to settle. Giada brought up possibly going back to California, but I think I would miss my family that I'm finally able to get to know here. Maybe we can figure out a way to be bicoastal, but we have plenty of time to decide. Right now, the only thing I care about is spending as much time enjoying my wife as humanly possible.

That's why this meeting at the prison needs to happen

today so I can finally put everything I came to Boston to do to bed. Jude's brother apparently has some pull with some political bigwigs and as a favor to Jude, his brother made a couple phone calls. Without having to wait to go through the normal channels, I'm standing inside the state penitentiary where Francesco Cataldi will be living out the rest of his days.

Francesco is led into a room normally reserved for meetings with attorneys, his eyes narrowing in confusion when he spots me leaning against the wall.

"Hello, Francesco," I greet as the guard attaches the handcuffs Francesco is wearing to the table in front of him.

When the guard leaves, Francesco is silent as he studies me. The man looks worse than the last time I laid eyes on him, his skin a pale shade of gray and practically hanging from his bones.

"You're not looking too well," I comment, taking a seat across from him.

"What the hell are you doing here, Luca? They told me I had a meeting with my attorney."

I shake my head from side to side. "Nope. Just me. I wanted to reintroduce myself to you."

His head rears back and he looks around the cement-walled room as though he doesn't understand what the hell is going on. That's fair. No one other than Giada and the capos, who are now under Finn's control, know who I am.

"I've always gone by Luca Bennetti, but my real last

name is Romano."

Francesco's eyes widen. The look on his face is similar to the one his son wore before I killed him. "You had my parents murdered. Wanted me dead alongside them."

He's too stunned to speak and looks at me as though he's seeing a ghost, or maybe he's recognizing my father in me for the first time.

"You little fucking prick. When Carlo finds out you betrayed our family for all these years, you're fucking dead. He won't stop until he finds you."

"Funny you should mention your son. He made some pigs very happy and full last I checked."

Francesco's face goes even more pale than I would think possible, considering it doesn't contain much more color than the walls around us.

"Your empire is gone. Your capos have made the wise decision to absorb their businesses into the Monaghan organization. It's over, Francesco, and you lost." I chuckle then stare the man in the eyes. "I thought it would take you lying in front of me in a pool of your own blood for me to feel like my parents' murders were avenged. But you know what? Knowing you're going to die here in pain and alone with the knowledge that your reign is now a cautionary tale to those who would dare fuck with my family is pretty fucking sweet revenge. There isn't a single person who is going to miss you or cry when you die unless, of course, it's tears of joy. Your wife's daughter will never have to fear you or who you're going to sell her off to because she married me, and it's now my life's mission to give her all the happiness and love you never showed her."

Francesco doesn't say a word as I lay everything at his feet. "Good fucking riddance, old man."

I stand and walk to the door, knocking twice to be escorted out. Francesco's back is to me as he stares at the wall. I don't need him to say anything to me; don't need any explanation or justification for his abhorrent actions through the years. I came to say my piece, and I'm leaving this hellhole lighter than when I walked in.

Giada and I are at Clovers, the bar I called all those years ago, looking for Cormac and finding my cousin instead. It feels so damn good to be here, surrounded by my family. I'm finally able to spend time with them without worrying about raising suspicion or being found out by Francesco or Carlo. Cillian and Finn are sitting at the table with me while Alessia and Giada are picking out songs from the jukebox. I'm admiring my wife's ass as she shakes it to the beat of the song when Finn interrupts me.

"So, Italy for three months, then where?" he asks.

I shrug and take a sip of my beer. "No clue. I've never had a vacation. Who knows, maybe Giada and I will decide to travel the world for the next few years." Between my money from Finn and the accounts Cillian was able to recover from the Cataldi estate for Giada, we don't have to worry about money for the next while, or maybe ever.

"Well, the offer stands. If you want to be part of my organization, I'll find a spot for you. Legal or otherwise."

"Thanks, cousin."

I've brought it up to Giada, and she says she's perfectly happy with whatever I choose, but all she knows is the darker side of this life. I want to give her something different.

Finn's eyes narrow on the front door when three men walk in. He turns to Cillian. "Go get Eoghan." Then he turns to me. "Fucking Russians."

Cillian nods and stands from his seat, heading to the back of the bar where Eoghan's office is.

"There're no fights tonight, Andrei. Not that you're welcome at any of them or in Boston at all, for that matter," he says when the three men approach the table. Finn leans back in his seat and opens his leather jacket, revealing the double holsters with a 9mm in each.

"We aren't here to cause problems, Finn," Andrei replies. "Our boss wanted us to come and pay our respects. He's sorry about the mix-up with the Cataldi girl."

That comment raises my hackles. "She isn't any of your boss's concern."

From the corner of my eye, I see Eoghan and Gemma come from the direction of Eoghan's office. His hair is a mess, and if I'm not mistaken, her sweater is on inside out.

"That's what he wanted you to know," the man says, briefly looking at me before turning back to Finn. "His plans to make his way into Boston have been put on hold."

"Tell him he'd better keep it that way. I'm not open to any new alliances with him or anyone from New York."

Andrei nods, looks at Gemma and then Eoghan, who looks mad enough to lay this guy out in the middle of his busy bar.

"You look familiar," Andrei says to Gemma. "Have you ever lived in New York?"

"Nope. And never plan on it," she replies, crossing her arms over her chest.

"Hmm. Could have sworn I knew you." Andrei turns and meets the gaze of every man standing or sitting in front of him. "I'll let you get back to your celebration. Have a good night."

The three men turn and leave the bar.

"That was fucking ballsy as hell," Alessia comments when she walks back to the table. "For all they knew, you could have shot them on sight."

"That's probably why Nikolai sent Andrei. He knows if Luca sees his face, he might do just that. And in Irish territory, he'd definitely get away with it," Cillian comments, staring at the door.

Alessia notices Gemma standing next to Eoghan and does a double take when she notes the state of her sweater. She shakes her head but doesn't call attention to what she sees before sitting next to Finn. Conversation resumes around us as I tuck Giada against my side.

"That kind of puts a damper on the evening," my wife says quietly.

I turn my head so I can speak softly in her ear. "That's okay. I was ready to get out of here anyways. I'd like to take you back to the penthouse and make you come at least twice more before we head to the airport in"—I look at my watch—"three hours."

Her tinkling laughter brings a wide smile to my face.

"You're something else, Luca Bennetti."

"Right back at you, Mrs. Bennetti."

The End

Thank you so much for reading Luca and Giada's story! If you enjoyed this story, I would be incredibly appreciative if you left a review where you purchased the book. Reviews are an amazing way to help indie authors get the word out about their stories.

Want to get to know more about the guys from the Black Roses? They have a series, too! And I have a prequel novella about a few of my guys when they were growing up in Shine. You can get that for fre by signing up for my newsletter at katerandallauthor.com. I promise, I'm not a spammer!

<u>Stalk me on my socials!</u>
<u>TikTok</u>
<u>Facebook</u>
<u>Instagram</u>
<u>Goodreads</u>
<u>BookBub</u>

Scan the QR code to follow me on all my socials and sign up for my newsletter!
Xoxo

ALSO BY KATE

The Ones Series
The Good One
The Fragile One
The Other One

The Black Roses MC
Linc
Jude
Ozzy
And more coming...

The Boston Syndicate
Finn
Luca
Eoghan
Cillian

Acknowledgements

First, I want to thank YOU for taking your time to read my words. I love Luca and Giada's story so much, and I so appreciate you coming on their journey with me. It means the world that you picked up this book for a few hours of getting lost in my world.

Thank you to the awesome team at The Next Step PR. Kiki, Megan and Anna are the best at what they do and I'm so fortunate to work with them.

Huge thank you to Victoria for making my stories make sense and always being up for a couple more stabby scenes! LOL. I'm so glad I found you and get to work with you.

And of course, Rose! You give so much care to my book babies and polish my words beautifully!

My sister-from-another-mister, Molls. There's so much that goes into keeping me partially sane while I'm in my oh-my-God-I-have-to-get-this-done-why-do-I-always-do-this freak out stage. You've talked me off many a ledge, sister. I love you.

Thank you to my amazing family. It's not easy living

with me (just ask my husband. LOL) but you make sure to keep everything moving along when I'm locked in my writing cave and only come out at feeding time. I love you guys to the moon and back times infinity.

About Kate

Kate is a lover of all things books. It doesn't matter what sub-genre, as long as there's a HEA, she's in. She started reading romance in high school and would hide novels in textbooks to read during class. Becoming an author was always a dream she had and finally decided to put pen to paper (or finger to keyboard) and write what she loves. She grew up in the beautiful upper peninsula of Michigan then became a West Coast girl where she lives with her amazing husband and hilarious son. She would love to hear from readers so check out all her socials and sign up for her newsletter so she can keep you up to date on her books and whatever other ramblings come to mind.